That was a night Megan would never forget

"Remember when we drove out to that pond?" Dev brushed back a tendril of hair from her face. "It was so hot that I took off my shirt and asked you to take off yours."

"And I told you big girls don't do that." Her lips barely moved; she was lost in the memory.

"But you eventually took it off," he whispered, moving in so close, a breath of air couldn't move between them.

"You were the one who took it off." Megan could feel the heat of his body sear her and she feared her own body's response. "Dev," she said in a faint voice, "I don't think this is a good idea."

He didn't stop pursuing her. "Why not?"

"Because we're divorced—"

"We may be divorced, Meggie—" he pressed closer to her until she could feel his full arousal "—but we're not dead."

ABOUT THE AUTHOR

The author of almost thirty-five novels, Linda
Randall Wisdom is well-known to readers of
Harlequin American Romance and romance
readers everywhere. Her lively stories, filled with
sexy heroes, humor and passionate romance, have
been delighting us for years—ever since she sold
her first book on her wedding anniversary, which,
Linda says, proves she was destined to write
romances. She and her husband and a houseful of
exotic birds make their home in Southern
California.

Books by Linda Randall Wisdom

HARLEQUIN AMERICAN ROMANCE

Don't miss any of our special offers. Write to us at the
following address for information on our newest releases.

Harlequin Reader Service
P.O. Box 1397, Buffalo, NY 14240
Canadian address: P.O. Box 603,
Fort Erie, Ont. L2A 5X3

LINDA RANDALL WISDOM

THIS OLD HOUSE

Harlequin Books

TORONTO • NEW YORK • LONDON
AMSTERDAM • PARIS • SYDNEY • HAMBURG
STOCKHOLM • ATHENS • TOKYO • MILAN
MADRID • WARSAW • BUDAPEST • AUCKLAND

Published June 1992

ISBN 0-373-16443-2

THIS OLD HOUSE

Chapter One

"I can't believe Gram would do this to me. She always told me I was her favorite grandson, then she turns around and ruins my life."

Devlin Grant reread the latest letter his company had forwarded to him from an attorney. It detailed a surprise legacy. So far, he'd read it three times, each time hoping the words would magically change. Each time, the neatly typed phrases said the exact same thing. After spending the day slogging through the rain-soaked mud and spending most of the night helping repair a bulldozer, he didn't need this bit of unexpected news.

"How could she do this to me?" he groaned again.

"Who did what?" Greg Foster, one of Devlin's fellow engineers, glanced over his shoulder at the creamy vellum stationery. "Law firm, huh? You in trouble, Dev? Should I go scrounging up bail money? Or is it just some babe suing you for breach of promise or paternity? You gotta be careful about those things, you know." Greg playfully punched his friend in the arm, looking pleased with his idea of a joke.

Dev shook his head. "None of the above. No, my grandmother died a month ago, and it seems she left me her house in Northern California." He grimaced at the greasy smudges his fingers left on the heavy stationery. He'd learned long ago nothing remained immaculate in the South American jungle.

Greg grinned. "*You* own a house?"

Dev nodded. "Hard as it may be to believe, old buddy, there are people in this world who own their own house and are happy doing it."

"Yeah, but they need the room for all their belongings. All of ours fit inside a duffel bag with room to spare." Greg dropped his hard hat onto the drafting table and leaned against the edge. "So, you going to settle down in one place and grow vegetables? Frankly, buddy, I can't see you as a happy homeowner."

Dev stroked his mud-streaked beard. He shifted his feet, feeling the aches and pains from a night in the field. "Maybe this is a sign, Greg. I've been thinking it's getting time to quit all this traveling and settle down in one place. Maybe even take that desk job corporate talked to me about."

"You? Hell, you don't even go to restaurants that make you wear a tie."

"I don't know, right about now, a normal life sounds pretty good to me." He tapped the letter against his hand. "Guess I should get on the phone and call this lawyer so I can get Megan's number."

"Megan?" Greg asked. "Who's that?"

Dev raked a hand through his hair. "Don't ask. *That's* a complication. It seems my grandmother left the house to me and someone else." He snorted derisively. "And that someone else happens to be my ex-wife."

Greg looked shocked. "After ten years of pouring out our guts over beers, you've never said a word about an ex-wife. Was it so bad that you don't even talk about her?"

"It happened when I was nineteen and stupid with raging hormones." Dev shook his head at the memory. "Trust me, Megan isn't someone you'd care to meet. Not if you want to keep your masculinity intact. Not to mention your sanity." He grimaced at the memory. "And if she wasn't bad enough, her family makes her look like Mary Poppins."

Greg winced. "That bad, huh?"

Dev thought of liquid brown eyes, a bright smile, Shirley Temple dimples and a soft voice that, at one time, made him crazy with desire. "She was pretty cute. I haven't seen her in fifteen years, and I'm damn glad of every one of those years. Trouble is, that cute exterior hid one of the hardest hearts a nineteen-year-old boy could ever come up against. By the time I came to my senses, I felt as if I'd lived ten lifetimes. I'm just glad I had my work to keep me sane afterwards. She bounced off to her ivy-league college, probably grateful I was out of her life and she was back to being her parents' little darling. I'm sure by this time, they've turned her into a cold, unfeeling clone of themselves."

Greg shuddered. "Sounds scary."

Dev laughed, but there was no mirth in the sound. "That's about it. Luckily, it didn't take us long to discover how opposite we were. It was just a shame we didn't find out until *after* the wedding. I tell you, I'd as soon have root canal rather than see her again. You see, old buddy, Megan Abernathy was, and I'm sure still is, a materialistic little twit."

"MEGAN LOUISE ABERNATHY, what is going on?"

"And hello to you too, Mother," Megan cheerfully greeted her mother while trying to cradle the cordless phone between her jaw and shoulder as she carefully folded a blouse and placed it in the suitcase she had laid out on the bed. She didn't need a genie to tell her why her mother called. "How is the Wells case going?"

"He was found guilty, of course. He received twenty years in the state penitentiary as he rightfully deserved," District Attorney Ellen Abernathy informed her daughter. "Don't try to change the subject, young woman. I called your office only to be told you're going to see a house you inherited. Funny, I don't recall any of our family dying recently." Her sarcasm was purposely laid on thick to imply she didn't appreciate learning this from a mere secretary instead of her only daughter.

Megan winced and silently damned her talkative secretary. Although, with Ellen's manner of interrogation, the poor thing probably hadn't had a chance! This was one conversation Megan had hoped to put off until after her trip. It didn't appear she was going to be that lucky. "I didn't exactly inherit a complete house, Mother, I only inherited half of one."

"That still doesn't answer my question. What relative died, and who inherited the other half?"

"Devlin Grant's grandmother, and we jointly inherited her house." Megan steeled herself for the expected response to her reply.

"What? It has to be some sort of sick joke, Megan. He's doing this because he wants you back," Ellen insisted. "I could tell that boy was trouble from the first time I met him."

"Mother, that 'boy' has probably grown up by now."

"I doubt it. His kind only manages to get into more trouble. For all you know he's in jail. Actually, I could do some checking and find out."

"No!" Megan's voice hardened. "Mother, this is purely between Devlin and me."

"If we hadn't gotten you out of that horrible marriage, who knows what would have happened. You would probably have six children and be on welfare." Once Ellen warmed to her subject, little short of a nuclear blast could stop her. "It must be some kind of plot. He probably wants to get even with you for the divorce."

"I can't imagine it would take him fifteen years to come to that decision," Megan said dryly, easily recalling the hellish events that surrounded her divorce. "After what happened back then, he probably wants nothing to do with me."

"Megan, you must listen to me. That Grant boy hurt you very badly back then. If we hadn't stepped in when we did, he would have turned you into some kind of camp follower traipsing off to foreign lands after him instead of staying in school and receiving a good education. Even if you did choose to use it to sell houses."

"I'm a broker specializing in commercial real estate," Megan corrected for the umpteenth time. Not that her mother ever listened. "There's a big difference between selling houses and entire business buildings."

"No matter, what I really want to know is why you think you need to see that man. What does Rob think about this?"

"Rob has nothing to say about this," Megan said firmly. "To be honest, I doubt I'll even see Dev. When I spoke to the attorney, he mentioned he hadn't even heard from Dev." She closed her eyes against a threatening headache. One always seemed to come when she had these kinds of conversations with her mother.

"Mother, I really have to go. Give my love to Father and I'll call you when I get back," she said swiftly.

"Megan, let us handle these legal matters for you. There's no reason for you to go up there." Ellen paused as if something occurred to her. "Dear, you're not having any problems, are you?"

"Problems?" Megan frowned as she threw a pair of Liz Claiborne bright turquoise walking shorts and a matching plaid shirt into the suitcase. "Problems with what?"

"You might be considered too young for a midlife crisis, but you have been acting a bit odd lately. Not at all like yourself. Perhaps you should make an appointment with your doctor. After all, this may be nothing more than a hormonal imbalance that can easily be taken care of with proper medication or a change of diet."

Megan swallowed the hysterical laughter that threatened to erupt. "Actually, I'm feeling better than I have in a long time. Now I really must go. Goodbye, Mother." She depressed the button, disconnecting the call. Barely ten seconds passed before the phone rang again. Without a guilty qualm, Megan quickly switched on her answering machine. "Sorry, Mother, but I'm not going to discuss Dev with you again."

She walked into the bathroom to gather up the cosmetics she'd sooner die than be without. She knew her mother would be less than happy to learn that if Megan did see Dev, she planned to apologize for what they had done to him. Fifteen years ago, he'd accused her of having no more feelings than that of a board, and now Megan intended to prove him wrong. *I'll show him I'm not the spoiled brat I was fifteen years ago!*

A smile softened her angular features as she thought of her inheritance. Sure, she'd loved Dev's grandmother, but she hadn't expected to be in the woman's will. And certainly not as the heir of a Victorian mansion on several acres of wooded property. But it must be beautiful, she thought. And maybe—just maybe—the answer to the restlessness she'd been feeling lately.

WHEN DEV WALKED THROUGH the house that had been his grandmother's and her mother's before that, he hadn't expected to feel such a strong tug deep down in his gut. His first intention when he received the letter was to fly up here, sign the necessary papers, arrange its sale and take off. And if all that could be accomplished without having to see, much less talk to, Megan Abernathy, so much the better. His intentions changed the moment he walked through the house. As he fingered the peeling wallpaper, gazed at the badly scratched hardwood floors and eyed damaged fireplaces, he began to visualize the house the way it must have looked years ago. He found himself wanting to see it looking that way again. "It's a sign," he murmured, running his hand down the badly scarred banister.

Dev wandered out onto the porch that wrapped around the entire front of the house with one post wobbling dangerously to one side. In deference to the unseasonably warm late-winter day, he rolled up the sleeves of his plaid shirt. He lit a thin cigar and gingerly placed a booted foot on the wood of the bottom rail. He braced his crossed arms on his thigh as he surveyed the yard overgrown with rose bushes more dead than alive and knee-high weeds and shrubs. The more he looked around at the neglected area, the more at peace he felt. For all his years wandering the world, this

was the first time he'd felt as if he'd finally come home
and a peace seemed to enter his soul. He didn't know
how he was going to do it, but he was going to persuade Megan to sell him her half.

The sound of a high-powered engine warned him his
time of peace and quiet was coming to an end. He
looked up when a silver BMW appeared at the top of
the drive. He didn't move from his spot as he watched
the car roll to a stop. Shade from nearby trees allowed
him to easily identify the driver, although he didn't need
to see the face. Around here, most people drove sturdy
American-made cars or heavy-duty pickups. There was
only one person he could think of who would drive a
status symbol.

"Well, well, well, look who left civilization to brave
the wilds," Dev said as he watched the driver climb
gracefully out of the car and walk around to the front.
He noted the poppy red T-shirt, a crest embroidered on
the pocket, tucked neatly into khaki linen slacks covering a too-thin body. Dark brown hair was brushed
back into a neat French braid that framed a narrow
face. Her pale olive skin was wildly flushed; obviously,
she hadn't had an easy time finding the place and now
looked frustrated enough to chew nails. The idea was
enough to make him grin. *Shoulder pads in a T-shirt,
yet,* he mused, drawing on his cigar as he watched her
walk toward him. *Even in the back of the beyond, she's
got to make a fashion statement.*

"This is *it?*" Megan looked around at the house that
appeared to be on its last legs with an expression of dis-
belief, mingled with horror. She tipped her head back
to look up at the shutters hanging on by a thread and
the warped boards curling outward. "*This* is the 'his-
torical Victorian mansion' we inherited?" She was so

stunned by the house's appearance, she didn't stop to realize she was speaking to a man she hadn't seen in fifteen years as if they'd just parted a day ago.

"Oh, it's not so bad. A little paint here, a few nails there and she'll look just fine. I don't know about you, but I've seen worse," he said lazily, tamping his cigar out on the railing.

"Are you sure this wasn't once owned by Norman Bates and his mother?" Megan fought to keep from laughing or crying at the cruel disappointment that coursed through her veins. All during her drive north, she had thought of a house fit for a queen. To learn that same house looked as if it belonged in a horror film seemed like a cruel joke. "I will say he's done a wonderful job of keeping the character of the place intact. I just bet the showers work beautifully."

Dev was surprised by Megan's sense of humor. He had expected her to throw a tantrum instead. "Hello, Meggie. I didn't know you'd be willing to venture out of lovely Malibu and Beverly Hills for the boonies. Didn't the guards stop you at the border and insist you return to rarefied air before you shriveled up to nothing?"

She threw her head back and looked him straight in the eye. She was completely undeterred by his standing so far above her. At the same time, she couldn't help but notice how well he fit into the rustic atmosphere with his Western-style shirt, faded jeans and scuffed boots. The fact that he also looked sexy as hell teased her senses before she firmly tamped them down. Even with the shoulder-length brown hair she remembered so well now cut to brush his collar and the sun-tipped beard, he looked as if he belonged in this wild background. His scent was devoid of cologne; only clean skin mingled with the woodsy aroma around them. That old zing in her veins was her first warning Dev had weathered the years much better than expected. "I thought I'd see if I could survive in air that wasn't smog laden. Surprise, I can still breathe." She held her arms out as if to say "Ta-da!"

His grin tolled the second warning bell. "Brave soul. Why don't you come on up and take a look at your inheritance." He caught her expression as she warily eyed the sagging steps. "Don't worry, the porch is completely safe. After all, I'm standing up here, aren't I?" He held his arms out.

She headed for the steps. "I wouldn't be surprised if you didn't mark the safe boards." She carefully climbed up, her eyes focused on each step as if afraid one would fly up and hit her in the face.

Dev shook his head, still trying to come to grips with the fact the cute but very spoiled girl he once lusted after and mistakenly married had matured into a beautiful woman who seemed to take the eccentricities of life more ably. "Don't tell me. You expected to find an elegant Victorian home complete with colorful rose bushes bordering the walkway."

She grimaced. "When one is informed one has inherited half ownership of a Victorian house on several acres of land, one naturally pictures said house in a certain manner. You can't tell me that you pictured it in this condition. It looks as if nothing has been done around here for decades." She swept her hand toward the front door.

"Since it hasn't been lived in for quite a while, I expected weeds, maybe a few broken windows, but I admit I didn't expect anything as dramatic as this." Dev's eyes slowly perused her from the top of her head down to the tips of her feet. With every breath he took, the light, sophisticated fragrance she wore suffused his lungs. "You're looking well, Meggie. I'm glad to see that you lost that baby fat you couldn't get rid of back then. You've sleeked down real nice. And didn't lose the boobs in the process, either."

She merely raised her head and looked at him. Not by word or manner was she going to allow him to unnerve her. Even if her hand itched madly to knock his block off. Baby fat! She never had baby fat! If it wasn't for that wicked twinkle in his eye, she would punch his lights out! "You're such a flatterer, Dev. I have to admit you're looking quite well yourself." Looking well? The man looked positively lethal! "You look as if you spend a great deal of time outdoors."

His blue-gray eyes danced with amusement as if he knew the reason for her stance and her polite tone. She had guessed he expected sarcasm and she had surprised him by providing the opposite. She was determined that, by the time the day ended, he'd see she had changed a great deal. Trouble was, she hadn't expected all these changes in him!

"I'm still with Hampton Construction. I'm a civil engineer now. How about you? Did you follow your parents' footsteps into the revered field of law the way they expected you to?" He studied the narrow angles of her face, noticing the dark lashes framing her chocolate brown eyes. Her pale olive skin and dark eyes were testimony of the hot-blooded Latin managing to mingle with the blue-blooded Abernathys sometime in the past. He always wondered if the person daring to add that passion somewhere along the line had been shot or just hanged for even thinking of diluting such an esteemed bloodline.

Megan shook her head. "Law is their love, not mine. I'm a commercial real-estate broker."

He looked her up and down, not missing one inch of her well-dressed frame. "My, my, a yuppie job for a real-life yuppie. You have to understand, we don't see too many of you out in the jungle." He glanced over her head at her car. "I just bet you've got one of those fancy phones in that machine, too, don't you?"

Megan swallowed her retort. He had no idea how much she hated those labels. Besides, her car phone was necessary in her business! "Oh, no, I'm not going to allow you to goad me into an argument. We haven't seen each other in fifteen years and I, for one, intend to keep this civilized." She flashed him the kind of smile she reserved for her well-heeled clients just before they practically begged to sign on the dotted line.

Dev looked at Megan even closer with frank male appreciation lighting his eyes. "Yeah, and I'd say those fifteen years seemed to have turned you into one hell of a woman, Meggie," he murmured. "I never knew yuppies could look this good."

She felt a blush warm her cheeks at his sensual undertone. A frank compliment from the man who used to call her a spoiled brat? Maybe an argument would be better, after all. She scrambled for a quick change of subject. "Have you looked inside the house yet?"

Dev nodded. "I just finished before you showed up. If you'd like, I'll take you on the nickel tour."

"Please, don't bother if you've already seen it. I'd prefer to look around on my own." She turned toward the door. "I gather it's still unlocked?"

"The door's warped, so you'll have to jiggle the doorknob and push with your shoulder. When you go upstairs, watch the third step. The wood's starting to rot away."

"I will." She pulled open the aged screen door and jiggled the door handle as Dev had suggested. She was aware he watched her from his post. She winced at the sound of creaking hinges.

"The hinges just need a little oil," Dev called after her.

"Or a bulldozer," she muttered, finally able to push the door open enough for her to enter.

The house was dark and forbidding inside and, for a moment, as she stood in the entryway, Megan considered taking up Dev's offer of a guided tour.

"Like something out of a nightmare, isn't it?" Dev spoke from behind.

Megan whirled around, her hand at her throat.

He smiled. "I figured you might appreciate the company."

"Fine, you can stand in front of me if a rat attacks us." She walked down the hallway, trying not to shudder when she glanced into the drawing room with its moth-eaten carpet and rags disguised as drapes.

"That probably isn't too far from the truth." Dev gestured toward the piles of rodent droppings on the kitchen floor. "I wonder how old these appliances are," he mused, resting his palm against the dingy stove.

Megan gave the room a cursory glance. "From the forties, I'd say. How long has it been since your grandmother lived here?"

He shrugged. "Mid-fifties, I think. I'm not sure. I always remembered her living in an apartment a few blocks from our house. Oh, I knew she owned property up here, but she never really talked about it all that much."

Megan looked up the narrow stairway leading from the kitchen to the upper floors. "How bad is it up there?"

"Carpet might as well be thrown on the trash heap. Mattresses nothing more than breeding grounds for mice. I found four brass head and footboards that only need a good polish job."

"How many bedrooms?" she asked absently, wandering out the back door and studying what must have once been a large vegetable garden. As she looked outside, a germ of an idea began to take hold and brewed before she realized what was happening.

"Eight, but only one main bathroom at the end of the hall. Master bedroom has a sitting room and an attached bath." Dev frowned at the expression on Megan's face. What was going through her devious little mind?

Megan gazed out over the overgrown yard, but she didn't see the weeds and brush. Instead, she saw rose bushes, perhaps night-blooming jasmine trained to climb up trellises adorning the side of the house, neatly clipped shrubs and white gravel walkways.

"Can't you see it? Wrought-iron lawn chairs circling glass-topped tables. Peacocks would add a nice touch, but they're so noisy. Maybe a few ducks and geese instead. A small pond would look very restful over there. The kind of pond you want to picnic beside."

Dev was lost in his own thoughts as he wandered around the yard. "Plenty of good fishing lakes up this way," he said to himself. "And I bet hunting's pretty good in the fall. You'd think there would be more decent places to stay."

"That one front parlor could be opened up more for a front desk and reservation area," Megan went on, clearly not listening to Dev, but it didn't matter because he didn't hear her, either. "The drawing room could be set up as a communal room, afternoon teas, evening wine tastings. I wonder what the zoning is for this area and how easily it could be changed if it had to. Did you get a chance to look at the foundation?" she asked in a louder voice while her mind raced with ideas. One thing she was known for was thinking quickly on her feet, and her ideas always formulated rapidly and rarely needed revision once done.

"It appears to be sound, although I'd have to crawl underneath to make sure, and I'm not all that experienced in that area. I couldn't see any outer signs of termites, something else that would have to be checked out by an expert. With a little elbow grease, this could be a showplace again," Dev said amiably, looking over the grounds. "Set up a game room with dart board and pool table, big-screen TV. Of course, I'd need a satellite dish. And I could run ads in hunting and fishing magazines."

"An elegant bed-and-breakfast inn, the kind of hideaway people would pay a small fortune to stay at," Megan said dreamily. "Old-world elegance, Laura Ashley fabrics for the bedrooms..."

"What?" Dev's shout intruded as Megan's words sank in and he realized how opposite they were from his own thoughts. "What do you mean 'an elegant bed-and-breakfast inn'?"

She turned toward him. "Why not? I realize it would take a lot of work and money, but I think it would be a wise investment."

He didn't know whether to burst out laughing or to howl in outrage. "One, this area is too remote for what you're talking about. Two, it's tailor-made for fishermen and hunters. The guy who runs the gas station said there's usually more sportsmen around here than accommodations. Three—"

"Three, you cannot even think of turning this beautiful house into some kind of hotel for dirty, smelly fishermen and hunters!" Now, she was outraged. "Besides, who would run it? Certainly not you. Not when you have the kind of career that sends you all over the world, and I can't imagine you'd care to give up something you've obviously worked so hard to attain."

"Maybe you're the kind of person to run one of those fancy inns, but I can't see you giving up your yuppie career to become an innkeeper," he challenged. "I can't imagine commercial real estate is exactly booming up here."

"I won't allow my half of this house to be turned into rooms filled with moose heads on the walls!"

"And I'm not going to allow *my* half to look like something out of *The Great Gatsby!*"

Megan's eyes blazed. "So what do you suggest we do to settle this?" Her sweet voice could slice steel. "Pistols at ten paces? Arm wrestling? Or shall we just draw a line down the middle of the house and we each do our own thing and see who succeeds?"

Dev exhaled a deep breath. "You are a very exasperating woman."

"It helps when you're in the real-estate game. Even more so when dealing with a cretin."

Dev stroked his beard as he gazed down at her. "So far, you're doing pretty good holding that hot temper of yours. I wonder how long it will last before you return to your witchy self."

Megan looked as if it was going to happen any second, then she regained her composure. "Let's just agree that we disagree and see what your grandmother's attorney has to say. Who knows, we both may end up the loser if the zoning laws prohibit a business venture. I'm sure Mr. Hawkins can answer any questions we might have."

"Sounds more than fair to me," Dev agreed, pleasantly surprised she hadn't blasted him. True, calling her a witch hadn't been the most polite thing to do, but there were much worse terms he could have used! He gestured for her to proceed him toward the side of the house, where he guided her toward a fairly new truck. "I'll drive."

"I have to lock my car," Megan protested, pulling back.

"I wouldn't worry. I doubt anyone would bother traveling up the hill just to strip that fancy yuppiemobile of yours." Ignoring her yelp of outrage, Dev placed his hand against Megan's butt and unceremoniously shoved her up into the passenger seat. Flashing a wicked grin at her outraged features, he closed the door and walked around to the driver's side.

Megan winced as country-western music blared out of the oversize speakers the moment Dev switched on the ignition.

"Sorry, princess, I never did like classical music," he shouted over the twanging guitars.

She managed, just barely, to give him a tight smile— all the time visualizing her hands around his neck, squeezing very hard. Yes, that did help relax her as nothing else did. For about two seconds. After that, she gave in and shut off the radio.

"There, now we can hear ourselves think," she declared brightly.

"If you say so." He revved up the engine before peeling out.

Megan was certain he did it deliberately. Anything to get her goat. Still, she had to admit the trip down the hill was much easier in the truck than the trip up had been in her small car.

"Do you have any idea why your grandmother left the house to both of us?" she asked, just to make conversation—and hoping to find the answer to a question that had been roaming around in her mind from the beginning. "It isn't as if she didn't know we were divorced."

"Considering all the uproar during that time she was more than aware of our split," Dev said wryly.

"You don't think she did this in . . . in hopes we'd get back together again, do you?" Megan asked haltingly. "You know, a reconciliation?"

Dev burst out laughing. "No, Gram had a lot more smarts than that. She was pretty vocal from the start how wrong we were for each other, so she wouldn't have tried that stunt. I don't know why she did it, and I guess we'll never know." He downshifted as the steep hill seemed to drop in front of them.

Looking down, Megan bit back a moan. She had never liked roller coasters, and while the truck wasn't traveling the rapid speed of an amusement-park ride, she could still get the idea of one. She would have closed her eyes if Dev hadn't been seated next to her. She'd die before she'd show him any signs of weakness.

"Kind of grabs the pit of your stomach, doesn't it?" Dev asked, not looking at her. The broad grin on his face revealed just how much he was enjoying the ride.

She turned her head. "I beg your pardon?"

"This hill. Can you imagine how many kids probably walked their bikes up here in order to have the thrill of coasting down?" He chuckled. "I know if I'd lived around here as a kid, I would have. San Diego didn't have hills like this one."

"You probably would have broken your neck the first time down." She drew a silent breath of relief when they reached the bottom.

"Yeah, probably. Still, a broken bone would have been worth it. I know one thing, that hill will have to be paved." He consulted the map lying between them. "Have you talked to this Ezra Hawkins yet?"

She nodded. "Right before I left. He said to call him for an appointment when I arrived. He mentioned he'd sent you a key and that you were on your way from South America, but wasn't sure when you'd get here."

"Then he's a lucky man to get us both at once." Dev skillfully steered around several large potholes. "Luckily, the project was almost finished, so I had no problem taking time off."

"What were you working on down there?" She was curious about his work that had been one of the main reasons for their split-up.

"A dam. The country needed a reliable water supply, and they figured a dam would help the present government stay in power. Before that, I was working on a bridge in a remote part of Spain, and before that, well, it all sounds like a repetition of one job done over and over."

"But that's what you wanted so badly. The travel, the excitement of building new things, seeing new places."

"Yeah, and I've done all of the above. Now I'm ready for a change."

"Such as a sports lodge?" Her lip curled.

"Why not?"

"Because you have wanderlust. I give you a year before you'd take off again."

His voice hardened. "Don't tell me what I have, lady, because you don't know me anymore."

"No, but I still remember all your arguments for working for an international construction firm. And you must be doing something right if you're now an engineer."

"Don't try to turn on the charm, princess. What worked fifteen years ago won't now."

At first she felt anger that he could so easily brush her aside, then she felt hurt that he didn't even want to give her a chance. Yet, she had to remind herself she hadn't given him much reason not to. "I'm just trying to make conversation. I would think they'd do that even in the jungle."

He shrugged as he tightened his fingers on the steering wheel. "Yeah, but we have other names for it that wouldn't be polite for your little ears. As for my working my way up, the company said I had a lot of potential and persuaded me to get my degree. I bet your parents would faint if they found out I'd made good after all. I'm sure they had decided I'd end up in the state prison sooner or later." He flashed her a challenging grin. "Hell, your mother probably would have begged to prosecute the case."

Megan winced because he had basically echoed her mother's words. Ellen had probably already contacted all law-enforcement agencies to make sure Dev wasn't a wanted man. Megan looked around when the truck abruptly stopped in front of a one-story frame building.

"The good lawyer Hawkins," Dev announced, shutting off the engine and climbing out of the truck.

Megan waited long enough to realize he wasn't going to open her door before pushing it open herself. Muttering under her breath about proper manners, she stalked up the walkway, reaching the office door the same time as Dev.

"We really should have made an appointment," she said.

He looked around the sleepy little town with few residents walking around. "I don't think we need to worry about his having a full schedule." He pushed the door open and stepped inside, a resigned Megan following him.

As Dev had assumed, the attorney was able to see them right away.

Completely bald except for a fringe of white hair over each ear, his slow, careful way of moving and a dark suit in fashion thirty years ago gave Ezra Hawkins the perfect appearance of the typical small-town lawyer.

"Maisie had me draw up this will several years ago when she came up here to check over the property," he stated to the couple seated before him. "She said she knew you two would be surprised she'd left the house to the both of you since you were divorced so long ago, but she had her reasons. Those she did not confide in me," he said with a sniff, as if upset she hadn't.

"Yes, that's something we've been curious about, also. How long do you think it will take for the will to be probated?" Megan asked. "You see, we've discussed renovating the house and turning it into an inn." She ignored Dev's snort of disgust as she flashed her winning smile at the elderly man.

The older man started. He fiddled with his spectacles before answering. "Turn it into a hotel?" He looked horrified at the idea. "Well, you see, one of our local citizens has instructed me to offer you a more than fair price for the house." He named a figure that, in Megan's mind, was much more than the house was worth.

"Why would anyone want to buy a house that's in such terrible shape?" Dev asked. "Does this person have the same idea we do or what?"

Mr. Hawkins coughed and took off his glasses, taking his time as he carefully wiped them clean with his handkerchief. "No," he muttered, performing his task very carefully. "No, she has no plans to do anything with the house other than tear it down."

Megan's smile was downright cold and calculating. She knew no one ever bought a piece of property to just let it stagnate unless there was an excellent reason for it.

"Mr. Hawkins, if you are to be our attorney, I would suggest you be completely candid with us." Megan spoke slowly. "Such as what is so valuable about the house another person wants to pay more than its market value? I would dearly love to hear your answer on that."

Dev looked at Megan with admiration in his eyes. "Very good," he breathed. "Wish I'd thought of it first, but then, my mind usually isn't focused on money."

"Shut up, Grant," she ordered then turned back to the attorney who was now visibly perspiring. This time her smile was pleasant and stubborn. "Take your time, Mr. Hawkins, we have all day."

He puffed up to his pompous self. "That is a personal matter and doesn't need to be any of your business."

"Oh, yes, it does." Dev leaned forward, fully prepared to apply physical pressure.

The older man glared back. "No matter what else, your grandmother always deported herself correctly. I suggest you remember your place here. It isn't all that secure. If I were you, I would sell the property and be done with it."

Megan sensed undercurrents here she couldn't fully understand and decided it might be better to back off for the moment. She stood up. "We'll take it under advisement, Mr. Hawkins."

Dev's face was a bright red. "I'm not finished here." His fists clenched tightly at his sides.

"Yes, you are, Devlin." She spoke to him as if to a small boy. "Come along." She lowered her voice. "Now."

"You'd be better off taking the money," Mr. Hawkins called after them. Dev's reply as to what Mr. Hawkins would be better off doing was decidedly profane.

"Don't push him too far, Mr. Hawkins. He tends to revert to his caveman beginnings when irritated," Megan kindly advised, pulling Dev out of the office and past a bug-eyed receptionist.

"What the hell is going on?" Dev exploded once they left the building and stood in front of the truck.

"We're regrouping and planning a new strategy." She looked around and, spying a sign advertising a coffee shop, she led him in that direction. "If they want war, they've got a war."

He rolled his eyes. "Wonderful. 'Yuppie scum wages war on town locals. Film at eleven.'"

Megan skidded to a stop and stalked back to him, straightening up enough to stand nose to nose. "Listen, bub," she said through gritted teeth. "If you say *yuppie* one more time, I'm going to pull your boots up around your ears, got it?" Her narrowed eyes promised him this was no idle threat.

Dev didn't blink. "Now that's the Meggie I remember."

Chapter Two

"What in the hell is going on around here?" Dev cast furtive glances around the small coffee shop as he and Megan settled at a table near one of the front windows. "The way they're looking at us, you'd think we were escaped convicts."

"Hmm?" Megan picked up the plastic-covered menu and studied it carefully. "Obviously, no one worries about fat and cholesterol around here. I just can imagine they cook everything in grease, too. I doubt they have any kind of mineral water to drink." She shrugged her shoulders with a defeated sigh. "Oh, well, you only live once." She frowned at Dev's furtive glances around the dining area. "What is wrong with you? You're acting as if people are staring at us."

"They are," he said under his breath, studying the tabletop as if something important was written there.

"If they are, it's because they can tell we're not residents. In a town this size, I'm sure everybody knows everybody else's business. Come on, see what you want to eat. My treat."

"You're awfully cheerful about this. Did you already change your mind about that offer we got?" He glared at her, not because he was angry with her, but because he didn't like the unsettled feelings she sparked in him. What had happened to the spoiled brat he'd divorced? She should be ordering him to take the money and planning what to do with her share. "Have you taken mind-altering drugs in the past fifteen years?"

She shot him an incredulous look. "What is with you?"

He buried his face in the menu. "Nothing."

Megan braced her arms on the tabletop. "I simply feel that the offer was much higher than the actual worth of the property, and no one does that unless they have an ulterior motive. I'd love to know what it is. Wouldn't you?"

Dev traced the rim of an empty coffee cup with his finger. "Are you trying to tell me there's a treasure hidden on the property or something? Get real, Meggie. That only happens in the movies."

"Not necessarily that, but there is something going on. People who want to buy property try to get a good deal, not pay more than it might be worth. Especially in an economically depressed area as this one appears to be. You felt the house's foundation looked pretty solid, so why would someone want to tear it down instead of renovating it?"

He shrugged. "Maybe they want to build something new."

"Maybe, but why offer so much money for it when they could probably buy other property for much less?" she countered, sitting back as a gum-chewing waitress dressed in jeans appeared at their table. "Yes, I'd like the cheeseburger with everything but onions, fries and a large diet Coke, please." Megan smiled at the young woman who busily wrote on her pad before turning to Dev and flashing him a bright smile.

"One more thing," Megan said to him once they were alone again. "Why would Mr. Hawkins refuse to name the buyer? If we sell the property, we'd find out then. Why is it such a big secret?" Having the sensation of being watched, she turned her head to find a grizzled old man staring at her. When she faced him fully, he gave her a broad wink and laughed heartily, slapping his billed cap against his thigh. "I think after we eat, we should go back and find out why someone would want the property so badly."

"Maybe this person wants to turn it into an elegant inn specializing in finger sandwiches with the afternoon tea."

Megan ignored his sarcasm. "Right now, I'm doing an excellent job of holding my temper. Don't push your luck."

Dev cocked his head. "You've changed, Meggie. No more flying off the handle at the least little thing. No more bitchy remarks. How long is this expected to last?"

She stared down at her manicured hands in her lap. "It wasn't easy, but I finally grew up," she said in a low voice. "I finally realized how horrid I was back then, and knew it was time to change." She lifted her head and stared directly at him. Sincerity was written across her delicate features. "I'm only sorry you had to be one of the casualties before I learned the error of my ways."

Dev blinked at this surprisingly candid announcement. "I can't believe what I'm hearing. You never thought about apologizing for your actions before. You preferred to put the blame on others."

"Not anymore." She looked up as the waitress set red plastic food baskets in front of them and explained she'd return with their drinks. "This looks wonderful.'' Megan picked up her cheeseburger and bit it hungrily, her eyes closed in bliss.

Dev's gaze was well and truly captured by the expression on Megan's face and the slow movement of her lips as she chewed. For a moment, he had trouble believing this was the same girl he'd been so disgusted with for so long. Before he could pull his gaze away, she opened her eyes, not missing his expression.

"Say, ain't you Maisie Grant's grandson?" A raspy voice from above intruded on their silent exchange.

Dev slowly tore his eyes away and looked up at the man who'd winked at Megan earlier. Iron gray hair stuck out in spikes around his ears, while a neatly pressed red flannel shirt and worn jeans covered a wiry body slightly bent with age. Although he had to be in his late seventies or early eighties, the man's spry manner made him appear younger.

"That's right, I'm Devlin Grant."

The man cackled merrily and drew up a chair, sitting down without waiting for an invitation. "We've sure missed that lady. She was something back then, a great lady, you know what I mean?" He chuckled, his pale eyes squinting at long-ago memories. "On second thought, you probably don't. Things ain't the way they used to be." He eyed Megan curiously. "And you've got to be the ex-wife. Got to say you're a looker. Yes, sir. You got class, too. I can see it. Maisie had class like that. But then she sure ran a classy place. She made a man feel like a king while he was there." He turned back to Dev. "We've been wonderin' when you'd be showing up, son. Some of us'd like to think you'd be openin' up the old house again, but we all know that can't happen now. Times and laws have changed, and I guess old Eunice St. Clair wouldn't be too happy if Maisie's Place opened up again. Eunice never did like Maisie or what she stood for. 'Course, Irene, my wife, wasn't too happy with Maisie, either, but she never treated her like dirt.''

Megan and Dev exchanged looks of confusion, each silently asking the other what this man could be talking about.

"Mr. ah—?" Megan looked at him questioningly.

"Brady. Harry Brady," he replied, extending his hand. "Lived here all my life and know more town skeletons than anyone. Was the town's only electrician till my retirement."

"Hello, Harry." Megan smiled as she accepted his heavily callused hand. "Then perhaps you could enlighten us a little. I'm afraid Mr. Hawkins didn't elaborate on a few things. What kind of business did Mrs. Grant run? A restaurant, a hotel—what?"

"A restaurant?" Harry hooted, slapping his knee. "That's a good one, missy, it sure is. Hell, no— Pardon my language. Maisie didn't run no restaurant. She ran a house. A good one, too."

"I know it's a house," Megan said slowly, wondering if the man was slow-witted or making a joke. Apparently, Dev had already understood the man's meaning. She noticed a look of dawning horror cross his face.

"Gram ran a *house?*" Dev choked.

Harry nodded. "Best damn house in the area. Actually, it was the only one, but she still kept it classy. We always said she didn't need the red light on the porch, we'd know where to find her."

The Coke Megan was sipping immediately trickled down the wrong way. "House? Red light?" she gasped. "Are you trying to tell us that the house— That it was a—" She couldn't bring herself to use the actual word.

Harry didn't have that problem. "Yes, ma'am, it sure was. Maisie's Place was a brothel."

"This is some kind of sick joke!" Dev exploded, heading up the sidewalk with ground-eating strides.

"Why didn't Mr. Hawkins tell us the house's history?" Megan said, panting, discovering her morning runs and gym workouts hadn't prepared her for this.

"I don't know, but I intend to find out." Dev's expression boded ill for the good lawyer Hawkins. The moment he reached the law office, he turned the knob and stalked inside. "I want to see Hawkins, now," he growled at the astounded secretary, who'd half risen from her chair.

"I'm sorry, but Mr. Hawkins is—" She wasn't given the chance to finish her statement. "Sir, you can't go in there!"

"Watch me." Dev threw open the door and entered, Megan on his heels.

"What is going on here?" The timid man looked up open-mouthed with surprise at the rude entrance.

Dev braced his hands on the desk and leaned forward. "Why didn't you tell us that my grandmother ran a whorehouse?"

Mr. Hawkins turned white. "I—"

"Mr. Hawkins, Dev's temper is not a pretty sight to behold. I suggest you don't try to put him off," Megan said gently, taking a position by the doorway where she could best watch the fireworks.

The older man lifted his chin. "We do not care to have this town remembered for having a house of ill-repute. Your grandmother may have been considered a fine woman among some, but she still ran an improper and illegal business," he said primly.

"That sure didn't stop you from taking her money all these years," Dev said darkly. "As for no one wanting to talk about it, I think you should have a talk with Harry Brady and his cronies, because they sure as hell remember that house. I want the whole story, now."

"Really, Mr. Grant. I do have a business to conduct here. And there's no more to say about your inheritance."

Dev slapped his palm against the desk, the sound sharp like a gunshot. "Now."

Affronted by such barbaric behavior, the attorney shuffled papers. "To put it simply, the house you and your ex-wife have inherited was a bordello since it was built in 1882. Your grandmother ran it from her mother's death in the late thirties until she closed it after the Korean conflict. She gave no reason for closing the house . . . nor any hint where she was going. I received letters from her on an annual basis regarding the house's upkeep. She didn't want it vandalized."

"You sure as hell didn't keep that agreement very well," Dev growled.

Hawkins's lips pursed in an expression of disdain. "She had once intimated that she would leave the property to the town when she died. Obviously, she felt she was having a last laugh by leaving it to you. But no matter, I have since spoken to my client, and she is willing to increase her offer another ten thousand dollars."

"Tell your precious mystery client that she can keep her money because we intend to not only keep the property, but to fix it up," Dev informed the lawyer with a grim smile. "We have ideas of our own for its use. I'm sure you can understand why I'll be looking for another attorney, one who will have my interests at heart.'' He spun around and exited as abruptly as he entered.

''You must make him listen to reason,'' Mr. Hawkins sputtered to Megan. ''That house has too many bitter memories for some of the townspeople. You cannot allow them to resurface.''

''Mr. Hawkins, I am in the real-estate business, and one thing I know is that a house with a shady past is a perfect drawing card for the public. If you want to keep your bones in one piece, I suggest you do as Mr. Grant suggests and send him the files. If you don't comply, I'll just have to sic my parents on you. They're both attorneys, and they could easily take you down without breaking into a sweat. You'd never know what hit you.''

Her exit was more graceful.

Once outside, Megan ran to catch up with Dev, who was opening the driver's door to his truck. She winced at the stream of curses spewing from his lips.

''What you're talking about is anatomically impossible,'' she commented, pulling open the passenger door and climbing into the truck's cab.

''By the time I'm through breaking all of his bones, it won't be,'' Dev muttered, revving the engine several times before putting it in gear. ''I can't believe this. My grandmother was a . . . a . . .''

''A madam,'' Megan bluntly stated, not backing off when he sent her a look fit to kill.

''I bet that will please your folks to no end. They thought I wasn't good enough for you before. With this piece of news, they'll be crowing with delight that they engineered our divorce.'' His boot pressed down on the accelerator.

Megan drew in a sharp breath at the bitterness lacing his voice. ''They can't be pleased about something they'll never know about. It's none of their business, Dev.''

"I can't imagine my father knowing about this and never saying anything," he muttered, practically racing down the road.

"If he doesn't already know, would you want to be the one to tell him?"

Dev didn't reply. The moment he braked to a stop in front of the house, he pushed open the door and climbed out of the truck.

Megan scrambled out and followed him at a slower pace. She found him sitting on the back steps, his head buried in his hands. She stood there for a moment, taken aback by the abject slump in his shoulders. She saw a vulnerability she was sure he wouldn't have displayed if he wasn't so upset.

"Dev?" She sat down next to him, placing a hand on his shoulder, gratified he didn't pull away. "I remember you once told me how much you loved your grandmother. Isn't that what really matters? Your memories of her, not what other people say and think?"

He looked up, his features twisted with inner pain. "No nasty jibes? No cracks about my grandmother making a living on her back?"

"I'm going to take your present state of mind under consideration. Otherwise, I'd be only too happy to give you a black eye," Megan retorted. "I admit that would have been something I might have said a long time ago, but that isn't me now. It seems you don't care to believe I might have changed over the years, and I don't intend to knock myself out to prove you wrong. Did you ever stop to think that you were luckier as a child than I was? Your grandmother baked chocolate-chip cookies for you. My grandmother's cook baked them for me, and then I was only allowed to eat one because they were bad for my skin. And I was only eight years old!''

A smile twitched the corners of his lips. "Fudge. Gram made the best fudge in the world."

Megan threw up her hands. "Whatever. All I'm trying to do is make a point. Why should it matter what she did before you were even born? It didn't affect you directly."

He chuckled and shook his head. "You're doing a pretty good job of cheering me up, Meggie."

She winced. "I'd prefer you forget the *Meggie,* if you don't mind."

Dev reached for a loose strand of hair curling around Megan's cheek. "You know, for two exes who once hated each other with a vengeance, we're talking pretty civilized."

"Probably because we're all grown-up now."

His dark eyes scanned her breasts, which were rising gently under the soft cotton. "Yeah, I noticed how grown up you are. You smell real good, too. Good and sexy."

She could feel her nipples peaking under his studied gaze. She shifted, feeling more uncomfortable by the moment. She was supposed to convince him she wasn't the same person of fifteen years ago, not grow aroused just because he looked at her! "We…ah…we need to talk about the house, not how I smell."

"Hmm?" He appeared very interested in the two nubs pushing out the bright-colored fabric.

Megan stood up, keeping her back to him. "I said, we need to talk about the house." She concentrated on keeping her voice strong and steady, then damned herself for it coming out soft and husky instead.

Dev leaned back against a post, lacing his fingers around a drawn-up knee. "You mean you want to talk about your elegant inn."

"No, I mean the house, in general. There's a lot of work that needs to be done before it could be converted to either an inn or sports lodge," she explained. "All of it basic before we get down to specific changes. Redone plumbing and wiring, new windows, wallpaper stripped..."

"Stripped, huh? I like that idea," he murmured, watching her through narrowed eyes.

Megan fixed him with a steely glance. "The kitchen floor needs to be replaced, the wood floors need to be sanded and refinished, the fireplaces cleaned, the garden redesigned. The house has to be painted inside and out, and that's only a portion of what needs to be done."

Dev nodded. "Fine. You're the expert in these matters. How much do you think all of that will cost?"

She closed her eyes and did some rapid calculations. "I can only give you a ballpark figure because it's not something I'm all that familiar with. Also, I have no idea what exactly needs to be done."

"Go for it."

She named a sum that left Dev gasping for air. "You're kidding, aren't you?"

Megan shook her head. "Materials are expensive, and labor even more so. You work in the construction trade, you should know that."

"Yeah, but concrete for a dam is a bit different than concrete for a driveway," he muttered, mentally tallying up his savings and finding them sadly falling short of her estimate. "Oh, hell, maybe we should sell it. You could use your half to buy yourself an elegant inn that doesn't need so much work.''

Megan looked up at the house with its peeling paint and warped window frames. She didn't just see a sadly neglected house. She also saw her chance at the change in life-style she realized she desperately needed rapidly dissipating. ''You know, you're right.''

''That's a first.''

She flicked her forefinger against the side of his head. ''Shut up and listen. What I'm saying is the kind of inn I visualized wouldn't work here, but your idea for a sports lodge would, and I'm willing to help you make it come true.''

He was instantly suspicious. ''How?''

''By putting up half the money for the repairs, or more, if necessary.''

''Why?''

''Because one of us should see our dream come true.''

Dev slowly shook his head. ''No. I want nothing from you because you feel guilty.''

She sat down beside him. ''This has nothing to do with guilt, Dev.'' Megan sighed at the knowing expression he flashed her. ''Okay, maybe a little guilt. You were handed a raw deal by me and my family. Now I'm in a position to help and I want to do it, no strings attached.'' Her voice softened. ''Dev, lately there've been days when I feel as if I'm burning out, and if I have to go out and show one more piece of property I'll scream. When all this came up, I saw it as the chance I've been looking for. My condo was a fixer upper and I know how to paint walls, hang wallpaper and sand floors. Anything else, I'm willing to learn. Please, let me help.'' The soft expression in her eyes echoed her spoken plea.

He couldn't have ignored her if he tried. He cocked his head as he studied her. "You're serious?"

Her gaze didn't waver under his regard. "Very."

Dev sighed. "I don't feel right about it."

She drew back. "You don't trust me. You think I'm planning a way to get your half of the house from you."

"Meggie, we've been together for only a couple of hours after not having seen each other for fifteen years. Back then, we were always ready to tear each other's throat out, and now you're acting like my best buddy. If the situation was reversed, wouldn't you feel more than a little uncomfortable about it?" he asked.

"I think the word you're looking for is *suspicious*. And it's understandable. If it will make you feel any better, we can find a lawyer and draw up paperwork to make it nice and legal, all aboveboard. We both know I shouldn't have even been named co-owner, but I wouldn't mind being your silent partner," she said softly, holding out her hand.

He grinned. "Silence was never one of your strong points." He stood up and clasped one of her hands between his own. "I'm probably only agreeing to this crazy scheme because I'm still suffering from jet lag, but I'm wiling to discuss your idea some more."

"I only have to make a couple phone calls." She talked so fast, her words almost ran together. "And I packed a suitcase, so there's no reason why we can't start the work right away."

"Hold on!" Dev grabbed hold of her shoulder to stop her flight. "I said we could talk this over some more, and for the time being that's all we're going to do." He dug into his pocket and pulled out a set of keys. "We need a walk-through to see what exactly needs to be done to each room."

Megan nodded as she dug through her leather tote bag for her Day Runner and opened it to the section holding blank note paper.

Dev looked at the overloaded gray leather appointment book and shook his head. "For someone who doesn't want to be called a yuppie, you sure have all the accessories."

"It's just an appointment book," she ground out. "Now let's get going."

"Still bossy, too." He unlocked the door and opened it, then grinned and shook his head in amazement. "You know, for someone who I was determined I wasn't going to allow to get my goat, you've really done a good job of it."

"At least you've gotten smart over the years and are willing to listen," she said, verbally jabbing him from the rear. "All right, let's take the kitchen first."

It took them over two hours to go through each room and detail the problems visible to the naked eye. They dreaded to think of what might be found behind the aging walls.

"There's definitely a lot to do here," Megan told Dev, as they settled outside, since there was nothing to sit on inside. "I noticed a hardware store in town, so we should have no problem getting the basics there and ordering whatever else we need."

"Wiring and plumbing need to be fixed first," he replied. "Think you can put up with some roughing it for a little while? I'm talking about camping out here in the backyard."

"Why do we need to rough it when we can just stay at a motel until we have some of the work finished?"

"One, because I don't intend to waste good money on a motel when I can put my sleeping bag anywhere." He ticked off on his fingers. "Two, there isn't a decent motel around for a good hundred miles. That's why I wanted to open the lodge, remember? Also, with the weather warming up, there's always a good chance of vandalism or someone breaking in to use the house for living quarters, as I suspect has happened during the past. Our staying here will take care of that."

Megan looked dismayed. "You really expect us to sleep here? On the ground?"

"Don't worry, I've got an extra sleeping bag you can use."

She shifted her feet. "But there are mice."

"That's only inside. Besides, a dab of peanut butter on some strategically placed traps and *snap!*" He rubbed his hand together.

She turned green at the mental picture. "I've just lost my fondness for peanut butter. All right, but I want my own room and you have to not only set the traps, but empty them, too. Deal?" This time she held out her hand.

"Deal." Dev took her hand and instead of shaking it, he lifted it to his lips.

Megan felt all the air leave her lungs as Dev's mouth caressed her knuckles. She remembered how she once thought of their former attraction as nothing more than the kind of instant lust two teenagers mistakenly viewed as love. At that moment, she was all for instant lust. "Funny, no one ever sealed a business deal with me that way before," she said huskily.

"That's because you never sealed a deal with me before," he murmured against her hand. "You know something, Meggie? You just might be right. I see the beginning of a wonderful partnership here."

Chapter Three

"I just know a man invented these floors," Megan admitted darkly, examining the third finger she'd injured during the last hour while prying up the kitchen floor tiles. "No woman would dream of inflicting this kind of pain."

"For someone who declared it would be a breeze, you sure do a lot of complaining." Dev appeared in the doorway, looking all too appealing in tight jeans, a tool belt slung low on his hips, his chest bare. His muscular skin, darkened to a teak brown from hours under a tropic sun, gleamed with sweat, and as far as Megan was concerned, he had filled out quite nicely over the years. Physical labor had added muscle to his arms and chest while leaving a trim waist and a body that looked as if it had been sculpted from steel. All of it added up to the kind of male form women drool over. "You said you had to replace the floor tiles in your condo, so what's the big deal here?"

"My condo didn't have fifty-year-old tiles. My condo isn't even fifty years old!" She jabbed the screwdriver under a loose corner of a once-yellow linoleum tile that was now a shade of ivory. She slowly pushed it forward, but a piece broke free and flew up in her face. She sat back on her heels and cursed the floor. "This floor is haunted!" She threw the screwdriver down. "I barely get a piece loose and it breaks off. I should say the hell with it and lay the new tiles over the old. It would be a lot easier."

"Naw, you'd just end up with a lumpy floor and the new tiles would curl up."

She braced her hands on her hips, unaware how comical she looked in her spread-legged position on the floor. "Tell me something—how come you know so much about laying floor tiles when you keep saying your expertise is building dams and bridges?"

"During one of my R and R periods, I helped a friend put a new floor in the kitchen and bathrooms." Dev looked off into the distance, his fingers absently scratching the crisp hair arrowing down his belly past the waistband of his low-slung jeans. Megan's eyes were fixed on his movements with something akin to hunger.

She was tempted to ask if the friend was male or female, but reminded herself it was none of her business. "I'll make a deal with you. You do the floor, and I'll work on the wiring," she offered in a bright voice.

His eyes twinkled with laughter. "You really want to work with Harry?"

"Harry? Such as the Harry who calls me 'little lady' every time he sees me?"

Dev nodded. "Yep, that's the one."

Megan sighed as she reached for the screwdriver. "For many years, the only electrician within a hundred miles."

"Fifty miles. He may be retired, but he knows more than a lot of people do." Dev squatted down on his haunches and fingered a loose strand of hair straying from her braid. "His brother lives two towns over, and Harry figures he'll be a big help when we start work on the plumbing. I'm sure you'll be grateful to have running water." His eyes wandered over her disheveled form.

"I know I look like a mess, but this job doesn't allow me to remain very clean." She eyed her filthy T-shirt and shorts with resignation.

"I don't know, I think you look cute with dirt on your nose." He tapped the tip with his forefinger then let it slide down to her cheekbone. "More human, less yuppie."

"I don't like you calling me that." Her voice came out a bare whisper of sound.

His face lowered until his mouth hovered a breath away from hers. "Then make me stop."

"Stop." Her lips barely moved.

"Not good enough."

Her stomach muscles quivered in response. The heat from his sweaty body enveloped them. "Stop, please."

His eyes darkened. "I never kissed a yuppie before."

"I'll introduce you to one." She couldn't remember ever wanting a kiss as badly as this one. Or fearing the consequences as much. They were supposed to be business partners, that's all. And all it would take to mess it all up was a kiss. She had to decide soon which path to follow.

"Dev, boy! I finally found those wires!" Harry called from the other room, oblivious of the tension shattered by his voice.

Luckily, the decision was taken out of Megan's hands. "I'm coming," Dev called back, keeping his eyes on Megan's parted lips. He rubbed his thumb across the slightly pouting lower lip. "Hold that thought." He straightened up and walked out of the kitchen without a backward glance.

LUNCH CONSISTED OF cold sandwiches on the run as Harry urged Dev to eat quickly so they could return to their work. Megan wasn't as eager to return to what she dubbed "the kitchen floor from hell." But she was stubborn enough not to give up, and she attacked the floor with a vengeance while brief snatches of Harry's stories about the old days reached her ears at odd times during the afternoon.

"Yep, even politicians were out here sometimes, though they usually just had a drink in the parlor or sat in on one of the poker games.

"Maisie was a good friend to everyone. She had a heart as big as Texas.

"I was in Germany at the time, but I heard they celebrated VJ Day as if it was New Year's Eve."

Dev's replies were low voiced and didn't carry as well as Harry's booming voice, no matter how much Megan strained her ears. She settled for humming under her breath as each tile started to lift a bit easier.

"Looking good."

Megan lifted her head, flashing Dev a smile of satisfaction. "I wasn't about to let this floor get the best of me. I just wish I could have it finished before it gets too dark to work. How's the wiring coming?"

Dev groaned. "Don't ask. It's worse than I thought it was, although Harry seems certain we'll be finished within a couple weeks." He placed his hands against the small of his back and arched his body. "I don't think I was meant to crawl around spaces made for a terrier. I don't know about you, but I'm in no mood to go shopping for dinner now. What would you say to eating out tonight?''

Megan looked down at her hands, turning them one way then the other. No matter how she looked at them, the once immaculately manicured nails were virtually destroyed. "Pam would be horrified if she saw these," she said sadly. "Now there's nothing left to manicure. I don't suppose there's any chance of a hot bath?" She knew his answer before she heard it.

"The plumber can't make it for another ten days."

She shrugged. "At least if I can't take a hot bath, you can't take a hot shower."

"I'll heat up some water for you on the barbecue," he offered, heading for the back door.

"My manicure is ruined, my hair will never be the same again and I'm going to have to settle for sponge baths," Megan mused. "So why am I not ranting and raving about primitive conditions? Mother was right. This has to be a hormonal imbalance. If I was in my right mind I wouldn't have stayed here more than an hour." She got up off the floor, groaning as sore muscles protested even her smallest movement. "I just know I'm going to end up a cripple from this."

Dev stuck his head around the screen door. "Guess I'll have to buy you some Gucci crutch pads, then."

She threw a damp rag at him but missed by a mile. "I hate Gucci!"

"YOU LOOK LIKE YOU'RE ready to fall asleep at any minute," Dev commented, cupping his hands around the match flame as he lit his cigarette.

"It's possible," Megan muttered, stretching her legs out in front of her. Dinner—even if it had been only fast-food hamburgers—had left her feeling content. She looked skyward. "It's so pretty up here. No smog, no traffic, no noisy neighbors. At first, the quiet kept me awake. Now I sleep better than I have in a long time."

A faint niggling thought wouldn't leave Dev alone. What if she got to like it up here too much and decided she wanted the house after all? What if all of this was just a sham to get his help in fixing the place up before she wielded her moneyed wand and took it all from him? He felt very uneasy at the thoughts racing through his mind. But instead of giving voice to them, he said, "You sound as if you're fed up with the good life."

"More like tired of it." The faint moonlight sent shadows across her pensive features. "There're only so many pieces of property you can show before they all start looking alike."

"I would think the hefty commissions you get would more than make up for it." His voice came out sharper than he intended. "I mean, all you do is drive people around and show them a building or piece of land and tell them why they need it."

"If only it was that easy," she retorted. "I handle office buildings, property zoned for commercial use and shopping centers. I spend half of my time on the phone finding properties to handle and the other half finding someone to buy them."

"If it's such a hassle, why not handle residential real estate. There must be more houses out there than commercial property."

Megan stared at him. "Are you trying to start a fight?"

"I'm just asking questions!" he snapped back.

"When you handle residential, you're doomed to follow couples through house after house while they find something wrong with each one of them. Nothing major, just enough to reject it. Then you have a couple buying an estate for eight point five million and the deal sailing through like a dream." She leaned forward to make her point. "Except during the final walk-through, the wife decides she doesn't want the house after all because she doesn't like the wallpaper in the master bathroom. Would *you* want to sell residential?"

Dev's mouth dropped. Eight point five million dollars for a house? Sure, he had read about mansions and estates going for millions of dollars, and it was natural someone as classy as Megan would handle high-priced real estate. He dreaded to think what commercial real estate could go for. No wonder she could so easily spring to finance all the repairs. Hell, she could probably afford to hire an entire crew to fix the place up! Which had him wondering why she was up here willing to ruin her fancy manicured nails and wash out of a bowl.

"Someone actually backed out of a sale because of wallpaper?"

"Yes, and I almost strangled the woman, but the man did whatever his 'little honeybun' wanted, so the deal fell through. The sellers were furious with me. They accused me of not trying to talk the buyers into taking the house anyway, so I also lost the listing. And I had talked to that woman until I was blue in the face. I even offered to wallpaper the damn bathroom myself if they'd take the house. When someone talked about a small shopping center that was having trouble selling, I decided to see what I could do. That's how I found my niche." She reached over and snatched Dev's cigarette out of his hand. "I smoked three packs a day during those times. I quit after I sold my first commercial property." She pulled the smoke deep into her lungs and promptly started coughing. "Thank goodness they still taste terrible to me."

Dev plucked the cigarette from her fingers. "Fine, you talked about your professional life, what about the rest of the time? You can't sell real estate twenty-four hours a day."

"Why do you want to know?"

"Because we're going to be working in close quarters for a while and it wouldn't hurt for us to get to know each other all over again."

"I have a full life."

"Meaning it's none of my business."

"Correct." She combed her fingers through her hair. "Besides, you don't hear me asking about your life."

"Probably because it's not as interesting. I seem to spend a lot of time in either mud or sand. Other than that, I do some traveling."

Megan smiled. "You've come a long way, Dev."

"Yeah, more than your parents would ever guess." Bitterness tinted the words. "I bet they're real disappointed their predictions didn't come true."

Her heart twisted. Would she ever be able to convince him to bury that part of the past? She had already seen that this mature Dev was a great deal more fascinating than the teenager she first fell for.

"Then be pleased with yourself for proving them wrong."

IT DIDN'T TAKE DEV LONG to learn that when Megan said she'd do her share of work, she meant just that. When she finished prying up the old kitchen tiles, she drove into town to choose new ones, even though he reminded her they couldn't be laid just yet.

"Oh, I know that," she admitted. "There's the counter space to be redone, walls to be painted and appliances to be replaced." She ticked each item off on her fingers. "Not to mention the appliances to tear out and the rewiring and plumbing. But it will give me a good feeling knowing they're here."

He looked around at the chipped sink with rust stains scarring the sides, a stove that was more black than white and the refrigerator that even he feared opening.

"I can't get to this room for a while."

"No problem." She wiped her hands down her shorts. "I thought I'd start steaming off the wallpaper in the downstairs rooms. There's plenty of other things to do," she assured him.

Dev frowned as he studied the once sand-colored shorts and light blue cotton blouse that probably cost more than his entire wardrobe. "You're ruining your good clothes doing all this."

Megan looked down at her clothes and wrinkled her nose. "If I'd known what I was getting into, I would have packed some old things."

"Get one of my T-shirts and a pair of cutoffs out of my duffel bag."

Megan looked surprised. "There's no reason to ruin your clothes, too," she protested.

"Mine don't have fancy names on the label," he said gruffly, turning away, wondering how a woman could work as hard as she had all day and still smell so good. "Just go ahead and help yourself to whatever you find." He backed out of the room before he gave in to his first impulse of burying his face against her neck to see if she smelled even better up close. And here he wanted her to wear his clothing! He wondered if his sanity was going to be able to handle it.

"I CAN'T DO IT." Megan's fingers hovered over the zipper of the canvas bag that held Dev's things. It was bad enough she had found herself hesitant to enter the room he kept his belongings in, but to actually rummage through his clothing and personal effects, even with his permission, sent strange tingles through her bloodstream. She looked around the room Dev had used as a catch-all. Since they both slept outside, his only stamp on the room was a bottle of after-shave and a battered leather shaving kit sitting on the old-fashioned chest of drawers. She didn't have to open the bottle to learn its scent. She only had to sit close to Dev first thing in the morning. It wasn't expensive, nor did it carry a fancy label, but that didn't matter because, in her eyes, it suited him perfectly.

She quickly unzipped the bag, groaning when she discovered his underwear lying on top. She gingerly probed until she found a T-shirt. She quickly pulled it out, dislodging the articles on top. Giving in to curiosity, she picked up a pair of briefs that were all too easy to imagine swathing Dev's lean hips. What man buys himself red underwear?

"I SHOULD HAVE STARTED AT the rear instead of the front." Megan stared, dismayed, at the large drawing room.

"Rear of what?" Dev stood behind her.

"I thought I'd clear out these rooms so I could start the painting and wallpaper." Megan walked through the room, picking up dust-covered throw pillows that still resided on an equally filthy settee. "I didn't realize how much clearing out this room needed. Unfortunately, all this furniture will have to go." She held the edge of one of the drapes between two fingers. A tiny shake caused dust to billow. She wrinkled her nose to keep from sneezing. "Dynamite would probably make the job go much easier. What is this?" She leaned over, looking at something on the floor.

Dev eyed the tempting sight of her rounded bottom. As his eyes lit on the settee, an imp of mischief whispered a daring suggestion in his ear. He didn't give in to his jokester side too often, but when he did... He rationalized it by telling himself this was the kind of opportunity not to be missed. He quickly straightened up and walked carefully into the room. "Well, there is something you could do," he said casually.

"What?" she asked absently, still trying to dislodge something attached to the molding. "Ugh! This is disgusting!"

"Well, why not throw it all out, like *this!*"

Megan screeched and almost lost her balance when a pillow hit her backside and burst open in a flurry of feathers.

"What was that for?" she demanded, spinning around and snatching the depleted pillow from the floor.

"Hey, you offered the kind of target no man could ignore." He grinned wickedly.

She narrowed her eyes. "Then I guess there's only one thing to say."

He stood before her with his hands on his hips, looking supremely male and pleased with himself. "What's that?"

"Ditto!" She reared back and hit his chest as hard as she could with another pillow, then hit it again. "And that's for daring to insinuate I once had baby fat!"

Feathers floated around their heads like white water droplets.

"I told you you sleeked down real nice," he said, defending himself as he quickly backed up, looking for another pillow.

"So what!"

"This is war, Meggie," he warned her as he grabbed another feather-filled weapon.

"You started it, you Neanderthal!" She squealed with laughter.

"Neanderthal, huh? If I'm one, you're a twit!" Dev hit her hard in the hip, causing her to slide several steps to one side.

"Twit!" Megan shrilled. "I'll show you!" She aimed for his face, but he dodged at the last moment.

By now, Dev had the light of battle gleaming in his eyes as he slowly advanced on Megan.

"Dev, what are you thinking of?" she asked warily, backing up two steps for his every one.

"What do you think?"

"I'm not sure." His fingers tightened on the almost-flat pillow she held at her side. Her chest rose quickly up and down from the exertions of their battle. "But I'd advise you to stop right there."

"Why? Am I making you nervous?" His question held all sorts of undertones she wasn't anxious to explore.

"Of course not." Her swift reply said otherwise.

He grinned. "I think I am making you nervous."

Megan silently groaned when she found her back literally against the wall. Dev didn't stop until he stood a fraction of an inch away from her, his palms braced against the wall on either side of her shoulders. There was no hope for her to escape.

"I never get nervous." Her denial came out soft and husky instead of self-assured.

He looked down at her face, now flushed a bright pink, then farther down to breasts covered by a soft black motorcycle T-shirt. "You give Harley-Davidson a new meaning." Standing this close to Megan, Dev could see her dark eyes retract to pinpoints—and he knew he was the reason. He leaned in more until their mouths almost touched.

"I gather you're conceding the battle," Megan murmured, keeping her eyes fixed on his mouth.

"Not exactly. I'm just changing the rules a bit."

"Oh?"

"Yeah." Dev tipped his head to one side. "Remember one hot July night when I borrowed my dad's pickup and we drove out to that pond?"

Her lips barely moved. That was a night she'd never forget. "Yes."

"And it was so hot your legs stuck to the seat covers because you were wearing those short shorts that barely covered your behind?"

"Yes." The word was a mere breath of air.

He flexed his fingers, itching to touch her. "I took off my shirt and suggested you take off yours."

"And I told you big girls didn't do that." Megan was lost in the memory.

He angled his hips a fraction of an inch closer until she felt his full arousal. "So I suggested we go skinny dipping 'cause the water would cover you up."

Her lips curved slowly. "And I said with the moon being full that night, I wouldn't have all that much coverage."

"And I said I wouldn't mind."

"And I said I would."

The tip of his tongue flicked out gently, tracing the seam of her lips. "You eventually took off your shirt," he whispered, moving in so close a breath of air couldn't move between them.

Megan could feel the heat of his body sear her. "You were the one who took it off."

"You let me.... Megan, are you going to slap my face if I kiss you the way I want to kiss you?"

She couldn't take her eyes off him. "Only if you don't kiss me within the next ten seconds." She braced her hands against his chest and slowly moved them upward. "My God, Devlin Grant, I never knew you to be so slow."

Dev took it from there, capturing her mouth with a potency that had to be illegal. Megan was powerless to resist, even if she wanted to. Her mouth opened under his, inviting his tongue into love play. His beard was a soft brush against her sensitized skin. She wrapped her arms around his neck, pulling him against her until she felt his arousal against her hip.

"I forgot how quickly you used to turn me on," Dev muttered, raining kisses across her face. "I'd look at you in those tiny shorts and tank tops you used to wear, and I'd want to take you right then and there."

"It appears I still can turn you on, and I don't even have to wear tight shorts and a tank top." She arched against his erection.

Dev groaned at the pleasurable pain of her softness rubbing against him. "Oh, hell, Meggie, you're killing me. I was wondering if you were wearing a bra under this shirt, and now that I know..." One hand traced a circle around her breast, blindly searching for a bra edge that wasn't there. "Damn!" he choked out.

She ran her tongue across her lower lip. "So what are you going to do about it?"

He refused to back down from her challenge. He caught her mouth in a deep, compelling kiss that rivaled the heat of the day. His hands ran down her back until they reached the hem of her T-shirt and pulled it up so he could feel her bare skin. Megan's moan of pleasure spurred him on as he stroked the silky skin, moving around until he found the edge of her breast and the hard nipple. Megan's tongue stroking inside his mouth was more than enough to send Dev over the edge as they both gasped for air and strained to touch each other all over. Her hands dove under his shirt, rubbing his skin in an erotic manner that only drove him crazier.

"Well, I never!"

The sound of a woman's voice, filled with disgust, tore Dev and Megan apart as effectively as a bucket of cold water would have.

Both were wide-eyed and flushed with unsatisfied arousal. They looked toward the doorway to find a silver-haired woman, tall and regal, staring at them with cold eyes.

"Did you find them, Eunice?" Harry's voice called from outside.

The woman's face, pinched either from age or habit, didn't change. "Yes, I did, and it appears this house's immoral influence has already taken root."

Chapter Four

She was a formidable woman from the top of her silver hair, swept back in a French twist, to the toes of her low-heeled, black leather pumps. Glacial blue eyes surveyed the feathers strewed across the floor and still floating around the disheveled couple like a soft snowstorm.

"Mr. and Mrs. Grant?" The voice was as icy as her gaze.

"I'm Devlin Grant. This is Megan Abernathy."

The older woman's nostrils flared a tiny bit. "I am Mrs. Eunice St. Clair. I've come to discuss with you my offer regarding the property."

"It isn't for sale," Megan said.

"Miss Abernathy." Mrs. St. Clair made the name sound like a four-letter word. "Everything and everyone has a price. It's just a question of finding it."

Dev's hackles rose at her tone. "Wrong, Mrs. St. Clair. I've never been for sale, and my ex-wife has more than enough money of her own, if you'll excuse my crude way of putting it. You should be glad we intend to turn this house into a paying proposition and put some new life into it. From what I could see of your town, you could use it."

"You shouldn't have called it a house," Megan muttered.

Eunice's body stiffened. "An abomination such as this should be burned to the ground. This house was a blight on the community for years. The memories resurrected will only cause old sorrows to surface."

"Mrs. St. Clair, Mrs. Grant closed this house in the fifties. I can't imagine too many people remember its history," Megan said, wondering at the reason behind the woman's vehemence.

"There's more than enough who remember. I'll increase my offer by another five thousand."

Dev turned to Megan. While he wanted to throw Eunice's offer back in her face, he knew he should consider Megan's wishes, too.

Megan turned to the older woman. "The property isn't for sale at any price."

"This is a small town, Miss Abernathy, with old-fashioned values we like to uphold. We don't approve of unmarried people living together, whether they've once been married to each other before or not. I also have a great deal of influence with the local businesses."

"Is that a threat?" Dev asked softly, too softly.

"Call it whatever you like." Eunice turned on her heel and walked out of the room. Moments later, they heard the purr of a car engine slowly fading away.

Dev exhaled. "She is not a nice lady."

"I think we just made our first enemy," Megan commented.

"I told you Eunice wouldn't be happy to find you fixing this place up," Harry said as he walked into the room.

"What kind of influence does she have around here?" Dev asked.

"She's the mayor's widow, district attorney's daughter and granddaughter of a state senator. The do-gooders in town consider her their patron saint."

Dev winced. "She have any influence with the hardware store?"

The older man looked apologetic. "The owner's her brother-in-law."

Dev swore long and hard. "What's the lady's problem? All we want to do is bring a little business to the town! You've got the fishing and hunting grounds, so why not utilize them more?" He paced back and forth, waving his arms for emphasis. "Hell, the way she's acting, you'd think we were going to open a gambling casino or worse!"

"As far as Eunice is concerned, anything built here would be bad," Harry told him. "I wouldn't worry too much. There's those who see your idea as a good one. The town's been slowly dying for years. More people moving out than moving in because there's no businesses. Maybe this will be a new beginning. Jed Lacey is already lookin' through bait-and-tackle catalogs. Figures he could start small in the back of his store and enlarge as time goes on."

"Only if we can turn this into a paying concern." Megan spoke the words the others were afraid to.

Dev turned to her. "Ready to go back to L.A.?"

"Not on your life!" She walked around the room picking up the tattered remains of the pillows. She grimaced at the idea of having to use a broom to gather up the scattered feathers as best she could when a vacuum cleaner would have sucked them up in no time. She hadn't realized how often she took the convenience of electricity for granted until now.

Harry shook his head as he followed her movements. "I sure don't envy you your job."

"You could always help."

"We've got wiring to finish," Dev said hastily.

Megan shot him a knowing look. "I'd be happier with plumbing."

"At least we made the outhouse habitable," he pointed out.

She flashed him a tight smile. "Yes, you did. Probably because I'm not the only one who has to use it."

Dev's wicked smile sent zingers straight to her stomach. "You forget, sweetheart, we he-men don't need the amenities you ladies do."

Megan silently ordered herself not to look at him when he flashed that sexy grin of his. Looking at him only reminded her of what had happened ten minutes ago, and what could very easily have happened if Eunice St. Clair hadn't shown up when she had. Megan firmly warned herself she shouldn't allow that to happen again, and to remember they were in the midst of a business deal. It should be kept that way, no matter what! After all, there wasn't any reason why this couldn't turn into a profitable enterprise as long as they both kept their minds on the task at hand.

"You can do it, Megan," she told herself during her trek to the kitchen to hunt up the broom. "You're known for always remaining cool under fire, so what's so difficult about watching yourself around one man. Even if that man is Dev. You've survived worse. After all, you're up here in the wilds, taking sponge baths and using an outhouse! After that, anything else should be a breeze."

"If you're that unhappy, you can always leave. No one's holding you here against your will."

Megan spun around so quickly the broom flew with her, the bristles connecting solidly with Dev's stomach.

"Oof!" His cheeks puffed up as he doubled over and grabbed hold of his stomach.

"Next time, give a person some warning!" She leaned the broom against the wall.

He sucked in much needed air. "Good thing you hadn't aimed that thing lower or I would have been singing soprano for the rest of my life."

"Considering you can't carry a tune, it might have improved your voice," she said without a hint of sympathy. "Now, what did you want?"

Dev's lips twitched. Megan in a snit was a sight to behold. He wondered what she'd do if he suggested another pillow fight. Trouble was, when he thought about pillows, he thought about an entirely different use for them. Considering their shared past, he wondered if libidinous thoughts regarding Megan were a good idea. But then, all he had to do was look at her wearing his T-shirt and cutoffs. Along with the firsthand knowledge she wasn't wearing a bra, libidinous thoughts were easier and easier to come by. "Harry and I are driving into town for some supplies. I thought I'd see if you need anything."

"Running water, a few one-hundred-watt bulbs and more mousetraps. If you can't come up with the first two, I'll happily settle for the third."

He nodded. "I'll pick up the traps."

Megan watched Harry's battered pickup rattle its way down the hill, then she started her sweeping.

"He's just another man, like any other," she told herself, then stopped and rolled her eyes. "And, Megan

Abernathy, if you believe that, you're really in trouble!"

"I CAN'T WAIT UNTIL the electricity is hooked up so we can be adventurous and cook on the stove." Megan dropped her paper plate from dinner into the large trash bag. "This camp stove you got is okay for a while, but you can't be too inventive with your cuisine."

"You forgot something—the new kitchen stove is a gas range."

She fell back, groaning loudly. "No, say it ain't so!"

"I could say it, but I'd be lying."

"You're a cruel man, Devlin Grant," Megan moaned.

"There's worse things. I once found a very poisonous snake inside my sleeping bag."

She repressed her shudder. "I check mine out before I get in."

"Bugs as big as rats that have nasty bites."

"That's what insect repellent is for."

He pointed his finger at her. "Jock itch."

"Luckily, I don't have that problem. For you, I'd recommend cornstarch. It prevents chafing."

Dev poured himself another cup of coffee from the pot sitting on the camp stove and carried it over to the wool blanket they used as a table. By sitting cross-legged on the corner, he could easily see Megan, who sat on the opposite corner near the Coleman lantern they used for their source of light.

"I have to give you a lot of credit, Meggie. I expected you to run screaming out of here after the first night. That you've lasted almost two weeks says a lot in my book."

She smiled. "I won't say it wasn't tempting to go out and find a piece of civilization. It's amazing how active the imagination gets after dark. I'd sleep inside where there're walls to hold off any unwelcome intruders—except for the mice in there."

"Most animals stay away from humans," Dev assured her. "Worst case, I have a rifle handy just in case one gets too stubborn. And if you're worrying about the furry critters' welfare, I prefer using tranquilizer darts instead of bullets."

Megan glanced around. "And if the furry critters turn out to be human?" She lowered her voice. "Or subhuman?"

Dev hadn't wanted to admit he had the same thoughts after Eunice St. Clair's visit. "Then they'll have a nice nap while being carted off to jail."

"You never did say what happened at the hardware store yesterday." She remembered the anger etched on Dev's features when he and Harry returned with an empty truck bed barely twenty minutes after they'd left. When she asked about the problem, Dev had brushed her off.

Now his face tightened. He could still hear the man's cold voice ringing in his ears, spouting ugly words about unmarried couples cavorting in sin, and how that house had shamed the town long enough, and no, siree, was he going to have a hand in bringing back more humiliation to the town.

Funny, what Dev thought about most during those disgusting moments were the episodes with Megan's parents when they also spouted words about his not being good enough for her. Back then, he had been too young to realize her parents wouldn't consider any man good enough for her. Instead, he had allowed his hair-trigger temper to erupt and, as a result, reveal just how wrong he was for Megan.

Although, he wryly reminded himself, Megan's temper wasn't much kinder than his. She had proved more than once what a little witch she could be.

He lifted his cup and drained the last of his coffee. "I told you. They didn't have what we needed."

Megan's gaze remained steady on his face. "You mean they wouldn't sell anything to you."

Dev shrugged. "Harry can get what we need through his brother—and probably at a better price."

He'd forgotten how cold liquid brown eyes could grow until he saw Megan's. Right now, they were cold enough to freeze Alaska. "The Abernathys have never backed down from a fight and I don't intend to be the first."

"For all I know, I could be a descendant of U. S. Grant, and if he could win a war, there's no reason why I can't do the same, so don't think you're alone with that line of reasoning," Dev told her.

"Don't go too overboard with the blue uniform and such," she said dryly.

His hand tightened on his mug. "I don't intend to let them run us out, Meggie. Not the way they probably drove out my grandmother. All right, maybe her occupation wasn't the kind a kid can brag about on career day, but she must have had her reasons to do what she did. If you listened to Harry, you'd think Gram should have been named a saint. According to him, she was instrumental in bringing in a local sheriff, setting up an emergency clinic and a day-care center for working mothers during World War II. He called her a woman ahead of her time."

Dev studied his hands still wrapped around the mug. "He told me Gram ran the administrative end of the business, not the physical. Under her supervision, fights were rare, drunkenness wasn't allowed and any defiance of her rules meant expulsion." His voice lowered as he reluctantly added, "He said she was one of the most beautiful women in the world and more than half the men in town were in love with her."

"It sounds as if she was well liked," Megan said softly.

His lips thinned. "By the men."

"It also sounds as if she was respected in a time when women were expected to remain in the kitchen and to raise children. Instead, she ran a business that left most women cold and hard toward others. From what you've said, she was one of the warmest people around, one who thought more of others than of herself. My grandmother believed in delegating work, not going out and doing it."

Dev looked surprised by the candid remarks meant to bolster him. "How come we never talked like this before?"

Megan laced her fingers together, then released them. "When you're nineteen, you don't think very much about talking. Back then, you feel there're more important things to worry about than wondering what's going to happen to us five or ten years down the road," she murmured. "I didn't turn serious about life until I realized I was reading articles warning me about the hazards of too much sun on the skin, cigarettes turning my lungs black and what cholesterol was doing to my arteries. After all that, I felt downright depressed!"

He smiled at that. "How difficult was it for you to quit smoking?"

She wrinkled her nose. "My secretary threatened to quit an average of ten times a day. I rearranged my closet twice a week and I alphabetized my pantry. I also ate my way through every one of the thirty-one Baskin-Robbins flavors," she said, chuckling. "I gained twenty-five pounds and horrified my mother so much she presented me with a membership to a local health club. After a week of running aimlessly around the club's indoor track, I tore a ligament. Naturally, aerobics were out. I tried swimming next and discovered I was allergic to the high chlorine content of the club's pool. We won't even discuss what happened in the weight room or on the racquetball court. Needless to say, they asked me not to come back."

Dev ducked his head, but his shaking shoulders gave away his mirth. He coughed in a vain attempt to disguise his laughter.

"The health club gave my mother a refund and suggested I stick to long walks. Between that, staying out of Baskin-Robbins and joining a ballet class that I could handle, I finally lost the weight and vowed to never touch another cigarette. There are days when things are so bad at work, I'd kill for a smoke, but so far, I've survived."

"Most places I've been at had drinking as the main source of entertainment," Dev told her. "After a few killer hangovers, I came to realize it wasn't my thing. A buddy of mine and I were usually working together on the same projects, so we'd always fix up a basketball hoop wherever we went. We played a lot of one on one. It kept us out of the bars and pretty much out of trouble."

Megan wondered if women were listed under the heading of "trouble," but she wasn't brave enough to ask. Especially when she would probably be told in blunt terms it was none of her business. If he didn't think a person didn't need to know something about him, he said so succinctly.

Although the silence surrounding them wasn't uncomfortable, she still felt the need to break it. To get them back on the footing she was fighting so hard to keep. "If Harry can't help us, I could make some calls to connections in L.A.," she said.

Dev looked doubtful. "The shipping costs would kill us."

"Not if they could have our orders sent from San Francisco, which is a lot closer to us." She grew animated as the idea mushroomed. "I can make some calls tomorrow."

He studied her in the flickering light. The immaculately dressed yuppie he had seen the first day had changed. Tonight, Megan wore a thigh-length, floral-print shirt with cream-colored leggings and bright pink socks. Had her legs been that shapely fifteen years ago? For a woman who had the worst luck practicing physical fitness, she had a good-looking figure.

She's past history, Grant, Dev reminded himself. *Remember the hell you put each other through fifteen years ago? Deep down, how do you know she isn't going to set you up for another fall? How do you know she isn't going along with your ideas only to take the place away from you when your part of the work is done? That's something her family would think of. You know very well if her folks have anything to do with it, they'd force you out tomorrow!*

He straightened up and walked over to the pan of water still warm from previous heating. He washed out his mug and put it away.

Megan watched his slow and deliberate movements. "No comment one way or the other?" She moved onto her knees. "Not even 'what a great idea, Megan,' or a flat out 'it won't work'? Surely you can come up with something to say."

His finger circled the rim of his mug. "If you're not careful, you'll sound like the boss on this project."

Her gaze bored holes into his back. "You make it sound like a crime."

"No, just that it's like always. The ones with the money feel they can call all the shots."

Megan leapt up. "Excuse me for wanting to express an idea." She stalked past him, only pausing long enough to snatch up her sleeping bag that lay near the fire they kept burning all night to discourage unwanted visitors.

He scowled at her. "Where do you think you're going?"

She didn't look back as she headed for the screen door leading to the kitchen. "I'll sleep inside tonight."

"You were the one to complain about the rats in there."

"I can deal better with the four-legged kind." Even half hanging off its hinges, the screen door gave a satisfactory slam as Megan abruptly pulled it closed behind her.

"Damn stubborn woman," Dev muttered, turning away. "If a rat starts nibbling on your toes tonight, don't come screaming to me. Thing is, if one did, it'd probably get ptomaine!" He picked up his sleeping bag and flipped it out before smoothing it over the ground sheet. "She hasn't changed. She still thinks she knows everything."

Maybe there aren't any underlying reasons behind her willingness to help. Maybe you're acting a little too paranoid, his traitorous mind countered. *If she can get a good price for the supplies, more power to her. Right?*

"What do you know?" he grumbled out loud, shucking his boots and jeans before sliding between the covers. "You haven't been right about one thing yet."

THE IDEA OF A QUIET countryside was a lie, Megan decided, shifting around until she got comfortable. Her foolish act meant she had no choice but to choose a sleeping place among the many rooms, so she chose the drawing room as the lesser evil. In her opinion, the upstairs was too scary at night, and no way would she return outside. With the bag zipped up as far as it would go and her eyes darting from one side to the other every time she heard the least sound, she doubted she'd get a wink of sleep.

"This is all his fault," she muttered. "We're supposed to be partners in this deal, and he acts like he's the only one who knows how to work on a house. He's not the one who ruined a perfectly good manicure prying up those damn tiles!" She stiffened at the sound of tiny feet scurrying across the floor overhead. "I hope a mountain lion eats his face." As the juvenile remark sank in, she couldn't help but giggle. Since she enjoyed watching horror movies—the scarier the better—her mental picture was easy to form. The trouble was, her imagination began to work overtime as she recalled movies dealing with haunted hotels where a ghostly guest would kill off any intruder, and from there her mind wandered through variations on the same theme. Either way, the intruder always met a nasty end after inflicting ghastly deeds on the victims.

"I should have known he'd just ignore my idea. He didn't listen to me when we were married, so why should it be any different now?" She smacked the small pillow with her fist, imagining it was his face. As she angrily listed his faults, she conveniently forgot that fifteen years ago the young couple only had two activities: arguing and settling their arguments with hot and heavy sex. All she thought about was how stubborn Dev was. If nothing else, her anger helped keep fear at bay and ensured her not running outside, right into the arms of Devlin Grant.

"SLEEP WELL?" DEV ASKED pleasantly as Megan walked outside the next morning, dragging her sleeping bag behind her.

"Just fine," she replied, flashing him a bright smile while trying to look everywhere but at the bare chest revealed between the unbuttoned folds of his red plaid shirt. She remembered when his chest had been almost completely free of hair. Now whorls of dark brown hair covered it very nicely. Her fingers itched to touch him. But she wasn't about to give in to her desires again.

For punishment, she replayed some of her mother's old conversations in her head. If anything could dampen a woman's ardor, it was memories of her mother lecturing her on what a good catch Rob was. Megan insisted she only considered him a friend, but that did nothing to stop her mother from viewing him as a suitable son-in-law.

Dev watched the play of emotions cross Megan's face. He was disgruntled not to see her looking as if she had sat up half the night. Damn her, did she sleep like a baby while he lay awake waiting for her screams so he could run in and act like the perfect hero? He felt like the perfect dolt.

"We're going to need groceries," he announced abruptly.

"I'll drive in and pick up what we need. If you like, I'll even practice my charm on the hardware-store owner. Perhaps I can wheedle a few basic things out of him." Megan poured herself a cup of coffee and helped herself to a bran muffin from the package she'd picked up the last time she'd gone into town for groceries. Dev insisted cardboard was tastier.

As she ate her sparse breakfast, Megan quickly made a shopping list and handed it to him. "Anything else you can think of?"

Dev looked the list over and penciled in a few extras. Then he plucked a piece of paper out of his shirt pocket and handed it to her. "While you're in town, you might as well make some calls to your friends and see if they can get this stuff up to us within three days. I wrote down the prices Harry can get. If they can do better, then go ahead and order them."

Megan looked down at the sheet of paper covered with Dev's distinctive scrawl. She didn't have to look at him to know it took a lot for him to do this. "I'll make the calls first thing," she murmured, picking up her leather tote bag.

"Don't take the hill too fast," he called after her retreating figure.

"Eat dirt and die!"

"Very mature, Abernathy."

Megan resisted the urge to race down the dirt driveway—after running over Dev, of course.

"I think they'd call it justifiable homicide," he yelled, easily reading the thoughts written across her face.

Once the BMW's dust settled, Dev cast his eyes upward.

"Gram, I hope you're happy you did this to your favorite grandson." He wondered if he'd be struck down by lightning if he shook his fist at the bright blue morning sky. "I was a happy man. A very happy man until you dared to die and make me half owner in this house with that witch. You didn't like her the first time you met. Wasn't there an easier way to make her life miserable without making me suffer, too?"

Yeah, right, you're suffering, Grant. You're out here with a gorgeous woman who still kisses like nothing else on earth. Okay, so you're leery about trusting her too much. Considering the past, you've got a great reason. And if she can get the parts for good prices, she's got one more argument if, later on, she decides she wants the whole show. So watch your back, old friend.

He stood in the middle of the yard, his hands resting on his hips, his head bowed as all sorts of crazy thoughts entered his mind.

"Why couldn't she have turned into a troll or something?"

Chapter Five

"We can't take your check."

Megan took a deep breath. Why wasn't she surprised the announcement was made in a flat, borderline-rude voice that didn't convey one hint of apology? "You've taken my checks before without a problem as long as I showed the proper ID," she said slowly. "I've shown you my driver's license and two major credit cards. What more do you want? My blood type is O positive."

The woman looked back stoically. "It's a new policy. We don't take out-of-town checks. You'll find the nearest grocery store fifty miles south," the woman informed her. "I heard tell they even take major credit cards."

"And naturally you don't." Megan tucked her checkbook back into her bag. Her cool smile was a sight to behold for the suddenly uneasy checker. "Then I guess we have two ways of dealing with this problem," Megan said. "I can either walk out of here and leave you with the nasty task of putting all of these things away, or I can pay cash." She pulled out her wallet and withdrew the proper amount of bills. "You do still accept cash, don't you?"

The cashier immediately looked at the store manager, who appeared stunned. He gave an abrupt nod of the head and stalked off.

Megan watched the box boy quickly load the bags and pack them into a cart. As she left the store pushing the cart, she smiled at the cashier. "Have a nice day." As she passed through the automatic doors, she muttered, "In a shark-infested tank."

Megan made a quick stop at the bank to cash a check. The teller acted as close to rude as she dared while Megan's smile grew more strained by the moment.

Her trip to the hardware store proved as fruitless as Dev's.

"Sorry, I ain't got nothin' you need," the thin-mouthed owner informed her.

She stared him in the eye. "No wonder this town is dying. If I had to deal with prigs like you, I'd leave, too. Mr. Grant and I are doing something that could bring new life into this town while all of you are fighting it."

The man's eyes narrowed. "That house is nothing more than an abomination to the town. It should be torn down and the land left to rot the way its occupants rotted."

Megan studied him, mentally figuring his age. "Don't tell me, you were one of their best customers." The flicker of expression in his cold eyes gave her her answer. "You hypocrite," she whispered, her narrowed gaze slicing through him like a heated knife. "You probably went up there every Saturday night and set the bedsprings squeaking a raucous melody."

"Get out of my store!"

"Gladly," she spat out, uncaring of their audience unashamedly listening to every word. "The air has gotten too foul in here.'' She stalked out, pushing the glass door open with the heel of her palm.

Megan's anger grew so strong inside her that as she looked around and spied the innocuous shingle hanging in front of a building she moved toward it, without thinking of what she might be doing.

''What are you doing?'' the secretary demanded as Megan walked past her desk. ''You can't go in there!''

''Watch me.'' She pushed open the door and entered Ezra Hawkins's inner office.

The older man looked startled by the intrusion. ''Miss Abernathy, this isn't—''

She planted her hands on top of his desk. ''I'll tell you what isn't,'' she stated. ''Let me bring up a few choice words I'm sure you'll understand. Discrimination and prejudice are the major ones. I've read about small towns where people help each other in times of trouble. Then there're ones like this, where people band together to protest what could be a very positive idea if they cared to look at it objectively. A small town with a small mind. Tell Mrs. St. Clair we aren't going to be run out and that if anything destructive happens, I'll have a big-city attorney up here so fast her tiny head will spin.'' She straightened up, dusting her hands on the back of her slacks as if touching the furniture here was distasteful to her.

''We don't cotton to threats, Miss Abernathy,'' Hawkins intoned, regaining composure once she'd put some distance between them.

''Oh, I never threaten, Mr. Hawkins. I only promise.'' Having said her piece, she left as abruptly as she entered.

Megan made a last stop at the gas station, hurriedly pumping gas into her car's tank before the attendant could run out and tell her they were closed. By now, she wouldn't put it past anyone. After giving him a slight smile, she handed the man the money and dug through her pockets for coins as she walked toward the pay phone.

"It don't work," he called after her.

She spun around. "Amazing. Isn't it a good thing I have a car phone." She climbed into her car and sped off, relishing the fact she missed the startled man's toes by inches as he jumped back.

"Maybe a Victorian inn would have been better here. They all have the right kind of thinking," she muttered, pressing down on the accelerator with more force than necessary. She immediately lifted her foot. "With my luck, I'd end up thrown in jail on a trumped-up charge." She waited until she was completely out of town before she pulled off to the side of the road and picked up her phone while digging through her bag for her Day Runner. Within moments, she arranged for the supplies to arrive within forty-eight hours. She even got them at a price better than Dev could hope for.

"You can't complain about this, Devlin Grant," she murmured, tucking the sheet into her bag and pulling back onto the road. "Because if you do, I will pull your head off and feed it to the first mountain lion I can find."

"YOU GONNA QUIT SPINNING your neck around to look out the window watching for that gal?" Harry squinted as he carefully replaced a section of wiring. "Hand me those needle-nose pliers, will ya?"

"She should have been back long ago." Dev dug through the box for the proper tool. "It doesn't take four hours to pick up groceries. If she was clothes shopping, I wouldn't expect her for a week. I can't imagine she finds grocery stores that fascinating.''

"Maybe she did decide to do some shopping. Women like to do that. Sure know mine does.''

"Meggie's idea of shopping is roaming through the stores on Rodeo Drive.'' Dev kept his eyes trained outside. "No, something happened. She said she was going to visit the hardware store. Knowing her temper, she probably got in a fight with the owner and got herself thrown in jail.''

"If she had, we would have heard by now.'' Harry carefully wrapped the wires together and placed them back in the wall.

"Not if they're holding her without bail. The lady has a mouth you wouldn't believe. She can emasculate a man in seconds.''

Harry's brow furrowed in a frown. "Does *emasculate* mean what I think it does?''

"In Meggie's case, worse. Much worse.'' Dev turned as he heard the powerful purr of the BMW. "It's about time.'' He set down his tools and walked outside, pausing beside the car as it slid to a stop. "Where the hell have you been?''

"If you don't yell, I'll tell you.''

He took a deep breath. "Meggie . . .''

She ignored his unspoken warning as she hopped out of the car and walked around to the trunk. "The grocery store refused to take my check.''

Dev swore under his breath. "You drove fifty miles to the next store?''

Megan shook her head. "They couldn't refuse my cash.'' She smiled smugly. "The man at the hardware store is not at all happy that I figured out he used to be a regular customer here. And thanks to my car phone, we'll have our supplies in two days." She smirked. "And you consider car phones a joke! My connection even asked for the first reservation when the house opens. He's an avid fisherman."

"And you did all this in four hours?"

She shook her head as she opened the trunk. "No. I also picked up some toiletries and work clothing for me." She began pulling out bags. "Plus another ice chest, several bags of ice and a couple of steaks for us to grill tonight. I don't know about you, but I'm sick of meals coming out of cans."

Dev's jaw dropped open in shock as he saw that the trunk and the back seat were filled with packages.

Megan turned to face him, the bags she was carrying swinging by her side. "Oh, by the way, Ezra Hawkins is going to claim I threatened him. Believe me, I didn't. I only made a promise." She turned toward the house again. "Want to bring in some of the heavier bags?"

"You threatened an attorney!" Dev had practically yelled, but he only received a wave of a hand as she walked through the open door. "Harry, want a cold beer?"

"The woman is nuts," Dev muttered, picking up three bags and cradling them in his arms. "Absolutely bonkers. No wonder she's never remarried. By the time she finished flapping that sharp tongue of hers, the poor guy wouldn't have any skin left."

"She got what we needed?" Harry walked out the door and took one of the bags out of Dev's arms.

Dev nodded. "Probably browbeat the guy until he gave in."

The older man chuckled. "She's somethin'."

"'Something' is right. I guess we should be grateful there's only one of her."

Harry scratched his head. "When I first saw her, I figured her for one of those city women who'd bitch and moan if she didn't have electricity and heat and running water. But Meggie hasn't complained once. No, sir. She's a gutsy lady. Considering you two are so friendly, I'm surprised you're divorced."

Dev laughed. "Let me put it this way. Our divorce has lasted longer than our marriage."

"But you were just kids back then. It's not as if you had anything of value between you." Harry knew they had divorced while in their late teens, but that was all Dev had said when first asked.

"I didn't have anything, but Meggie did, and her parents wanted to make sure I didn't try to get anything from her. By the time we entered a courtroom, we hated each other so much it's surprising one of us hadn't committed murder."

Harry clucked his tongue and shook his head. "Never could understand these people who look at marriage as something that can be dissolved by a judge's words and a piece of paper. When I was growing up, I was taught marriages were for better or worse and when things got worse, you just stuck around till things got better again. Shame how everything is so disposable nowadays. Plates, diapers, marriages..."

Dev nudged the door open with his hip. "Yeah, well, that's the nineties."

"Slowpoke." Megan passed him in the hallway on her way back outside. Within seconds, she returned carrying more packages.

"What all did you buy besides groceries?" Dev demanded, setting the bags on the kitchen table.

"I told you. Toiletries and some work clothing for me. I can't wear yours all the time." She breezed past him.

He thought of the way his denim cutoffs fit her so well. They never looked that good on him! "You don't see me complaining."

"I'd just feel more comfortable wearing my own clothing."

"Instead of you flitting around the countryside, we could have used your help here." Deep down, Dev knew he was acting like a jerk, but, dammit, the woman had that way of looking at him as if he didn't have the brains of a flea!

"Harry doesn't believe women should fool around with electrical wiring," she coolly informed him, slapping a white bag into his hand. "So I did the womanly thing by going shopping." She stalked out of the kitchen with her head held high.

"Damn fool woman," Dev muttered, eying the bag warily, as if afraid a snake was in it. He wouldn't put it past her. He opened it carefully and peeked inside. Allergy capsules. She had obviously remembered that the rose bushes were bothering him and had picked up pills for him.

He looked around at the old floor tiles stacked neatly in one corner while boxes of the new tiles lay in another. The Formica counters shone and the cabinets were free of old paint, revealing lovely wood. "Damn fool me."

As much as he hated apologies, Dev knew he was going to have to make one. And if he was smart, he'd do it immediately.

As he approached the room Megan kept her clothes in, he heard the muttered curses she was angrily heaping on his head. He winced at one particular method of torture Megan wanted to subject him to.

"The woman is evil," he sighed. "There is no way she can be sane."

"What are you mumbling about?" She appeared in the doorway, her hands braced on her hips.

"I wanted to apologize for what I said. I shouldn't have said what I did when you've been willing to do more than your share," he blurted out. "And I wanted to thank you for picking up the allergy pills for me."

Megan studied his face, looking for insincerity. He stared back at her. All anger left her body as something else began to fill it. First, there was that old tingle deep inside that slowly radiated outward. Then the room temperature seemed to rise. Not a lot, but enough to catch her attention. And, unfortunately, Dev's.

"Meggie?" His voice was husky, questioning.

She looked as if she was going to step closer to him, then quickly changed her mind. "It isn't a good idea."

He was the one to step closer. "Why not?"

"Because, considering everything, we'd probably end up in a fight," she said bluntly.

He looked down at her crisp new jeans with the factory-induced faded look, a turquoise T-shirt tucked neatly into the waistband. A faint lacy pattern was discernible under the soft cotton top. His eyes mirrored his disappointment that she was wearing a bra. "And maybe we wouldn't. We didn't that time down in the drawing room."

Her eyes darkened with the memory. "Only because Mrs. St. Clair interrupted us."

"Yeah, but we'll never know, unless we try again." He effectively trapped her against the wall.

"We're too volatile together. It wouldn't be safe." There was no mistaking the sorrow in her eyes. But along with that was a stubbornness Dev could easily read. "We're better off remembering this is a business deal between us."

He leaned forward and brushed his lips across hers several times. Each time, her lips parted a fraction more. "Yeah, we're volatile, all right," he whispered. "Except it has nothing to do with arguing. Don't you remember that old saying, Meggie? 'Make love, not war.' The former would be a lot more enjoyable."

"Dev, boy, we've got a lot of work to do before the day is over." Harry's shout could be heard all through the house.

Megan almost collapsed with relief. At the rate Dev's verbal seduction was going, she would have been a goner in about three more minutes.

"I still have things to put away." She expected Dev to step back and was unnerved to see he had no such intention.

Dev grinned. "We're not finished yet, darlin'," he drawled. "But since there's a third party in the house, I'll let you go. We can always take this up later."

"In your dreams, Grant," she muttered, pushing past him.

"I figured we were getting real close, what with wearing the same clothes and all," he called after her retreating figure.

Her steps faltered. His comment forced her to realize he'd been wearing the same cutoffs she'd been wearing.

"I won't even dignify that with an answer." Her haughty tone was enough to freeze the air around them as she practically ran down the hallway and out of sight.

Dev didn't stop grinning. "Ah, but, sweetheart, you just did."

MEGAN WENT IN SEARCH OF the most physical task she could find. After their last confrontation she needed something that would force her to think about anything but him. In the end, it turned out to be cleaning the mold and mildew out of the master bedroom shower so she could chip out the grout and pry off the old tiles.

"No wonder my cleaning lady demands so much money," she groused. "If I had to do something this disgusting on a regular basis, I'd expect to be paid a small fortune for my services, too."

She was doing fine with keeping Dev out of her mind until a mental picture of them sharing this shower came to mind. She just started scrubbing harder, as if the cleaner would erase the image at the same time. It didn't help.

"I WANT TO STAND UNDER a hot shower for at least an hour." Megan pulled her braid free, combing the crinkly strands with her fingers. "Then I want to fill the tub with equally hot water and soak for another hour. I don't care if I look like a prune afterwards, I'll be clean."

"You don't want much, do you?" Dev studied his sandwich with varying degrees of distaste. "How come when it's your turn to cook, we get peanut butter and jelly sandwiches?"

"Probably because I don't cook. Correction, I can't cook. Besides, you claimed you only wanted a snack while you got the stove going for the steaks." Megan opened a can of diet Coke and drank thirstily. "Do you have any idea how awful a filthy shower smells?"

He sniffed. "Somewhat like you?"

A look of disgust crossed her face as she lifted her arm and sniffed her wrist. "Ugh! I smell like mold!"

Dev tightened his lips so he wouldn't laugh at Megan's horrified expression. He sensed any laughter on his part would invoke physical violence on hers. He looked away and coughed into his hand. As it was, it'd taken several hours of hard labor to stop thinking about that lace outline against her T-shirt. And just when he had succeeded, it was time to knock off and he was confronted with that same picture.

"Maybe some of that French dusting powder of yours will kill the smell," he suggested.

She looked as if she wanted to cry. "Nothing will kill this! This is the kind of smell that never comes out. It just lingers, making people think of dirty locker rooms when you walk past them."

"Some people like the smell of dirty locker rooms. Although, I wouldn't mind if you'd stand a bit more downwind."

Megan moaned softly and drew her legs up against her chest.

Dev bit into his sandwich and gamely chewed the gummy concoction. "You honestly mean you can't cook anything?" His words were a bit garbled. "I thought you only fixed sandwiches because they were quick and both of us were sometimes too tired to care what we ate."

She fixed him with a telling look. "My only cooking is done with a microwave. And as we don't have any electricity yet, that's a moot point, isn't it?"

"I thought you said you got straight A's in home ec."

Megan was surprised he remembered that little piece of information from so many years ago. "Those straight A's were the sewing part, not the cooking."

He set his sandwich back on his paper plate. "Yeah, I can see why."

She bristled as she jumped to her feet. "And you think you do any better?"

"You don't complain the nights I cook," he pointed out.

"You warm up cans of Campbell's soup! How much in the way of brain power does that take!"

"Obviously more than you have since you don't seem to have even that talent."

Megan's eyes narrowed to slits. "In about two seconds I'm going to hit you."

"If you do, I'll burn your steak to a crisp—and you know very well you hate your steaks well done."

That stopped her cold. "For someone who vowed to erase me from his personal memory banks, you've retained a lot of old information."

"Things just pop out every so often. I didn't think it was a crime." Dev leaned over her, resting one hand on the counter, effectively trapping her against the edge. "Come on, admit it," he coaxed, "you remember stuff about me."

"Nothing."

"Sure you do."

She looked him square in the eye. "Zip."

He help up his forefinger. "Not even one tiny little thing?"

Megan shook her head. She didn't care if lightning struck her dead. There was no way she was going to admit long-buried memories were surfacing a bit at a time. While her memories of a boy paled considerably in comparison to the flesh-and-blood man standing in front of her, a few of the others were still enough to get the juices flowing more than she cared to think about. It took a lot of willpower, but she managed to keep her gaze filled with indifference. Considering he was so close to her she could smell the warm, slightly sweaty tang of his skin, it wasn't easy to picture him as someone who ranked just above the role of a stranger.

"My life has been very full," she said finally. "Thinking about the past is low on my list."

"Don't hold it in, Meggie. Just let it out. Don't worry about hurting my feelings," he ground out, feeling more than a little irritated that she could sound so cool and indifferent. He straightened up and stepped back, needing to put distance between them. Megan may smell like a locker room, but she was still a very sexy woman. He tried to put it down to being without feminine company for a long time, but it didn't work as well as he'd hoped. Dammit, couldn't she have thought about him at least once? Would it have hurt her? The least she could have done was lie to him! After all, they had been married. He ignored the tiny voice chanting that he hadn't exactly been in mourning all these years.

Megan took a deep breath as she eased her back from the sharp edge of the counter. "Perhaps we do have unresolved feelings between us, Dev, but that isn't the issue here. Your ego is injured because, deep down, you hoped I would have cried buckets of tears over you. If you recall, we both were only too happy to regain our freedom. I came up here—"

"Because you felt guilty," he chimed in.

She nodded. "Yes, but also because I wanted to tell you that face-to-face. I've been going through a lot of transitions in my life lately and I felt time away from my territory, so to speak, would help me put things into their proper perspective. Working on this house has helped. And seeing you again, seeing the changes in you has also helped me see that my parents and I didn't do any irrevocable damage. I'd be the first to admit that my parents are more than a little overpowering. Once I gained some common sense in that area, I taught myself to deal with them. Now I'm teaching myself to deal with me.''

"I'm still not used to this new you. I mean, there hasn't been one screaming tantrum because you hadn't gotten your way,'' he murmured, studying her.

"I told you, I grew up. I don't know if it can be done, but I'd like to think we can end up friends.''

Dev's face creased in a smile. "That would be a new experience for us, wouldn't it? We were lovers before we really knew all that much about each other. And we were married before we grew up. I guess since we're business partners, the least we can do is keep it on a friendly basis. Yeah, I'd like to see that, too.''

Megan beamed. Maybe this would all work out after all and she could walk away with her sanity intact. "All right. Now, I have a few things to do before it gets too dark to work, and I just heard Harry's truck return.''

Dev nodded and turned as if to leave the kitchen. Just as quickly, he spun back around and hauled Megan into his arms. Before she could voice any form of protest, he covered her mouth with his, kissing her as thoroughly as a man could, until he felt her grow limp in his arms. Keeping a broad smile on his face, he gently put her from him. "Just sealing our friendship.''

He walked out, leaving a shaken Megan hanging on to the counter edge. She gripped it tightly, taking deep breaths until she felt her respiration rate return to as close to normal as possible. Even then, she found it difficult to focus her eyes. She wiped the back of her hand across her forehead, unsurprised that it came away damp.

"If that's how he seals a friendship, what he does in a more intimate relationship must really blow a woman's socks off. Along with a few other items of clothing."

Chapter Six

"It's amazing how much dirt can accumulate in a house closed up for almost forty years," Megan said with a sigh, looking around what had once been Maisie's bedroom.

Dev remained in the doorway. "We took all the mattresses and furniture beyond help out to the dump, so that leaves you plenty of room to work in."

Megan smiled, recalling the colorful curses as Dev and Harry wrestled the furniture down the stairway and into Harry's truck.

She eyed the peeling wallpaper with water stains obscuring the delicate trailing rose design. "Thank goodness you two finally finished the rewiring. I can use the steamer to get this mess off."

"Yeah, we're starting work on the plumbing today. Harry's brother is driving out to help us." Dev grinned. "I'd hate to hook up pipes and discover that flushing the toilet turned on the shower instead."

"Just make sure you hook up the hot water to the hot and cold to the cold," Megan advised, plugging in the wallpaper steamer unit. She turned around in time to catch his frown. "What's wrong?"

He shrugged, clearly uncomfortable with his train of thought. "It's just that this was Gram's room, and I can't help but wonder..." His voice trailed off and he looked off into the distance, lips tight with feeling.

Her heart melted at his sad discomfort. "Dev, don't do this to yourself. From what Harry has said your grandmother was a fine woman. And it didn't seem that she...that anyone ever..." She grimaced. "I think I'll quit while I'm ahead."

From the beginning, it hadn't been difficult to see Maisie's past was a sore point with Dev. Megan had watched him keep a deliberate distance from the upstairs rooms, and even from the drawing room, except for the day of their impromptu pillow fight. She wondered how he managed to hold his tongue while working with the garrulous Harry, whose chief occupation, besides all-around handyman, was to talk about the good old days at Maisie's Place. She wished she had the courage to walk over and put her arms around him. But while Dev still enjoyed tormenting her with quick, heated kisses and brushing his fingers across the back of her neck when she least expected it, he didn't do anything to invite the idea of comfort.

A memory suddenly intruded. She recalled long ago when they walked out of the courthouse after hearing their divorce had been granted. Megan had looked over her shoulder. People swarmed out of the courthouse, walking around his still figure. Dev stood there looking very much alone. She wondered now if he was aware of the few times he had revealed his true feelings.

"Once the windows are washed, the wallpaper replaced and the walls painted, it will look like a new room," she said brightly, hoping she could divert his thoughts. "Working in here will be a pleasant change after the bathrooms."

"I guess this isn't what you expected when we started all this restoring," Dev said quietly.

"My hands and nails will probably never be the same again, and I'm certain I'm suffering from permanent curvature of the spine from bending over," she said flippantly. "But I have to admit it's a challenge and, strangely, a lot of fun."

He stood there studying her for several moments. The expression on his face was so serious, Megan started to get worried.

"Dev, are you all right?" she ventured, holding out her hand.

He blinked several times before turning his head and looking at her as if seeing her for the first time. "I'm learning a lot, too," he said quietly. Before she could question him further, he walked away, shouting something to Harry.

Megan found her enthusiasm a bit dampened as she returned to her exploration of the large bedroom and adjoining sitting room. She'd already pulled down the sapphire blue velvet drapes and now threw open the windows to allow fresh air inside.

Megan went to work in the sitting room first. By using a rag-covered broom, she attacked the spiderwebs, coughing and sneezing her way through her chore.

Slapping the broom against one particularly stubborn web, she hit a corner of the fireplace and was stunned to see one of the stones fall onto the floor. She picked it up, planning to replace it when she noticed the hole was more than just an empty space. She crouched down and peered inside. The square interior was filled with some kind of package. "There better not be anything alive in there.'' She screwed up her courage and reached inside, touching oilcloth. She pulled the package out and carefully peeled back the covering to find several slim leather-bound notebooks. ''What do we have here?'' she murmured, opening one of the books.

''Maisie's book of thoughts for 1944'' was written in a delicate script across the inside cover.

Megan flipped through the other books, discovering they bore the same inscription for different years.

''A diary,'' she breathed, leafing through a few pages before closing the last book. Excited with her find, she quickly ran to the door, prepared to share her discovery with Dev. Then she stepped back. Something warned her Dev wouldn't be as excited as she was. Before she could change her mind again, she quickly rewrapped the books and stashed them back in their hiding place, the stone firmly lodged in place.

For the rest of the day, Megan's mind was more on the hidden journals than on her work. Every time she heard Dev's voice or laughter in the distance, she wondered if she shouldn't tell him, after all. Eventually, she decided to skim the books first, and if there wasn't anything damaging in the contents, she'd give them to Dev and urge him to read them. ''Megan, you are so clever.'' She mentally patted herself on the back.

''Clever at what?''

Her shriek left her lips before she could stop it. She spun around, her hand covering her breast.

''If you ever do something that horrible again, I will rip your heart out,'' she gasped.

Dev looked astonished by her vehemence. ''What did I do?''

She gulped much needed air. ''Scare me half to death. I didn't hear you come in.''

"I made enough noise for a herd of horses. But you seemed deep in thought. So, what were you clever about?"

"Scraping this paint off without harming the wood underneath," she said quickly.

Dev stood there in his loose-hipped stance, studying her face for something undefinable. Megan watched him with the blandest smile this side of the Mississippi. Thanks to her quick thinking she doubted he would find out the truth. "Is there anything wrong?" she asked with incredible innocence in her voice. "Do I have dirt on my face?" She reached up to touch her cheek.

He shook his head. "No." He appeared reluctant to leave, although he wouldn't step over the threshold. "How's it going in here?"

She gave a nonchalant shrug of the shoulders. "Coming along slowly but surely. After I finish the downstairs rooms, I want to work in here."

"You can work where you want." His features tightened as he looked around. "Thanks to Harry's brother, we should have running water in the downstairs bathroom by the end of the week. What's going to take the most time is replacing all those old copper pipes." He made a face. "We probably would have been better off tearing the place down and starting fresh."

"That would be like tearing down the Lincoln Memorial!" she protested.

"It doesn't have to worry about plumbing and electrical problems."

She didn't hesitate. "If you don't feel you can continue with the house, I'll buy out your half and finish it myself."

Dev had a difficult time holding on to his temper. He still had vague suspicions that Megan might be trying to wrest the house from him. Although she hadn't even intimated anything like that, it still occasionally gnawed at him. And lately, his nerves were a bit jangled as he became more and more familiar with the house his grandmother once owned and used as a place of business. By refusing to admit it bothered him, keeping everything in had left him sometimes difficult to deal with. Such as today. "Thanks for the offer, but no thanks. I doubt you could run a sports lodge," he scoffed. "You'd probably want to serve the guests finger sandwiches and offer white wine with dinner." With that, he walked out.

"Finger sandwiches! You ingrate, I could probably do a better job than you," she shouted after him.

"Twit," he called over his shoulder.

Megan's scowl furrowed her brow as she returned to her paint scraping. "Twit," she mumbled. "This from the man who once thought Stradivarius was a division of Levi Strauss."

"THAT WOMAN IS ENOUGH to give a man ulcers," Dev grumbled to himself as he strained and pulled to loosen a stubborn length of pipe. His anger gave him the needed extra strength.

"To hear you talk for the last hour, people'd think you don't like the girl," Harry commented around the cigar he was chewing on.

"There're days when I could cheerfully throttle that little she-devil." The veins in Dev's arms bulged from his exertions.

"Then why'd you marry her?"

"Lust, pure and simple. She had a way of wiggling her behind when she walked that left a guy panting."

"Like I said, why'd you marry her?" Harry grinned. "Why not just have some of that free love all the kids want?"

"Free love was back in the sixties. We were into doing our own thing and as much a rebel as I was back then, some traditional part of me insisted on marrying her instead of just having a hot-and-heavy teen affair." Dev found himself uncomfortable with discussing Megan like this with a man who, for all he knew, had had an affair with his grandmother!

"I like Megan," the older man announced. "She's got a good head on her shoulders. And she isn't afraid of hard work."

Dev swore under his breath when a ragged piece of the pipe end scraped his forearm. "Yeah, she has her good points, as few as they are."

"'Pears to me you're still sweet on her."

Dev gritted his teeth. "I learned my lesson about women like Megan a long time ago. They're better off playing shallow games with shallow men and not bothering to learn anything about real life."

"So if you dislike her so much, why did you let her stick around and help fix the house up?"

"Because I didn't have the money to buy her half, and she had the money to pay for the renovations."

"Some people would say that makes you shallow to be willing to use a woman's money like that."

Dev turned his head so fast, he almost suffered whiplash. Harry stood behind him looking as innocent as a newborn babe. "It's a business deal, that's all."

"Business deals have been known to get personal," Harry pointed out, still talking around his cigar.

"We're making sure this one won't be. Ten to one, once the house is finished, Megan will run back to her yuppie friends and fast-lane career."

Harry shook his head.

"Now what?" Dev asked, exasperated.

"That doesn't sound like the Megan I've gotten to know."

"Believe me, that's her all the way." But the more Dev thought about his disparaging words, the less certain he felt. He knew he had said some cruel things about Megan. Things she didn't deserve, considering all the hard work she had put into the house so far. No matter how hard he tried to deny it, he had to admit Megan had truly grown up and that the new Megan was a hundred percent improved.

"Just think about it, boy," Harry went on. "The Megan you remember was young, probably impetuous, someone used to following her folks' lead. She hadn't learned to stand on her own feet yet. Maybe I didn't know her back then, but I'd still say it wouldn't hurt you to consider that."

Dev looked at the older man with new insight. "Harry, you old coot, are you trying to play matchmaker?"

"Me?" He chuckled. "Hell, my wife would tell you I'm about as romantic as a fence post. Naw, I just don't see any use in the two of you squabbling when you're both working toward the same goal—to see this old house be something again. Maisie would be proud of the two of you doing all this."

"I still say you're trying to play Cupid," Dev playfully accused, punching the older man's arm lightly.

"No, but if shooting arrows in your butts would accomplish something, I'd probably try it."

MEGAN WAS SO TIRED, she was past exhaustion. She sat propped against the doorway joining the master suite's two rooms as she looked around at the interiors now blissfully dust and cobweb free. Her back ached, her hands were dry and cracked, and her nails were...well, they just weren't there. She made a mental note to use extra hand cream that night.

"You've been busy."

She lifted her head, aware she probably looked as tired as she felt.

"I don't talk to people who call me a twit."

"What if that person apologizes for calling you a twit?"

She rolled her tongue around her cheek. "Okay, and you're not really an ingrate. As for being busy, that's an understatement. If you weighed the dust and dirt I've swept out of these rooms, you'd see the ton marker rise sky-high," she told him, not bothering to move.

Dev walked over and crouched down in front of her. "You've got dirt on your face," he said softly while his eyes catalogued every inch of her face. "And I really do apologize."

"I have dirt everywhere," she corrected.

He lifted one hand and inspected the ragged nails and the skin cracked from exposure to harsh cleansers. "You should wear rubber gloves."

She grimaced. "They made my skin itch. I'll just use lots of cream tonight."

Dev lifted his head. "Maybe the budget should be stretched to include some help for you." His soft voice washed over her like a warm shower.

Megan shook her head. "No, actually, I'm happy doing all of this on my own. Oh, there're days when my muscles tell me how crazy I am and I start thinking about a month at a spa, but it doesn't matter." She laughed at the skepticism showing in his face. "Honest, Dev, it doesn't. I'm honestly enjoying myself."

"I just hate to see you ruin your hands." He brushed his lips across her reddened knuckles.

A harsh breath slammed against her throat at the whisper-soft touch. For a moment, she couldn't think of a reply. She stared down at his downcast head. Her fingers itched to brush that unruly lock of hair away from his forehead. "Some tender loving care and they'll be fine. Believe me, this work's a lot more fun than dealing with demanding clients and guzzling Maalox by the gallon."

Dev frowned. "Is your work that high-pressure? You never said it affected you that badly."

Her shoulders rose and fell in a fatalistic shrug. "It's all part of the game."

"Endangering your health isn't worth any job."

"Hey," she murmured, now having the courage to cradle his bearded chin with her palm. "Don't do this, Dev. My parents like to rant and rave about how I would have been better off practicing law. Yet my dad has a peptic ulcer, and my mother still gets hives before a new court case. They just don't see that we all deal with our work in different ways." Her fingers lingered over his cheek.

All he had to do was move his mouth a fraction of an inch and he could taste her, Dev realized. Move it a bit more and he could taste her mouth. Find out if it was still as sweet as it was the first time he kissed her. He wanted her to turn back into that deliciously wanton creature he had once held in his arms. The one who had always made him feel like the biggest stud alive. He looked up and saw her answer in her eyes. She wanted that just as much as he did.

"Dev?" she whispered, using her tongue to dampen her lips.

He leaned forward and repeated her movements. Her soft moan filled his mouth as he leaned forward even more to deepen their kiss. His hand snaked under her shirt and found her breast, smooth and warm to the touch. She sighed as he rolled her nipple between his fingers. It was so right! So perfect! Just as he always remembered during that time when they were young, in lust and—

"Stupid." Without thinking, he'd said the word out loud, heedless of the consequences.

Megan reared back as if she'd been slapped. "Stupid?" She stared at him. *"Stupid?"*

Dev grimaced, silently cursing his big mouth. "Meggie, I wasn't talking about us, here and now."

"Of course, you weren't." Her words dropped acid sweet on his head. "It was nothing more than an error. The word just happened to pop out of your mouth. It's just like that fairy tale when frogs popped out of the ugly princess's mouth every time she spoke. I'm sure she didn't think, either. Do us both a favor and leave before I take the broom handle to the back of your hard little head!"

The determined gleam in her eyes sent Dev out faster than any number of verbal warnings would have.

Megan barely blinked before Dev disappeared from the room. "That man always could put his size-eleven foot in his size-four mouth without too much effort," she muttered, pushing herself away from the door-jamb. "It just goes to show that maturity doesn't necessarily control all parts of the brain."

Chapter Seven

"You still mad at me for speaking first and thinking afterwards?" Dev asked.

"No, I just stopped and considered the source." Megan stabbed her fork through the lamb chops Dev had barbecued.

He winced every time the tines penetrated the tender meat. He had an uneasy feeling she was visualizing the fork stabbing him instead of the meat. "So, you get a lot done today?" he asked with false cheer.

"Maisie's room is about as clean as I can get it. I'll start steaming the wallpaper off tomorrow." She picked up the two plates and shoved one of them at Dev's chest. Unfortunately, the paper plate only bent.

Dev noticed Megan ate her meal with the same deliberate grace she used with all her tasks. Funny, he had never thought of a woman eating as erotic, but there was something about the way Megan did it that tightened the muscles in his stomach and sent his mind wandering through other ways she could use those perfect white teeth. He shifted his body, now uncomfortably aware just how tight his jeans had become in the past few moments. He was grateful the lamplight was dim enough to hide him from her sharp eyes. Wouldn't she just love to make some smartass comment on his present state of arousal! Amazing how one woman could send him through a wide range of emotions. Some of them dealing with murder. The others dealing with beds instead of guns. Maybe even a shower or whirlpool bath. Yeah, all that swirling water could create some real interesting situations! He shifted around and cursed under his breath. He really had to get his mind off sex! As if that was possible with her around.

"What is wrong with you?" Megan demanded. She frowned at him as she snatched the paper plate and plastic utensils from his hands and carried them over to the trash bag.

"What do you mean?"

"You've been sitting there for the past ten minutes groaning and muttering under your breath. I've asked you the same question three times, and all you've done is ignore me." She made quick work of their trash and tied the bag up tightly.

"So what did you ask?"

She muttered something very uncomplimentary under her breath. "I asked if Harry and Charlie will be here tomorrow or not."

"Yeah, they'll be here." He paused, noticing how her dark hair was highlighted by the lantern. "You want to know what I was really thinking?"

"It was probably something private."

"Private about the two of us." He shot to his feet and walked over to her. "I was thinking how sexy you look in those jeans and how that T-shirt shows off the body I want to find out about all over again."

Megan's breath slammed against her chest. She tilted her head back to look better at his taut features. "Dev, no." Her warning was weak in her ears.

"It's not that easy, Meggie," he bit out. "Especially when you're wearing that sexy perfume and displaying flashes of lace at odd times. I'm not dead. I'm a man who hasn't been with a woman for a long time." The moment the words left his mouth, he knew he'd made a major error.

She reared back. "So you're basically saying I'm convenient."

He knew he was going to hate himself in the morning. But how else was he going to be able to keep her at arm's length? "Yeah."

Her smile told him she didn't believe him. "Well, then, let me give you something to think about." She wrapped her arms around his neck and pulled him down for a kiss that involved lips, teeth and tongue. The kind of kiss that left a man so hard with arousal, he could easily shatter into a thousand pieces. The kind of kiss no red-blooded man could ignore. By the time she finished, Megan had made sure the air around them crackled with sexual vibrations. Then stepped back. Dev looked as if he'd gone through a major battle. "Pleasant dreams." She gathered up her sleeping bag and flashlight.

"Yeah." He sounded shell-shocked.

Megan hid her smile of triumph as she walked into the house. For once, she was the victor, and it felt so good!

Despite that good feeling she lay sleepless for over an hour, staring up at the ceiling in the master suite, trying to make sense of the shadows on the surface from the moon shining through the windows.

"Maybe some reading would help." She turned over and flicked on her flashlight, then crawled out of her sleeping bag and headed for the fireplace's hiding place.

After selecting the journal with the earliest date, she settled back in her sleeping bag to read.

March 4, 1937.
Only three months into this year and I have turned twenty-one and lost my mother. She told me on her deathbed she didn't expect me to keep the house open. What an odd word to use as a description. Yes, this is a house. A house holding ten women. Women who couldn't find any work in this depressed area and, therefore, came to my mother seeking help. And she gave it. She watched over them like a mother hen. What a shame so many didn't know her like I did. She had a beautiful speaking and singing voice, loved nature and read the classics. Yet, the so-called "good women" of the town shunned her and treated her like a deadly illness. No wonder she sent me away to school. Had they no idea she was so ill this past year? More likely, they didn't care. If it hadn't been for Barney's compassion and his letter begging me to come home, I would have learned of Mother's illness too late. And, I'm certain, she would have made sure I never learned of her well-kept secret—that she ran a brothel. I don't hate her for choosing that life. After all, it appears it has been the occupation of our female ancestors of the past several generations. And, for all I know, it will be mine, because someone has to keep this house running.

October 31, 1937.
Wouldn't the "good women" of the town be surprised to know the newest "fallen woman" chose to remain a virgin until the right man came along.

Their icy stares don't upset me as much as make me
pity them. After all, it's their husbands who come
to visit my ladies. Mother was right. If they paid
more attention to their husbands, they wouldn't
come see us at all. Although, some of the clients
are single men like Barney. Except he isn't a client.
He is a very dear friend who gives me so much as
we spend evenings listening to classical music and
discussing books. He admits he hates to see me
work as a madam, but he also understands my
need to look after Mama's ladies. But I've seen the
truth in his eyes when a man walks in and thinks
I'm for sale. Still, I never turn him away the times
he comes, and if he's still there for breakfast, it's
my business and my business only. Because I will
never take any kind of help or money from the man
I love. The man I gave my innocence to because I
knew he was the right one to accept my gift. He
made it so beautiful for me that I'm glad I waited
for him.

Megan smiled. "Oh, Maisie, you were only a woman
in love." She quickly turned the page, eager to learn
more about the mysterious Barney. She wondered if he
was still alive.

December 31, 1937.
I told Barney he mustn't come back. I'm so in love
with him, but I can't allow him to ruin his political chances. Not when he's come so far and could
even run for governor. He needs to marry the right
kind of woman, and it's a well-known fact I'm not
that kind of woman. His father made that only too
clear when he came here to try to buy me off. I felt

sick that he thought I could be bought off, and I refused his money. I didn't bother to tell him that I loved Barney enough to give him up. It hurts so much, I know I will never recover. But I will go on, because there will be one more life to depend on me in seven months. I carry on the family tradition of bearing my child out of wedlock. But I will survive, because I know the child is a result of great love, and because my child's father is the man I gave my virtue to. No other man will ever mean as much to me, because you can only truly love once.

Megan swiped at the tears streaming down her cheeks. "Oh, Maisie," she whispered, sniffing several times. "You were convinced your bloodline was destined to always love and lose. I guess Dev's and my divorce only confirmed your theory, didn't it?"

Megan closed the book and rewrapped it, making sure it was secure in its hiding place before she snapped off the flashlight and settled back under the folds of the down sleeping bag. Her mind raced. What if her and Dev's coming here was to change history? To show that there were second chances?

Could they?

"I'M SORRY."

Dev turned around so suddenly, drops of hot coffee splashed on his wrist. He swore under his breath and wiped the drops off with the other sleeve. "Sorry for what?"

Megan stood a short distance away, looking bedraggled, as if she had slept little the night before. Just as Dev had lain awake wishing he hadn't told hateful lies to Megan.

"Some things should be done for certain reasons, not just to prove a point," she said softly. "Dev, fixing up this house has become very important to me. I can't really explain why. Maybe because it's forcing me to display talents I didn't know I had. But if we can't work together without the battles, I'll leave. No guilt trips, no reproaches. After all, this really should have been your house. All I ask is that you don't hang moose heads on the parlor walls." A tiny smile flickered on her lips.

He couldn't believe his ears or the dismay he felt at the idea of Megan leaving. "You'd just walk away without a word?"

"I may have done things in my past I'm not proud of, but I've never lied to you. Yes, I would leave."

Dev searched her face for clues, but there were none. Her eyes were red rimmed, but otherwise clear. Her features were a bit pale, but composed. He knew she meant every word she'd uttered.

"Hey, lady, if you think I'm going to hang all that wallpaper you've planned, you've got another think coming." He forced his tone to be light. "If you think you're leaving me with everything, you'll soon learn I can dismantle your car in five minutes." He noticed her shoulders visibly relaxing with relief.

"Let's just take it one day at a time," he suggested. "Considering everything, we've done pretty well so far, right?" He held out his hand, although he would have preferred sealing the bargain with a kiss.

She slipped her hand into his. "All right."

Their hands remained clasped for a moment before Megan slowly pulled back.

"There's more coffee?" She nodded toward the pot.

"Sure." Sensing this was the perfect time to also back off, Dev ambled into the house. "I already had my breakfast, so I think I'll get to work. No reason I can't get the rest of those downstairs pipes pulled out before Harry and Charlie show up."

As the screen door slapped against his back, Dev could feel Megan's eyes on him. For the rest of the day, he felt as if he carried a mark on his skin.

"MR. GRANT, YOU CANNOT continue your work." Ezra Hawkins stood before a grim-featured Dev who was looking like a little boy called before the school principal.

"Give me one good reason why not," Dev spoke in a soft, but very lethal, voice.

The older man nervously wrung his hands. "Because you don't have the necessary permits."

"Ah, hell, Ezra, when did that ever matter around here?" Harry snorted. "All we're doin' is replacin' some wirin' and plumbin'. It's not as if we're building the house from the ground up. And we have all the paperwork we need."

The attorney straightened up and looked down his officious nose at the other man. "Building permits are necessary, Harry, and you know it. Your participation in this could cost your license."

Harry narrowed his eyes. "How much is Eunice payin' you for this?"

"I am not being bribed. After all, I represent Mr. Grant and Ms. Abernathy, and I only have their best interests at heart."

Harry spat into the ground, dangerously close to Ezra's highly polished wing tips. "I remember Dev here telling me he found himself a new lawyer to take over the paperwork on the house. And Meggie already has enough lawyers in her own family, she wouldn't be adding another one. Nope, the way I see it, the only interest you have is in your own pocket, and Eunice is the only one willing to line it."

"If work isn't stopped immediately, there will be no other recourse but to have the sheriff out to close you down," Ezra warned.

The attorney jumped when Dev reached into his back pocket.

"Then it's a good thing I applied for the necessary paperwork, isn't it?" He slapped the papers into Ezra's hand so hard, the man winced. "I think you'll find everything in order."

Ezra looked through the papers. "We had no idea." Dismay filled his voice.

"There's no reason you should. Although after what I've seen and heard, I wouldn't be surprised if Eunice St. Clair doesn't have ears in the county courthouse," Dev said grimly. "You tell that old bat for me that I don't appreciate the way Megan has been treated in town. She's a lady to the bone. Just as my grandmother was a lady. If I hear any more talk . . ." He left the rest of his threat unsaid, but no less understood.

The lawyer immediately backed off, dropping the papers to the ground as he did so.

"I'm only doing my job," he said, defending himself, feeling braver as the distance between him and Dev lengthened.

"Doing Eunice's dirty work is more like it," Harry told him. "Just as you've done it for the past thirty years. Come on, Ezra, show some backbone. Show you're a man after all."

"The permits will be verified." With that parting shot, Ezra climbed into his aging Pontiac and drove off.

Harry shook his head. "Ezra always was a wimp."

"They mean to stop us any way they can," Megan spoke up as she approached them. She'd remained on the front porch during the confrontation.

Dev stared at the dust trail Ezra's car made as it went down the hill. "They won't succeed."

She walked over to him and laid a hand on his arm. The muscles tensed under her touch. "You didn't have to stand up for me," she said softly. "But I'm glad you did."

"These people are so damn close minded, they can't see the truth in front of them," Dev muttered. "We're giving them a chance to give a dying town a new life, and they prefer to remain stuck in the last century."

Megan's fingers dug into his arm as she tried to lead him away. "Come on, Grant, we've got a ton of work to do, and daylight is getting away from us," she urged.

He smiled. "Slave driver."

"I learned it from the best."

They stood there smiling at each other, as if sharing a private moment. They had no idea Harry watched them with a knowing grin on his face. "For a divorced couple, they sure like to look at each other a lot."

MEGAN FROWNED AS SHE reread the words and sensed the pain behind them.

July 2, 1938.
I have a son. He is the most perfect baby I have ever seen, and I love him dearly. I wonder what is going on at the house. For Barney's sake, I went through my pregnancy in San Diego where no one would know me. I found a wonderful doctor who thinks I am a widow of a military man, as does the owner of the residence hotel I am staying at. I will

not have my child suffer any slurs. My mother was able to protect me, and I will do the same for my child. I only wish Barney could see his son, but that is even more impossible now. The man I love more than life itself married a proper woman the day his son was born. I only pray that he will be happy.

"Oh, Maisie, it seems as if Barney didn't love you as much as you loved him," Megan murmured, finally turning the page. "Maybe you were better off without him."

September 20, 1938.
You'd think by now I'd be used to being an object of speculation. The "good women" of the town would dearly love to know who William's father is. Not that I'd give them that satisfaction. It shows how much many of them trust their husbands as they study William's face looking for the least similarity. It must pain them to see only me in his face. Ironic how much he looked like his father at birth, then started to resemble me more than Barney as he grew. I dread the day I'll have to send him away in order to keep him safe. I now only see Barney at a distance. He looks so unhappy. I hear his wife is only interested in helping him further his political career and that he'll be running for town mayor next year. The last time I was in town, I ran into him when I left the pharmacy. I could tell by the look on his face he knew William is his. I did the only thing I could even though it almost broke my heart. I barely nodded and walked past him. I refuse to subject him to the gossip mill.

Megan read several more pages, then her eyelids began to droop with weariness. It took all of her remaining energy to turn off the flashlight. Just before she fell asleep, a thought occurred to her.

"Maisie, you had to know there could have been a chance these journals could fall into the wrong hands when you left here almost forty years ago. Why did you leave them behind?" Megan asked the empty room. She knew she wouldn't receive an answer, but it helped just to say the words out loud. Hopefully, she would find the answer in a later journal.

She stretched her jaw in a huge yawn as she settled down in the sleeping bag. If she wasn't careful, these late nights were going to catch up to her with a vengeance.

"I just bet Dev is out there sleeping like a baby," she muttered, curling up on her side. "And snoring loud enough to drown out all those crickets. And tossing and turning so much, you'd think there was an earthquake." She stared wide awake into the darkness. "And mumbling in his sleep. I hate him."

"WHAT ARE YOU DOING UP there with the flashlight on most of the night?" Dev asked, walking up behind Megan as she carefully peeled off the soggy wallpaper she had just attacked with the steamer. Her portable CD player played golden oldies in the background. "Are you using it as a nightlight to keep all the ghosties away?" His teasing grin wobbled under her warning glare. "Of course, maybe you're working up there or something."

"Or something." She returned to her work. "Isn't Harry calling you?"

"Nope, he and Charlie are cleaning up before they go into town. I figured I'd go along with them, and thought I'd see if you wanted anything."

Megan thought for a moment and shook her head. "Not a thing."

He nodded. "We shouldn't be gone long."

She smiled. "You're just getting out of work."

He grinned back. "Hey, whatever works."

Megan continued working until it started to grow so dark she had to turn on a light. She looked outside, but found no sign the men had returned. At first, she wasn't worried until an hour passed, then another. She was ready to get into her car and drive to town when Harry's truck appeared at the top of the hill.

"It's about time," she muttered, walking toward it. A chill invaded her system when she realized only two men were in the vehicle.

Harry climbed out and walked toward Megan.

"What happened?" she demanded.

He winced. "There's no way I can say it easy, Meggie. Dev's in jail."

Chapter Eight

"You have to understand, little lady, that we don't hold with assault and battery on our good citizens around here," the grim-faced sheriff told Megan.

From the moment Charlie and Harry broke the news to her, she wasted no time in herding them back to the sheriff's office.

By the time she stormed into the building, she was hopping mad. Mad at Dev for getting thrown in jail on some crazy charge. Mad at Harry and Charlie for allowing him to get into a fight and get arrested. And right now she was downright furious at the sheriff for calling her "little lady."

"The way I heard it, the other man threw the first punch and Mr. Grant was only defending himself," she argued, determined to keep her composure at all costs and, for the first time, regretting not attending law school. She remembered her mother once saying the best way to win a case was to remain cold and deliberate. Megan was determined to use her temper on better things—such as Dev.

The man leaned back in his swivel chair and propped his booted feet on top of his desk. "That's not the way

I heard it. I heard Grant broke one man's front teeth and almost broke another man's arm.''

Her eyes narrowed to dangerous slits. "Dev Grant may be a lot of things, but a hothead isn't one of them. He doesn't start fights, he only finishes them."

The man's gaze, centered on her breasts, didn't waver. "He started one this time."

Megan bit back the nasty words, and instead said, "Fine, how much is his bail?"

The sheriff nodded his head several times in thought. "Well now, hard to say. He's pretty dangerous to the community. I'd hate to let him out only to have him start up trouble again. Who knows what would start up next time."

"Trust me, Sheriff, I'll make sure he doesn't get into any more trouble." Megan bit out each word. "And he'll remain out on the property."

He leered. "Way I hear it, a lot happens out there after dark. No wonder the boy got into a fight over you." His eyes roamed over her body with disturbing intensity.

Megan resisted punching the man in the eye. She decided there was only one way to win this battle. She reached forward and picked up the phone.

"Hey, what're you doing?" he demanded, trying to grab the receiver, but she kept it out of his reach. "That phone's for official business only."

"This is official business. My mother is a district attorney with a great many connections in this state. I'm sure she and my father know a lot of people up here who can assist us in straightening this out with a minimum of fuss," she said mockingly. "If I recall, there's a Judge Thornton on the bench in this county. He's a very by-the-book man who doesn't appreciate trumped-up charges."

The sheriff scowled as he finally succeeded in snatching the receiver out of Megan's hand. "Hundred-dollar fine and he doesn't come into town for the next thirty days," the man said tersely. "I ever see him step one foot off that property of yours, I slap him back in jail for a long time."

Ten minutes later, Megan was leaving the sheriff's office with Dev right behind her.

"Look, Meggie, it isn't what you think."

She gestured to the truck bed while Harry and Charlie waited in the cab. "Of course, it isn't. You got that black eye from a fly attacking you."

"Come on, Meggie, give me a break."

She leaned forward. As long as she held on to her anger, she knew she would survive. Seeing Dev walk through the door leading from the jail cells, his face scratched and bloodied, an eye rapidly turning bright tones of black and blue and his clothes torn beyond repair, she had wanted nothing more than to throw her arms around him and pamper him. Then she had wanted to kill him.

She gritted her teeth and remembered the tiny hints the sheriff had dropped regarding the reason for the fight.

"I just laid out a hundred dollars, which you will pay me back, to spring you from a place I probably should have left you in. I had to listen to some Neanderthal of a lawman call me 'little lady,' and I lied through my teeth to get you out on bail. Now get in that damn truck before I tell them to drive off and leave you here." She climbed into the cab and slammed the door behind her.

Harry leaned out of the driver's side window. "She's pretty mad, Dev. Better do as she says."

"Yeah," he muttered, slowly climbing into the back and sitting against the cab's wall. "Great, she's mad, and I'm the one in pain."

Dev was convinced Harry's truck hit every pothole. He told himself he wouldn't be surprised if Megan was directing the older man over every hole in the road. He groaned as tender muscles protested the rough treatment.

"Last time I'll fight some big ape to defend her honor. She can do well enough taking care of herself." He uttered several imaginative curses as he felt new bruises heaped on the old ones from the bouncing truck. "A few well-placed words from her and the guy would have dropped like a rock."

Dev was more than ready to climb out of the truck the moment it skidded to a stop in front of the house.

"You better put something on that eye to get the swelling down," Harry advised, watching Dev practically crawl out of the truck bed. "I don't know how Cal could get that punch in. He's usually pretty slow with his right."

"Yeah, well, he got lucky."

Megan stood at the foot of the steps with her arms crossed in front of her chest. Her foreboding expression was enough to make Dev think more than once about turning tail and running for his life. Standing up to that idiot who'd made lewd remarks about Megan was a snap compared with dealing with Megan in her present frame of mind. Dev managed a brief grin, but discovered even that hurt.

"Just remember, I did defend your honor."

"And how did your opponent fare in this battle?"

Dev sighed and shifted his feet. "He . . . ah . . . he was a bit bigger than me."

She looked suspicious. "How big?"

"About six foot five or so. Built like a mountain, with a fist like a pile driver."

She arched an eyebrow. "And what did this cretin say to cause you to get so angry you threw a punch at him?"

He looked off in the distance. "I really don't care to repeat it."

Megan looked beyond his shoulder to Harry and Charlie standing expectantly by the truck. "Did you overhear the conversation before the fight?" Both men nodded. "Then what was said?"

Harry's face reddened. "No, ma'am, I'd never say those words to a lady."

A knot formed in her stomach. "Pretend I'm not one."

Harry shook his head. "Meggie, Cal's words were downright disgusting. He'd had more than a few beers, and he wanted to get Dev's goat."

She stared at Dev's bruised face. "It appears he did an excellent job of it."

"We'll see you tomorrow, Dev," Harry called out, quickly climbing back into the truck, with Charlie just as fast on the passenger side. The truck wheezed its way down the hill.

"Cowards," Dev muttered, watching their escape.

Megan sighed. "Come on, let's get that eye taken care of." She walked into the house and headed for the kitchen, where they now kept the camp stove. She set out a pan of water to heat. "Those clothes aren't good for anything more than rags." She hunted through the box of extras and pulled out some antiseptic and a strip of cloth she'd picked up at a remnants table. She frequently tested the temperature of the water and once it was warm enough, she took the pan off the stove.

"Meggie, I'm really sorry you had to talk to that idiot they call a sheriff," Dev told her, sitting down at the table.

"He was an experience I wouldn't care to repeat," she admitted, carrying everything over to the table. "Dev, what kind of fight were you in?" She gasped, staring at the scratches on his chest visible after he'd pulled off his shirt.

He looked down. "Oh, these are from good old Cal's girlfriend. She was screaming that I was hurting her baby and got into the act. Man, she had the longest nails I ever saw. They were like cat's claws."

"Maybe we should get a vet's certificate to prove she's had her shots recently."

Megan doused the cloth with antiseptic and dabbed at the scratches. Dev hissed through his teeth and swore under his breath as the fiery liquid covered the open wounds.

"If there's a fight between the two of you, I've got my money on you," Dev told her. "Ow! Damn! That stings!" He tried to evade her, but she held fast on to his arm to keep him still.

"Good, that means it's working." Her eyes glittered like dark diamonds. "You were a fool to go up against someone so much bigger than you. You could have ended up in the hospital." She poured more antiseptic onto the cloth and rubbed a little more vigorously this time.

"Hey! Watch it!" He jumped. "What're you trying to do, kill me?"

"Don't give me any ideas," she said grimly, trying not to stare at the variety of rapidly darkening bruises scattered across Dev's torso. She blinked to hold back her tears. "You're going to be in a lot of discomfort tomorrow from those bruises."

"Wanna kiss them and make them better?" he asked glibly.

"This is not something you can brush off with a joke, Devlin Grant," she said hoarsely. "You have a black eye, bruises and scratches. For all we know, you could have a broken rib or two."

"I'd know it."

She looked at him with horror. "You mean you've broken them before?"

"Meggie, in my line of work, broken bones aren't all that uncommon."

The tears now ran down her cheeks unchecked. "This lousy town will do anything to run us out. What's going to happen next? Are they going to show up in the dead of night and burn us out?"

"They might, as a last resort."

Megan slammed the bottle down on the table. "You're saying we could have a war on our hands just because we want to give this house a new life? Oh, no, they're not going to get away with it." She tossed the rag down after the bottle and spun on her heel.

"Where are you going?" Dev watched her snatch up her purse.

"I'm going to stop this before it goes any further."

He stood up. "Megan, don't do anything foolish."

She didn't look back as she flung open the back door. "I don't intend to, but I'm not going to allow this adolescent behavior to continue, either."

Dev started to hurry after her, then cursed fluently under his breath as his sore body protested his quick movements. "Dammit, Megan, get back here!" he roared. "I won't bail you out if you get thrown in jail!" He could already hear the car pulling away, and he reached the front yard in time to see the car's taillights off in the distance. "Damn fool woman. She can just stay in jail until I'm damn well ready to bail her out."

He stomped back into the kitchen and grabbed the bottle of whiskey he kept for emergency use. Right now, he considered the time a very big emergency.

MEGAN'S FURY ESCALATED as she reached the outskirts of town. She didn't have to think twice about her destination. She may have only seen the house once, but it wasn't difficult to find. After all, there weren't many Old South mansions in the small dying town. She braked to a quick stop in front of the house and hopped out of the car. As she stalked up the walkway, she didn't bother noticing the immaculate lawn and brightly colored flowers that dotted the front of the freshly painted white house that seemed to glow in the early-evening light.

She kept her finger on the doorbell until the door was opened by a dark-haired woman wearing a gray dress and white apron. The woman gasped as Megan rudely pushed past her.

"Excuse me, but you can't go in there. Mrs. St. Clair has guests," the woman protested.

"Good, the more witnesses, the better." Megan followed the sound of voices and grasped the double doors. She threw them open and walked through with all the drama of a good entrance.

Eunice St. Clair smiled coolly. "I don't believe you were invited."

Megan ignored her words and walked to the head of the table until she stood just a hair away from Eunice. When one man rose as if to interfere, Eunice gestured to him to sit. Megan slapped her palms down on the table causing one woman to jump and squeak with fear.

"You certainly don't believe in showing your elders respect, do you?" Eunice didn't look the least bit intimidated.

"No matter what the age, respect has to be earned. Eunice, you're really ticking me off," Megan told her in a soft, deadly voice. "And I'm not a nice person when I'm ticked off. You've allowed what should have been a private battle between us to get out of hand. Tonight's activities proved just how out of hand it's gotten. Now, I'll put up with a long drive to a grocery store and bank and having to deal with suppliers out of the area, thereby denying your 'good citizens'—" she spat out the words "—the revenue. That's no skin off my nose. But I have an idea that circulating dirty rumors about Dev and myself is more your style. Because I'm certain that's what started the fight tonight." She leaned in closer to Eunice. "You call off your trained puppets and let us do what we came here to do—bring a lovely old house to life."

"Do something even better," Eunice said in an even voice as she faced her opponent. "Sell me the property and all your troubles will go away like magic."

Megan's lovely face hardened. "Let me give it to you straight. If Dev or I are hassled in such a vicious manner again, I won't bother reporting it to the sheriff or even going to the county, I'll come to the source—you." Megan straightened up, not taking her eyes off the old woman's face. "You don't want me for an enemy, Eunice." With that, Megan walked out without a backward glance.

Eunice remained in her chair, hearing the muted sounds of the front door opening and closing, then the roar of a car starting up before a squeal of tires rent the air. A tiny smile curved her lips. If nothing else, Eunice St. Clair recognized—and respected—a formidable enemy. She wanted to make sure she won not only the next battle, but the entire war.

"WHERE THE HELL HAVE YOU been?" Dev loomed over Megan the moment she stepped inside the kitchen.

"Out." She threw her purse onto the counter. "Do you want some dinner?"

"Please." He shuddered. "I'm already in enough pain. I don't want to add heartburn to the list."

He was surprised when Megan smiled instead of remaining angry at him.

"Then you're lucky there're still a few places in town that're willing to take our money." She went back outside, then reappeared with a flat cardboard box in her hands. "Extra large with beef, mushrooms and extra cheese. I even picked up a bottle of wine. I figured after today, we needed—no, deserved this treat."

Dev could already feel his mouth watering at the unexpected treat.

"If I knew this was all it took to get a pizza out of you, I'd've gotten beaten up sooner." He pulled out paper plates and plastic cups.

They both dove into their dinner. Between bites, Megan said, "I went to see Eunice St. Clair. I told her if she tries anything again, she'll have me to reckon with. She knew I meant it."

"You did what . . . ? Talk about a crazy stunt, that's the worst thing you could have done. She could have had you arrested for trespassing!"

"You could have done better?"

"I sure wouldn't have gone to Eunice St. Clair's house and threatened her."

"I didn't threaten her. I merely made a promise. Besides, her playing God in this battle of wills could have left you seriously hurt," Megan pointed out. "I wanted her to know we were on to her games and we weren't going to allow it to go on any further without retaliation. If necessary, we'll get the proper permits and buy ourselves a couple of rifles for protection."

Dev looked at Megan as if he had never seen her before. "I can't believe I'm hearing this from the woman who used to spout all the reasons for private citizens *not* owning firearms. And here you're not only talking about owning one, but firing it."

She looked at him squarely. "I don't appreciate people telling me what I can't do. And I especially don't like grand dames who think they can own a town just because they've been here forever. She needs to be shown the world has come a long way since her day."

Dev rubbed his forehead. "Megan, you're getting a little too radical, even for my taste."

"Oh, yeah? While I waited for our pizza, I heard people talking about the fight. I also heard what Cal said to you. I'm sure I was meant to overhear, and little did they know I'm glad I did." She looked down, searching for words. "Dev, if these people have their way, things will get more vicious. We're going to have to hold on to our tempers or we'll both be in jail."

"I wasn't the one who stormed Eunice St. Clair's house and told her off."

Megan grimaced. "Maybe it was a bit much, but I was so furious. She had to know she either has to back off or pay the consequences. I think she got the message."

"But do you think she's going to back off?"

Megan released a long, drawn-out breath and slowly shook her head. "Hopefully, she'll consider the consequences before trying anything again."

Dev chuckled. "That's my hot little lady for you." He slid the chair around the table until he sat next to her, then reached out and pulled her into his lap. "My heroine," he murmured, circling her waist with his arms. "You charged in like a mighty Amazon warrior to stand up for me."

She could feel the warmth of his hands radiating through her cotton shirt and concentrated on not relaxing against his touch. "I just got so angry, I needed to vent it against the people who caused the trouble to begin with."

He ducked his dead and nuzzled her ear. "There're other, more pleasurable ways to deal with your emotions," he said huskily, nibbling the earlobe dotted by a tiny sapphire-stud earring.

Megan felt her breath rush out of her lungs. It appeared Dev hadn't forgotten how sensitive that part of her body was. "You've had a rough night." Her voice came out raspy instead of clear. "You need your rest."

"You gonna rest with me? After you kiss my bruises better, that is," he murmured, grazing the soft skin of her throat with his teeth.

She gulped in much-needed air. "Dev, this isn't a good idea."

He didn't stop his nibbling. "Why not?"

"Because we're divorced from each other."

"But we're not dead." His hands smoothed their way under her shirt. "No, you're most definitely not dead. Not with skin as warm as yours."

She forced herself to remain calm under his stroking hands. "We don't even like each other."

Dev's hand gripped her chin and forced her head around so that she had to face him. "There are times you drive me so crazy, it wouldn't be difficult for me to think about killing you. And there's other times when you get on your high horse that I think about knocking you off it, but I have never said I didn't like you," he stated clearly.

She studied his eyes, fascinated by the streaks of blue blending with gray. Memory told her the more gray his eyes were, the more aroused he was. She didn't have to consider the hardness of his body under her hips or the way his hands tightened on her face as he watched her to tell her just how much he wanted her. She only had to look into his eyes. She'd never had an idea how strong certain memories were until now. "You called me a twit."

His lips traveled lightly over hers, moistening them, parting them. "You have been a twit. Besides, you called me a Neanderthal, so we're even."

"Being called a twit is worse," she whispered, unable to stop herself from linking her arms around his neck, waiting for his kiss to deepen.

He kept the touch light and teasing. "That's only because you've never been called a Neanderthal."

Her lips parted even more, inviting as much as he was willing to give. "We still shouldn't do this," she said with a sigh, even as her body screamed, *Do it, do it!*

"Sure, we should. The night is young, the air is sweet and we are both very ready, willing and more than able." His fingertips gently pressed against her skin in a slow circular motion, moving upward and trailing gently across her breast, deliberately leaving her aching nipple alone.

"That's what I'm afraid of, that I'll be too willing," she confessed, keeping her arms loosely circling his neck and her mouth a bit out of range. She knew by now just how seductive Dev's kisses were. "When I came up here, I knew I was taking a chance. I thought the moment you saw me, you'd probably order me to get out of your sight. I had no idea the attraction could be so strong. The thing is, I don't like to play games with my emotions." Slowly, reluctantly, she drew her arms away from him. When she tried to stand up, his hands tightened their grip, then loosened.

"I'm not playing a game with you, Megan," he said quietly, looking up at her. "I didn't expect this attraction to each other, either. But our denying the truth won't work."

Megan took a deep breath. Desire for Dev was something she couldn't allow to grow. Their shared past had been rocky; there was no guarantee their history wouldn't be repeated, and this time, the wounds would be even bloodier. She had to do something, now, to diffuse the situation. There was only one way to do it. "Dev, I've been involved with someone in L.A. for the past year. It's pretty serious."

For a moment, anger flared in the deep gray eyes, then cooled.

"You *think* you're involved with a man, Megan, my love," Dev whispered, chucking her under the chin. "Thing is, if you felt that strongly for another man, you wouldn't be up here with me, and you definitely wouldn't have responded to me the way you just did.

NO RISK, NO OBLIGATION TO BUY...NOW OR EVER!

GUARANTEED

PLAY "ROLL A DOUBLE" AND GET AS MANY AS FIVE GIFTS!

HERE'S HOW TO PLAY:

1. Peel off label from front cover. Place it in space provided at right. With a coin, carefully scratch off the silver dice. This makes you eligible to receive two or more free books, and possibly another gift, depending on what is revealed beneath the scratch-off area.

2. You'll receive brand-new Harlequin American Romance® novels. When you return this card, we'll rush you the books and gift you qualify for ABSOLUTELY FREE!

3. Then, if we don't hear from you, every month, we'll send you 4 additional novels to read and enjoy. You can return them and owe nothing, but if you decide to keep them, you'll pay only $2.96 per book—a saving of 43¢ each off the cover price—plus only 49¢ delivery for the entire shipment.

4. When you subscribe to the Harlequin Reader Service®, you'll also get our newsletter, as well as additional free gifts from time to time.

5. You must be completely satisfied. You may cancel at any time simply by sending us a note or a shipping statement marked ''cancel'' or by returning any shipment to us at our expense.

The Austrian crystal sparkles like a diamond! And it's carefully set in a romantic "Key to Your Heart" pendant on a generous 18″ chain. The entire necklace is yours free as added thanks for giving our Reader Service a try!

DETACH AND MAIL CARD TODAY!

HARLEQUIN "NO RISK" GUARANTEE

* You're not required to buy a single book—ever!
* You must be completely satisfied or you may cancel at any time simply by sending us a note or shipping statement marked "cancel" or by returning any shipment to us at our cost. Either way, you will receive no more books; you'll have no obligation to buy.
* The free books and gift you claimed on this "Roll A Double" offer remain yours to keep no matter what you decide.

If offer card is missing, please write to: Harlequin Reader Service, P.O. Box 609, Fort Erie, Ontario L2A 5X3

Business Reply Mail

No Postage Stamp Necessary if Mailed in Canada

Postage will be paid by

HARLEQUIN READER SERVICE
PO BOX 609
FORT ERIE, ONT.
L2A 9Z9

Canada Post
Postes Canada
125

DETACH AND MAIL CARD TODAY!

That tells me that relationship is about as hot as an ice cube. Do the guy a favor and let him find another woman,'' he advised as he slightly straightened up. "Now, these battered old bones need their rest. See you in the morning.''

Still stunned by his words, Megan could only stand there speechless and watch him walk outside. She opened her mouth, fully prepared to argue with him. Instead she closed it. Maybe because she knew she couldn't convince Dev of something she had never felt for Rob. And now knew she never would.

Chapter Nine

"I can't sign off your work when your permits aren't filled out properly. You won't be able to continue until you straighten this out."

Frustrated with this new turn of events, which sounded about as phoney as a three-dollar bill, Dev spun around, pushing his fingers through his hair. With each passing day, he grew angrier at the so-called powers-that-be who tried to control him.

"When we applied for the permit, we were told everything was in order," he gritted out.

The smaller man puffed up like a rooster in a feeble attempt to stare Dev down. It didn't work. "The man who signed this permit doesn't work for the county anymore."

"So what? He worked there when he signed it."

"Down, Rover." Megan patted Dev's back. "Mr. Carson, isn't it?" The man's head bobbed up and down. "Now, when Mr. Grant and I applied for the permits to redo the plumbing and electricity, Mr. Sanders was a duly authorized agent for the county. It is my understanding that as long as the permits are signed by the proper people, there are no problems. The electricity and plumbing was brought up to code. Isn't that what's important? We followed the steps to the letter, so I can't see where there could be any problems."

"He didn't have the authority to sign this," Mr. Carson stubbornly maintained, slapping the paper with his hand.

"He did when he signed it," Megan pointed out, determined to be just as stubborn.

"Come on, Ralph," Harry growled, taking his cigar out of his mouth. "You and I both know there's nothing wrong with those permits. Why don't you just sign off the work and get back to your poker game going on over behind the fire house."

Ralph Carson wasn't about to back down now. "The work has to be done by a certified electrician and plumber."

"It was." Harry jerked his thumb backward at Charlie. "And if you don't think Charlie is qualified, I don't know why you had him install the new toilet in your guest bathroom."

The other man hemmed and hawed, but finally grudgingly scribbled his name across the bottom of the paper. "You just better have all the proper permits for the actual construction work."

"All signed and sealed," Harry assured him, draping an arm around the man's shoulder and escorting him back to his car. "Now, why don't you go on and harass someone else so we can get back to work."

Mr. Carson stopped long enough to look back at the house. Megan knew exactly what he saw. While there was indoor plumbing and working electricity on the inside, the exterior still looked like something out of a horror movie. "Give us a couple of months and you won't know the place," she said breezily, flashing him the smile that never failed to charm difficult clients.

Mr. Carson was not charmed. He scowled at her as if she was the bearer of bad news. "A house with this kind of history should be torn down so the land can be put to good use."

Dev stepped forward, looking fierce, the smaller man backed away. "It will be put to good use if the damn town will get their heads out of the ground and realize an inn will bring in much-needed income," he said darkly.

"I should think you'd have good memories of this place, Ralph." Harry's smile was sly. "I remember you coming out here every Thursday night to see Adele. And the way I hear it the two of you didn't do much talking, either!" he cackled.

Ralph Carson threw Harry a lethal glare before he marched to his car and got in, slamming the door after him. The car sped down the hill with a cloud of dust following it.

"Harry, you make more enemies that way," Charlie said. "Besides, you were wrong."

"What do you mean 'wrong'? I told him like it was," he insisted.

"Maybe, but Ralph didn't see Adele on Thursdays. He saw her on Tuesdays. Remember? Sam Wilson saw Adele on Thursdays like clockwork 'cause that was Doris's night for canasta."

Megan glanced at Dev, then looked away. She bit her lip to keep from laughing. She was pleased to notice he didn't look uncomfortable at the talk about his grandmother's profession. Maybe he was finally coming to terms with it.

"It sounds as if Adele was a popular lady," Megan murmured, walking back to the house. She slanted Dev a teasing look. "Come on, big guy, and I'll console you with a cold can of Coke."

"Some offers just can't be refused. 'Course, I'm hoping you'll offer a great deal more by the time we get up there."

"In your dreams, Grant."

"That does seem to be where all the action has been lately."

Dev started to follow, then stopped and looked back at the two older men. "Who did my grandmother see?" The last word came out as a sneer.

Harry looked up. "Why, son, Maisie didn't have any clients. She just ran the place. She took care of the bookkeeping and the girls. That was all. I heard that when she first took over, she let it be known she wasn't available, so to speak."

Dev looked unsure whether to believe him or not, but the man's expression indicated he spoke the truth.

Charlie shook his head. "Though some of us did think she might have had a gentleman friend. Oh, not that kind," he hurried on when he saw Dev's grim expression. "I mean someone she was serious about. There were rumors, but no one was sure who it was, and she was real discreet. She didn't allow the girls to flaunt themselves in town, and she always acted like a real lady, though to me, it wasn't acting. She was a *real* lady. Most of the wives could have taken lessons from her on how to act."

Megan thought about the mysterious Barney written about in Maisie's journals and knew better than to bring him up. She had been so tired the past couple weeks, she hadn't been able to get much reading in, but she vowed to get back to it that night. Dev still preferred to sleep outside since the weather was nice, so she still had the house to herself after dark.

"At least, we have the work signed off," she told him in an effort to divert his attention. "We should celebrate. The hardest part's done."

"Wanna bet?" he said grimly, clearly still thinking about his grandmother. "How many rooms have you been able to finish?"

"Two," she had to admit.

"And how many more do you have to do?"

"More than I'd like to think about."

"And why is that?"

Megan rolled her eyes. "Because you said there're some walls that need to be torn down and replastered or whatever, plus all those walls you, Harry and Charlie tore out to replace wiring and pipes and whatever that need to be rebuilt," she went on. "And now you get to put up new walls, along with tearing down a few more old ones. I don't envy you your job."

"Since there isn't much you can do, you can help us."

Her smile felt stiff on her lips. "I don't think so."

"I do. Don't worry, there will be lots of little things you can do to help out. Carry out the rubbish, hand us tools—we can keep you plenty busy," he assured her as the foursome entered the kitchen. Dev opened the door to the industrial-size refrigerator that had been delivered a few days before and extracted cans of soda for everyone.

"Okay, I know it's grunt work," he went on, tipping his can back to take a drink, "but it's important grunt work."

"It's dirty work, Meggie," Harry added. "Real dirty work. But we can use the extra pair of hands."

She held hers up. "No problem." She smiled gamely.

Dev grasped her hands and turned them over. Something lurched in the pit of his stomach as he remembered the polished young woman who had driven up the hill more than two months ago. In her place was a curly-haired waif wearing jeans cut off above the knee and a T-shirt with a torn sleeve. When he raised his head, his scowl displayed his displeasure. "I thought you were wearing rubber gloves."

"I told you I can't." She tried to tear her hands from his grasp, but he merely tightened his grip. "Dev, please," she whispered, slanting a glance at Harry and Charlie, who were watching with great interest.

Dev hid a grin as he looked down at her flushed features. "Something bothering you?"

This time she was able to break free. "Yes, you," she muttered, moving out of harm's way. "Now if you three are finished playing your little macho games, we can get back to work."

Dev grinned at Harry and Charlie. "And *she* talks about macho? Okay, where shall we start?"

"Upstairs," Harry suggested. "We haven't worked on the master bedroom yet."

"No!" The moment the words left her mouth, Megan realized her mistake in speaking out so vehemently. "It's just that I'm sleeping in there and I'm not too keen on breathing in plaster dust all night." She hoped she sounded more positive to them than she did to her own ears.

Dev looked at her curiously but didn't challenge her statement or recommend she merely move to another room. "Then we'll start on the front rooms and work our way back."

"That room that used to have green-flocked wallpaper sounded as if rats are still in the walls." Megan wrinkled her nose with distaste.

"Better pick up some more traps," Dev decided. "All right, the boss says we need to get back to work, so let's get at it." He set his now-empty soda can on the counter and walked to the door. The two older men followed suit. Harry paused in the doorway and turned to Megan.

"You two are going to have a mighty fine place here when you're finished," he told her. "If I were you, I'd think about sticking around."

"That's Dev's dream. I'm just here to see it accomplished, then I disappear in a puff of smoke like a fairy godmother," Megan said crisply, but she didn't sound as convinced as she would have liked.

"Not even if he needs you?"

She smiled wanly at Harry's gentle question. "Dev hasn't needed anyone, especially me, for a long time. Please don't look for something that doesn't exist."

"Maybe it does. All you have to do is look hard enough to see the truth."

Megan smiled after his departing figure. "Oh, Harry, you're such a sweetie that I don't have the heart to tell you it won't do you any good to act like Cupid in overalls. It's only in the movies and in books that the boy and girl get back together and live happily ever after."

"I'M TOO OLD FOR THIS," Megan moaned, dropping her aching body into a kitchen chair. "When you talked to me about cleaning up and carrying things out, I figured, fine, a little sweeping, a few boards. Not half the wall!"

"At least we broke the wood up into manageable pieces for you," Dev pointed out.

She shot him a look fit to kill. "Yeah, maybe for somebody whose arms are six feet apart." She stretched her arms over her head in an attempt to ease strained muscles and groaned when they refused to cooperate. "I hate you."

Dev straightened up from his slouched position against the kitchen counter and held out his hand. "Come on, I've got a treat for you."

"No, please, I just want to sit here and die quietly," she whimpered, batting his outstretched hand. "You're a sadist, Devlin Grant. You are a slave driver, a downright meanie."

His coaxing voice was pure seduction. "You'll like this idea. Trust me."

"Ha! I'd sooner trust a weasel!" She glared at him.

He traced abstract patterns on her knee. "How do you relax overexerted muscles?"

"My bathtub has a whirlpool."

"Would a bubbling hot spring suffice?" he crooned, allowing his fingers to move upward.

She slapped his fingers. "I said—" She looked suspicious. "You're not kidding, are you? Because if all you mean is a pan of water you're blowing bubbles in through a straw, I'll—"

He hastily interrupted her threat. "There's one less than a mile from here. Charlie told me about it today. He said it's on the property, but few people know about it. It's secluded, well off the beaten track and as good as a whirlpool." As he explained, Dev grabbed her fingers and tugged her to her feet.

Megan didn't want to believe him, but the idea of hot water that didn't have to be heated on a camp stove was vastly appealing. "I can't believe anything like that is around here and no one knows about it. That would be too good to be true."

"No one's bothered to come out here since the house was closed," Dev pointed out. "Charlie only remembered it today when I said something about missing hot showers. So, are you game?"

"Real hot water?"

Dev nodded, now remaining silent and allowing her to make her own decision.

Her face fell. "I didn't bring a swimsuit."

"I don't have one, either. Besides, your underwear probably covers more than most of those bikinis do nowadays."

Megan knew Dev was right. Her underwear did cover more than her bikini would have. "All right, but if you make me walk all that way and we discover this spring has dried up, you'll be a dead man."

He held his hand up in the Boy Scout pledge. "You got it."

"You were never a Boy Scout."

"Hey, I swore I'd quit calling you a yuppie, and I haven't, have I?"

"Not in earshot, no. All right, give me a few minutes."

Megan went upstairs, groaning on every step. She rummaged up a towel and the biodegradable soap campers used. She was determined to take full advantage of an abundance of hot water. Dev was already waiting by the kitchen door with a rolled-up towel under his arm when she returned downstairs. Megan carefully blanked her thoughts as she looked at the tall man wearing only a pair of faded jeans that clung to his body like a second skin, a provocative tear in the denim displaying sun-browned skin. He hadn't bothered wearing a shirt, and Megan had to admit a man with a physique like Dev's shouldn't ever bother with one.

"Ready," she declared a shade too brightly. Dev's knowing smile told her he noticed the direction her eyes had traveled and that he hadn't minded her visual journey one bit.

"Let's go, then." He gestured for her to leave first.

"No wonder no one goes out here," Megan muttered five minutes later as she ducked to avoid another low-hanging tree limb that threatened to decapitate her. "They'd have to be Daniel Boone to find their way. I thought you said it wasn't far."

"It's not." Dev held back another limb so she could safely pass. "If you'd stop flapping your mouth, you'd hear the water."

Her glare was useless since heavy clouds obscured the moon. She silently vowed to get even with him for that crack later. Who knows, if the water was deep enough, she might be able to drown him. "All I hear is the wind and the usual night sounds," she said softly.

He bent over and whispered in her ear, his warm breath skimming over the sensitive skin. "What you're hearing, sweetheart, is the sound of bubbling water, not the wind."

Her breath was stolen from her lungs at his endearment and his moist caress against the top swirl of her ear. She was grateful for the darkness since it kept him from seeing her lick her suddenly dry lips. Although, yes, if she cared to look closely, she could see his eyes gleaming and teeth flashing white—like a wolf staring down his prey. She suddenly wished she hadn't thought of that analogy. "Do you think there's anything dangerous around?"

"Besides me?"

She elbowed him in the stomach, sad to realize she couldn't even make a dent. "You know very well what I mean."

"You're perfectly safe."

"Yeah, right," she muttered, stepping forward. She immediately misstepped and would have fallen flat on her nose if Dev's hand hadn't swiftly grabbed her wrist and kept her upright.

She swallowed her embarrassment. "Thank you."

His chuckle grated on her suddenly tender nerves. "Wouldn't want you to hurt your gold-plated rear end. You better let me lead the way." He didn't release her hand as he walked surefooted along the narrow, overgrown path.

Megan continued ducking out of the way of attacking tree branches until Dev stopped so quickly, she almost bumped into him.

"Charlie didn't do it justice," he said softly.

Megan moved around Dev only to stop short as she gazed at the large pool of bubbling water with tendrils of steam rising above it. The area surrounding the pool was overgrown, presenting a vision of a wild jungle that befitted such a pool. A small waterfall allowed fresh water to flow into the pool. With the clouds now barely obscuring the moonlight, it looked lovely and wild at the same time.

The perfect place for a love tryst. The thought suddenly popped into Megan's head. Had Maisie and her lover come here? Had they swum in the water and, perhaps, made love on that grassy edge that looked as soft as a feather bed? The more she tried to banish the questions, the more they intruded. And it didn't take much imagination to picture such a scene.

She shook her head violently to toss out those thoughts. What was wrong with her? Dev was her ex-husband and her business partner, not a prospective lover! Although, if memory served her right, he had been incredible in bed. Not to mention on the couch. In the shower. Then there was that time when they—

She gasped and quickly fanned herself with her hand. It didn't lower her internal temperature one bit.

"Are you all right?" Dev asked, noticing her flushed face.

"Just a little winded from the walk," she said weakly. "I didn't expect to have trees jump out and try to trip me."

"Stay here for another minute." He investigated the perimeter and once assured there were no furry visitors present to ruin their swim he nodded his satisfaction and reached for the metal button on the waistband of his jeans.

Following suit, Megan quickly pulled off her T-shirt and shorts. Wearing a cotton camisole and bikini pants she walked over to the pool's edge and dipped her toes in. The water bubbled around them and felt like a warm bath. Still cautious, she eased her way into the water.

"This is wonderful!" she said with a laugh, splashing the naturally heated water around her shoulders. "I only wish we had known about this sooner. To think I've put up with having to warm pots of water on a camp stove when this was within walking distance. Why couldn't Charlie have told us sooner?"

Dev took a more vigorous approach as he literally dropped into the water. "Sure beats using the hose in the backyard," he agreed, ducking his head under the water and shooting straight up. He used his hands to wipe the excess water from his beard and hair. The remaining droplets shone silver among the darker hair on his face. To Megan, he looked primitive and dangerous. Not to mention very sexy. "Although now that the plumbing is hooked up, you can have all the hot water you want."

"Wanna bet?" she shot back. "There's one minor problem you forgot about."

"Oh?" He seemed to enjoy her infectious spirits as he made his way closer to her.

"Yeah." Megan stepped farther into the water until it lapped gently around her shoulders. She stretched her arms over her head and lay back until she rested on the water as comfortably as if she were on a waterbed. With Dev in such close quarters, that was a thought to firmly keep out of her head. "It's nothing important. Not really all that significant, but we kind of need a hot-water heater to get all that hot water you've been fantasizing about."

"Augh!" Dev's groan was laced with laughter. "One more thing to worry about!"

"Actually," she said, drawing out the word, "two things."

"Two?" He frowned.

She nodded as she tread water. "Two. Someone still has to come out and check the well."

Dev swore aloud. "It's a conspiracy!"

"And you thought you were so smart," Megan teased, using the heel of her hand to splash water on him. "Now you know why I'm the brains of this outfit and you're the brawn."

"Hey, actions like that mean war, lady." With mock grim purpose, Dev dove after her.

Megan squealed and tried to swim away, but her actions weren't as fast as Dev's. Before she could take more than a couple strokes, his arms were around her waist. He twisted her around and pulled her toward him.

"Dev, we'll go under!" she protested, having no choice but to grab hold of his shoulders as their bodies started to sink until he scissor kicked a few times to keep their heads above water. Her nipples tightened in reaction as they brushed against the crisp mat of hair swirled across his chest.

"No, I'd never do that."

Her gaze flew upward at the serious tone in his voice. "Dev?" Her voice was hushed, questioning. Was playtime over?

He looked down at her face. "Will you hit me if I kiss you?"

Her arms lifted to encircle his neck. "I'll only hit you if you *don't* kiss me."

His head lowered until their mouths just barely touched. "I may not be a gentleman, but I do know when not to keep a lady waiting," he breathed, just before his mouth fully covered hers.

Chapter Ten

Dev's kiss was both familiar and new. The boy who had once kissed her with youthful passion that had sent her young heart aflutter had grown into a man who knew which of her pulse points generated the most response, and he used them all shamelessly. The face was rougher yet softer at the same time, his beard caressing her face with a velvet touch. Funny, she never used to like beards on men before. Until she first saw Dev.

His tongue stroked her lips apart before dipping inside to savor her taste. She moaned her acceptance and felt the heat rise up through her veins until she felt as if she were on fire inside and out. And only Dev could put it out.

"Dev," she breathed, combing her fingers through the wet silk of his hair. She tipped her head back and closed her eyes to better savor the rioting sensations racing through her body.

He grasped her legs, lifting them up until they were wrapped around his waist. His hands roamed over her back, finally settling in a heated caress across her buttocks. "Can't you say more than my name?" he teased, the rasp in his voice telling her that even a kiss shared between them was enough to fan the flames. "Come on, try to say a few words for the audience."

She managed a brief smile. "You are insane, Dev Grant. Anything I say would come out as pure gibberish."

He looked down at her breasts. The water had turned her camisole transparent, and her nipples showed through the thin fabric. "Did you wear this to drive me crazy?" he demanded huskily, covering one breast with his palm.

She opened her eyes and looked into his. She couldn't be anything less than honest. "I'm not sure. I wouldn't be surprised if it wasn't unconsciously deliberate."

"I think you did." He looked at her face, so lovely, and her body sleek like a seal's. He wanted to take hours to discover what changes time had wrought. In his arms wasn't the girl he once married, but a woman. A woman he wanted to make love to. A woman who, judging from the glaze in her lovely brown eyes, wanted him just as much.

"Dev, if we stay like this much longer, we'll drown," she whispered, wiggling her hips against his.

He groaned as he felt her softness brush against his erection. "Meggie, if you keep that up, I won't last very long."

She gifted him with that womanly smile that had spelled men's downfalls over the centuries. "Do you want me to stop?"

"Nothing doing!"

This time he wasn't gentle with her. He crushed her mouth with his in a deep, soul-stealing kiss.

If the water around them had been hot before, it turned to steam as Dev and Megan shifted their mouths from one angle to another to better taste each other.

Their tongues danced, catching droplets of water dripping down their faces. Megan moved closer, rubbing her aching breasts against Dev's chest. What happened next, neither would know. Suddenly the water closed over them.

"What happened?" Megan gasped as she broke the surface of the water. She used her fingers to slick her hair back from her face.

"I think we both got a little overexcited," Dev said wryly.

Megan paddled over to him and kept treading water as she circled. "What happened to your briefs?"

He grinned. "Saw no reason to bother with something so unnecessary."

Her laughter rang clear in the night. "You haven't changed at all, Devlin Grant."

"Yes, I have. If I knew back then what I know now, I would have fought that divorce." He appeared just as surprised by his blunt statement as she was surprised to hear it. "I wouldn't have let you go so easily. I would have been willing to wait for us to grow up."

Megan's lips parted. "It was better we had the chance to grow up on our own, Dev."

"I don't think so, Meggie."

She made her way to the edge of the pool where she could sit down. The water lapped just above her breasts as she leaned backward, resting her weight on her hands. "Dev, it's natural we would feel this physical pull. After all, we've been lovers before and we know what excites each other."

"Married lovers."

She slowly nodded. "Tonight we're in a situation that fairly screams of wild, uninhibited sex."

He stiffened. "Is that how you see this? Sex, not making love."

Megan looked away. Should she tell Dev how much she wanted him—and risk complicating matters? Or should she lie and say there was nothing wrong in a little sex between two ex-spouses? But she didn't want to lie to him. They had shared too much since they began work on the house. Shared more than a business relationship. Until now, all those touches and kisses before had been nothing more than a way to tease their senses.

"What if this is nothing more than our being thrown together in the heat of the moment?" she asked huskily.

"Is that what you really believe?"

"No, but it sounds good, doesn't it?"

Dev made his way over to her and settled down next to her. He reached out and brushed his knuckles across her cheek. "You've really grown up, Meggie. You never used to be so philosophical."

She covered his hand with her own. "I don't want to see either one of us hurt. We hurt each other enough before, why continue?" She only had to look at his expression to know he didn't want to talk about common sense. The clouds left shifting shadows on his face, but she had no trouble reading his thoughts.

"Know what? You worry too much." His mouth hovered over hers. "We were always good together, Meggie. Didn't you ever wonder if we still would be? Don't you want to find out if we can make it better?"

"Yes." She sighed. "I won't lie to you, Dev. I want you. And not because I feel I need a lover, but because of you. They say you don't forget your first lover." She traced his cheekbone with her fingertips. "Over the years I've wondered what you were doing, if you had found anyone to love and if you were happy. I think what I was really wondering about was if you were happier without me."

"I never bothered to find anyone else to love," he replied quietly. "I'm afraid you won't like me as much when I tell you I preferred not to think about you."

If she was hurt, she gave no indication. "I didn't expect you to pine away for me, Dev. We did the best thing by parting before we could destroy each other."

He shook his head. "Maybe it was for the best. I went on to do what I wanted to do, and you lived the life your parents wanted you to." A trace of bitterness coated his words.

"You forget, they wanted me to be a lawyer." She used her forefinger to trace a meandering line down his throat to the hollow where a drop of water still nested. She lapped it up, feeling his body shudder under her touch. She smiled. "How could I tell them I don't even like to watch *Perry Mason* or *L.A. Law* much less live the real thing? So you did one good thing when you came into my life, Devlin Grant. You showed me there were alternatives."

Dev stood up and put his hand out. "Had enough of the water?"

She ignored his outstretched hand as she looked up at him. "I'd planned to take a long-awaited bath and shampoo my hair. Why, is there a time limit on how long we can stay out here? Didn't you tip the pool man enough to let us have privacy more than fifteen minutes or so?"

He smiled ruefully at her light teasing. "I'm quickly discovering the more I look at you in that sheer excuse for underwear, the more I want to make love with you."

Her nerves jumped at his words. "No hot lust, no jumping on each other's bones?"

He placed his fingers over her lips. "I'm talking about two adults powerfully attracted to each other, willing to take that very important next step."

Megan didn't say another word. Instead, she lifted her hand and placed it in his.

He gently pulled her to her feet and led her back to where they had dropped their clothing and towels.

"We would probably be more comfortable on a large bed with silk sheets," he said as he laid out the towels.

"You slide around on silk sheets." Then when she felt his gaze, she said, "I read it somewhere."

"Don't you dare do or say anything to ruin this," he warned.

Megan stretched out on the towels. "Now that I have you where I want you? Not on your life."

Dev looked as if he wasn't sure whether to look relieved or suspicious as he lay down next to her. "This thing is downright dangerous," he accused playfully as he drew his finger down the narrow camisole strap to the sweetheart neckline. He drew the garment slowly over her head, then curled two fingers around the narrow bands of her panties and slid them down her legs. He rained kisses on every inch of silky skin he revealed, working his way back up to her mouth. "If I'd known something like this was under my T-shirts, I probably would have gone crazy."

She ran her hands across his shoulders and down to his waist. "Don't you dare think about stopping for at least the next twelve hours."

"Whatever the lady wants, the lady gets."

Megan soon discovered Dev had an incredible arsenal of kisses to tempt her senses. Not the deep soul kisses of before, but light and teasing ones that left her aching and begging for more. Every time she reached out to touch him, he moved out of her way, softly explaining that this was all for her, for her enjoyment. When his mouth found her nipple, she bit her lower lip to keep back her screams of delight. His teeth nibbled their way back up her chest and neck, and by the time he covered her mouth, Megan was almost insane with desire. He placed himself in the cradle of her hips, pressing down until he rested against her hot and hard.

"I want you inside of me," she breathed.

"Not yet. We still need to reacquaint ourselves with each other. Find out what we like and dislike."

"I like what you're doing just fine as long as you don't stop," she gasped out when she felt his fingers stroking between her legs. She gripped his upper arms so hard, her fingers dug into his skin.

"That's it," he murmured, pleased with his efforts at arousing her. Who would have ever believed cool, calm Megan could turn into a volcano. He wanted to have her tell him she had never responded to any other man like this. He wanted this to be only theirs. "Oh, Meggie, once we start, there's no turning back."

"I'm the practical one, remember?" She deliberately allowed her fingers to brush against his hardness, then encircle it. "No more talking, Dev." She guided him toward her, lifting her body to entrap him.

The moment Dev thrust inside Megan, he knew he was lost. He looked down into her eyes, luminous in the moonlight that now spilled fully out over them as if the clouds refused to allow them to try to hide from each other.

Their bodies moved in a languorous rhythm that required no stopwatch, no time limit. As far as they were concerned, they had all the time in the world, and they were intent to utilize it as they rediscovered old rhythms and made new ones.

Dev dipped his head, presenting Megan with the kind of kiss a boy gives to a girl the first time. The kind of kiss that began their relationship fifteen years ago. A relationship they both instinctively now knew hadn't disintegrated back then, but had been put on hold until the time for them was right. Then, as desire escalated, his kisses turned hot and hungry, as if he couldn't get enough of her, and their bodies moved together faster and faster.

Megan gasped as the first wave of ecstasy overtook her body. She dug her fingers into his back, uncaring if her grip bruised him. She felt as if she needed to hold on to something solid or she would fly into a million pieces.

"Dev?" She was breathless, as if she'd gone to a place where air was a precious commodity.

"Let it go, Meggie," he urged. "Give in so we can go together." He gritted his teeth with the knowledge he couldn't go on much longer. But he wasn't going to leave her behind. They'd already started sharing, she would continue as they went.

Megan was past hearing as she felt all the nerve endings in her body explode. She couldn't take her eyes from Dev's contorted features, nor could she close them as she felt a darkness overtake her. She couldn't remember ever experiencing anything this intense before, and she wondered if she'd survive. She wasn't certain, but she thought she screamed his name when the world imploded around them.

"Wow," Megan moaned once she found herself back in the real world.

"Yeah." Dev rolled over onto his back and drew her with him until she lay sprawled across his body.

"I wish you'd thought of that sooner. I think a rock is permanently embedded in my back." She sighed with relief at his fingertips pressing along her spine.

"Bitch, bitch, bitch," he said lazily. His grin grew larger by the second. "I have to be honest, Meggie. I don't remember us being this great fifteen years ago. Maybe age has its compensations after all."

"Stop with what happened fifteen years ago. We're here and now." She yawned. "Let's concentrate on that." Even with the aftershocks still pleasantly rocking her body, she wanted Dev again. "Except, this time," she drawled, moving over him fully, "let's change places."

Dev laughed. "Honey, you might be able to forget about the fifteen years, but my body hasn't. I can't recharge my batteries as easily as I used to."

She straightened up until she straddled his hips, one shapely leg on either side. "Well, then, I'll just have to see what I can do to jump start your motor, won't I, ace?" she purred, nuzzling the flat copper nipple until it rose up to a hard nub under her searching lips.

Dev never knew what hit him.

"YOU'RE GOING TO HAVE TO post rules for the guests using that pool," Megan said, not giving a hint that the idea of anyone using *their* pool was sacrilege in her eyes. "Such as it's completely off-limits. Say there're snakes in it or something."

"No problem. We just won't tell anyone about it," Dev announced, keeping his arm draped around her shoulders as they walked back to the house. "I don't think some people's hearts could handle its magical properties."

Megan smiled with satisfaction. "Good."

"You going to come back outside? We could zip our sleeping bags together," he suggested. There was no doubt they would spend the remainder of their nights together after tonight.

"Or you could sleep inside where bugs can't drop onto your face in the middle of the night. It's even nicer now that we have indoor plumbing." She tickled the back of his neck.

Dev paused. "Maybe one of the front rooms that still has an intact wall."

"What's wrong with the room I'm in now?" She already knew the answer to her question. She just wanted to hear him admit it.

Dev didn't say anything until they reached the backyard, and then he waited until they entered the house and stood in the kitchen. He switched on the overhead light and looked down at Megan's waiting figure. Right now, her wet hair curled riotously around her face and her clothing was damp from the soaking they indulged in after the second time they made love. Her skin was flushed a faint rose and her eyes were still languorous. She had never looked more beautiful to him. Incredibly, he wanted her again.

"Don't push the issue, Megan," he said quietly with gentle force. "Please."

She thought about the hiding place in the fireplace and the still-unread journals. Perhaps it was better they used a different room. She couldn't afford for him to find the journals just yet.

"Why don't you go outside and get your things while I set up that first room at the top of the stairs," she suggested. "It gets the morning sun—we'll need it to wake up."

Relieved she didn't try to pursue the subject, he dropped a kiss on her lips. "I can probably come up with something better if I put my mind to it."

"If I were you, buster, I'd use something other than my mind," she tossed back.

Megan practically ran upstairs so she could make sure the stone protecting the journals was secure before she moved her things into the other bedroom. Now she'd have to find another way to read the journals without Dev finding out about them.

As she gathered up her sleeping bag and dragged it down the hall, she told herself this was a new turning point in her life, something still very fragile that would have to be nurtured. She promptly put out of her mind all the plants her black thumb had killed over the years. A relationship wasn't a plant, anyway.

When she returned for her clothing, she stood in the middle of the room with the armload threatening to fall at any moment. "You obviously loved someone very special, Maisie," she said softly to the woman's spirit she sometimes felt still inhabited the space. "I'm only sorry you couldn't keep him with you forever, because from what you've written, he was the best thing to come into your life. Don't worry. I'll make Dev see the truth, I promise."

"You promise what?"

She turned and found Dev standing in the doorway. He stepped forward and took her clothes out of her arms.

Her fingers tracked their way from the first shirt button all the way down to the button peeping over his waistband. She wiggled her fingers between the fabric folds until she found warm, bare skin. "I promise to give you the kind of night you only dreamed about before." She winked, looking incredibly naughty and very sexy.

Dev brightened at the prospect. "Maybe I better rush out and buy a bottle of multivitamins."

She tugged on his waistband and pulled him toward her. "Don't worry, you'll do fine without them."

"SON, IF YOU AREN'T careful you're going to drop that sledgehammer on your foot," Harry warned.

Dev lowered the heavy hammer that seemed to have increased by a hundred pounds since he'd first picked it up a few minutes ago. "Yeah, well, I didn't sleep too well last night."

"Shoulda made use of that pool I told you about," Charlie advised in his slow, even voice as he surveyed the wall already torn out by their morning efforts.

"We did," Dev muttered then snapped his mouth shut.

Both older men stared at him with amazement. Surprisingly, neither pursued the subject.

"What, you guys slacking off again?" Megan walked into the room with a slight trot to her gait.

"You've been mighty chipper all day," Harry drawled.

"The sun is shining, the birds are singing and all is perfect with the world," she replied brightly. "That jerk at the hardware store didn't give me a bad time when I bought those nails for you. Of course, it might have had something to do with the ax I held at the time," she mused, sending Dev a sly smile. "I also bought a hot-water heater, which'll be delivered day after tomorrow, and arranged for our phone to be connected tomorrow morning. I have to say the house is finally starting to take shape. I can't wait until we can start painting outside. It's going to look so great when we finish!" She patted Dev on the cheek. "Poor baby, I don't think he slept very well last night," she informed the other men. "We also didn't have any coffee in the house, and Dev's not worth a plug nickel without his morning coffee. I took care of that, too." She pulled a pair of work gloves out of the back pocket of her jeans and pulled them on. "Back to work for this grunt." She began piling pieces of plasterboard in the wheelbarrow. In no time she had the wheelbarrow filled and she wheeled it out the door.

"How does she do it?" Harry demanded of Dev.

"I have no idea," he muttered, forcing himself to pick up the sledgehammer again, carefully lifting it over his shoulder. "That woman has more energy than ten people. She must suck it out of others and use it for herself."

Harry and Charlie exchanged a silent, telling look.

"Maybe you better take whatever she does to get your own energy level up," Harry advised with a sly grin.

"I don't think so." Dev uttered an oath of exasperation. "We going to get these walls torn down today, or just stand around jawing about Megan?"

"Tear down walls," Harry said immediately. "That's what we're here for. Megan, get a move on," he shouted out the open window. "The boss is rarin' to go."

He grinned broadly at Dev's muttered curse. He and Charlie had been trying to play matchmaker from the beginning. Charlie's suggestion about the pool seemed to have done the trick.

MEGAN DIDN'T GIVE A DAMN she couldn't whistle. She just felt so good she had to do something and her singing voice was even worse than her whistling. She pushed the wheelbarrow down to the edge of the front yard and dumped the debris on the pile waiting to be trucked over to the dump.

She didn't need a mirror to see what she looked like. Having overslept that morning, she contented herself with pulling her hair up in a haphazard ponytail and pulling on one of Dev's T-shirts with her jeans. Makeup wasn't needed to emphasize her glowing eyes and skin. If her face was dirty, she didn't care. She was too happy.

She had no idea what time she and Dev had finally fallen asleep. She hadn't cared because she had been too busy enjoying the freedom of exploring his body. "I better let him get some sleep tonight," she told herself, turning the wheelbarrow back toward the house.

She had just reached the front steps when the sound of a car engine alerted her to visitors. "It better not be Eunice or that idiot of a sheriff here to ruin my good mood," she mumbled, trying to see beyond the cloud of dust obscuring the car. She looked up to see Dev looking out the window. He looked grim, as if fearing the worst. Megan gave him a reassuring smile. "Don't worry, I'll protect you," she cooed, blowing him a kiss.

His lips curved then straightened again. Megan turned around to see the reason for Dev's mood change. She recognized the sporty red Mercedes immediately and wanted to stamp her feet and scream her outrage. What was he doing here? More importantly, why?

She uttered one of Dev's favorite curses.

The man that stepped out of the Mercedes looked like a male copy of Megan when she first arrived. Crisp pleated khaki slacks, salmon knit polo shirt, leather deck shoes, the latest in designer sun glasses, blond hair perfectly styled as if the late-morning breeze wouldn't dare blow one strand out of place and an orthodon-tist's dream of a smile.

"I'm going to be ill," Megan moaned at the same time Dev uttered his own opinion of "die yuppie scum."

"Is that who I think it is?" Dev's low voice reached Megan's ears.

"Yes."

"Did you invite him?"

"No."

"What do you intend to do?"

She watched the man talk toward her. "Before or after I break his arms?"

"Good, you'll save me the trouble."

"Honey, what has happened to you?" The man's drawl was pure upper-crust East Coast. "You look as if you just climbed out of a rag bag." His gaze swept up and down her body.

"What are you doing here?" Megan demanded.

"I missed you," he admitted, stopping abruptly about a foot away from her, as if afraid of getting dirty. He couldn't hide his shock as he whipped off his sun-glasses and took a better look at her. He still kept a careful distance. "Megan, I was wrong. You look more like the little match girl!"

"When you're renovating an old house, you can ex-pect to get a little dirty." She was grateful for that dirt because she knew he wouldn't dream of touching her. "I still want an answer, Rob. I never mentioned where I was going, so there can only be one person who would tell you." She made a mental note to murder her mother when she got back to L.A.

"Your mother is worried about you," Rob ex-plained, looking around the still-overgrown yard and the rose garden beyond. His expression of distaste rang out loud and clear to his audience. "You can't tell me that you're actually staying here and working like a common laborer?"

"I'm doing my part, and I'm proud of it." She flinched when she heard the front screen door slam. She didn't have to turn around to know Dev had walked outside. She could feel his energy force, remarkably renewed from a few minutes ago.

"Is there a problem?" Dev stopped beside Megan. Not once did he take his eyes off the other man. With his bare chest and jeans covered with dust and scuffed boots, he looked like a dangerous thug.

"No problem, Dev, this is Rob Peters. Rob, Dev Grant, my partner," Megan said, making hasty introductions.

Rob started to put out his hand then reconsidered when he noticed the filthy work gloves Dev hadn't bothered to remove. "So, you're Megan's ex-husband." Rob's brief smile said he could now understand why the marriage failed. His expression turned to one of confusion when he looked at Megan. This urchin before him was not the woman he'd been seeing for the past year.

"Yeah, well, we're pretty busy here," Dev drawled, knowing he was acting like the roughneck Rob saw him as, but didn't care. Just as long as he left...alone. "So whatever you've got to say to Megan, could you get on with it so we can get back to work?"

"What I'd like to say can't be said here." Rob continued smiling in the way that set Dev's teeth on edge. "Basically, her mother has asked me to bring Megan home. She's been worried about her, and Megan has hardly called her while she's been up here." He shot her a look of faint reproach. "We all care about you, Megan."

"I don't need that kind of 'care,'" she said between clenched teeth. Her mother had sent him up here like an errand boy to retrieve a package. And she was the package!

Rob looked taken aback by her anger. "Megan, you have a lot of responsibilities back home to consider. Your boss is threatening to fire you if you don't return by the end of the week. After all, he was kind enough to give you a lengthy leave of absence, but you can't abuse his generosity." Rob had no idea how pompous he sounded.

"Jerry threatens to fire someone at least once a week," Megan tossed back. "Besides, he's a jerk to work for. As for my mother, she has no right to send you up here. I'm old enough to dictate where I go and how long I stay. You can tell her that for me. I'm sorry you made the trip for nothing." She knew she didn't sound sincere, but all she wanted was for Rob to leave. The tension in Dev's body was fairly radiating outward.

Rob glanced worriedly at Dev. "Megan, you don't belong here," he said in a low voice. "Can't we go somewhere and talk about this? I've really missed you."

Megan hated that he tried to make it sound as though they shared more than they ever did.

"There's really nothing to talk about, Rob." Her voice gentled. She should have known he never took her subtle hints. She should have been more direct from the beginning.

Rob's forehead creased in a puzzled frown. "But your mother said you were missing me just as much as I was missing you. That's why I drove up. We also have that charity function coming up in a week. You said you'd go with me, remember?''

"What he's missing is a few screws if he can't understand plain English," Dev muttered, shifting from one foot to the other.

Megan placed her hand on Dev's arm. "Why don't you go inside," she murmured. "I'll take care of this."

He looked from one to the other. "And you tried to make me believe you were going hot and heavy with him." His sarcastic voice reached only her ears.

"Please, Dev."

He nodded jerkily and walked back to the house. Megan turned back to Rob.

"Is there something going on I should know about?" he asked once Dev entered the house.

She shook her head. And she used to enjoy this man's company! Had he always been this dense? Or she that blind? Had she only dated him because he was suitable, the kind of man she preferred being seen with? One who would never dream of getting his hands dirty or doing any kind of physical labor other than batting around a tennis ball?

"Nothing that's any of your business," she replied. "I never promised you anything, Rob. I never intimated there could ever be anything between us. So please do us both a favor and go back to L.A. Tell my mother—no, I guess that's something I should do myself." She sighed heavily.

"You've changed, Megan. I don't think I know you anymore." He looked sad. He looked beyond her at the house that looked disreputable. "I can't believe you actually think you can make something of a house that looks as if it would fall down at any moment. It doesn't even look safe to be inside."

She smiled. "Yes, I have changed, and for the better, I might add. I'm not the same woman you knew. And to be honest, I'm glad I'm not. As for the house, it's sturdier than you think. Just like people. I'm learning that there's more sides to me than I ever imagined, and I'm beginning to like myself again."

He looked confused. "What do you mean like yourself? There was never anything wrong with you before. Did that thug tell you that?"

Megan almost laughed at the description. "No, Dev had other words to describe me, and they were all true. I don't want to live a plastic life again, Rob. I want it to have good old-fashioned value, and I can't find that back there. Even if I did go back now, Rob, I wouldn't be the same person, and I doubt you'd like this new Megan as well." She looked over his shoulder at his car, his pride and joy, then back at him. "Go home, Rob."

Chapter Eleven

December 7, 1941.
The Japanese bombed Pearl Harbor early this morning. When I heard the news on the radio, I could only curl up in a chair and cry at the number of lives lost. Someone thinks Richard Brown is on the *Arizona*. Not Richard. Such a sweet loving man. He came in here to play poker with some of the other men and sometimes he'd play the piano. Such sweet sad songs he played. I will miss him. Barney stopped by after church. He told me he's enlisting in the army. He hasn't told his family yet because he knows they'll try to talk him out of it. His father has enough political influence to keep him home, but he said he has to fight. I wanted to beg him to stay, to not leave me, but I know this is something he feels compelled to do. Instead, I smiled bravely and told him he will be in my prayers every night.

January 5, 1942.
Barney left for boot camp today. I wanted so badly to go into town to see him off, but I knew it would

be better if I remained home. We don't think his wife knows about me, but we won't take any chances. And I refuse to make things any more difficult for him. His family is already upset that he enlisted. Poor Barney. They should be proud of him instead of acting ashamed he insisted on going overseas. Perhaps I should have sold the house years ago and we could have gone away and made a fresh start. But life can't be lived with a lot of "should haves." I'll just pray for his safe and speedy return.

"Who was Barney, Maisie?" Megan whispered, keeping her arms well out of the bath water. She knew she was taking a chance bringing the journal into the bathroom, but she'd told Dev she wanted some time to herself while she relaxed in a well-deserved bubble bath, now that the water heater had been installed, the gas lines hooked up and the well approved. "I can understand why you didn't dare use his last name, but I wish you could have given a hint. Come on, one little hint." She skimmed pages, reading on about the scares concerning Japanese submarines parked off the California coast, food-and-gas rationing and war-bond rallies. She smiled as she read about Maisie's frustration with the lack of nylons, how she used makeup and pencils to draw a seam along the back of the leg. Especially, how much she missed coffee and chocolate. And Megan felt like crying as she read Maisie's sorrow over the town's losses each time a family received a telegram from the War Department and more women appeared in black.

A pounding on the door startled her so badly, she almost dropped the book into the water.

"Hey, you almost finished in there?"

"No!" Megan leaned over the side of the deep, claw-foot tub, hurriedly wrapped the journal in a towel and jammed it under the tub.

"Does that mean I can come in?" The doorknob rattled before he opened the door and peeked in. "Look what we have here, a mermaid. How much bubble bath did you pour in there?" He scanned with frank male interest the high mound of pearlized bubbles surrounding Megan. "Did you leave any hot water for me?"

"If you don't mind smelling like Red by Giorgio, you can join me," she invited, picking up a handful of bubbles and blowing them at him.

He was already shedding his clothing, dropping it every which way as he advanced on the tub. He stepped into the opposite end, wrinkling his nose at the fragrant bubbles. "Something tells me this tub is going to become pretty popular," he commented, resting his arms along the rim and leaning back.

Megan grinned. "You know, you look cute with all those bubbles."

He made a face as he reached out and pulled her toward him. "I don't know why I let you do all these horrible things to me," he grumbled good-naturedly, rubbing his cheek against her shoulder.

"Horrible things?" she questioned, cocking her head to one side to provide him better access.

"Yeah, making me walk all that way to a hot spring we weren't in more than two minutes before you seduced me, then keeping me up all night so I couldn't get my work done the next day. It's becoming a pattern, you know. Then, if that isn't bad enough, you crack the whip while I install the hot-water heater just so you can have bubble baths." He turned her around so her back rested against his chest. "Then you lay around in here while I'm out there working my butt off."

She turned her head so she could see his face. A face she loved more each day. "You were working at making a lot of noise," she commented, wiggling her hips until she sat snugly between his spread thighs. His arms wrapped around her in a warm embrace. "It's very difficult to relax with all that hammering and swearing. What were you doing out there?"

"You'll find out soon enough."

She stroked the back of his hand, idly tracing the wisps of dark hair. "Do I get a hint?"

"Nope." One of his hands found its way to her breast, covering the wet globe and rubbing her nipple to a rosy prominence. His other hand traveled lower under the waterline until he touched her damp heat. His fingers combed through the dark thatch of hair before cupping her intimately and beginning a slow, insistent rhythm that took her breath away.

She closed her eyes and lost herself in his sensual touch. "This isn't fair," she gasped.

"Why not?" His lips traveled across her nape left bare by her hair pinned on top of her head.

"Because I can't do anything to you."

"Don't worry, when the time comes, I'll allow you to return the favor," he murmured, fastening his teeth on her damp skin. "Did I ever tell you how good you taste?" Right then, she couldn't have answered if her life depended on it. He didn't bother to wait for one. "You do, you know. You taste sweet and tart all at the same time. And you always leave me wanting more." He nuzzled the curly strands of hair falling down. "You turn me on, Meggie."

She moaned and tried desperately to turn around, but he refused to allow her to move as his fingers continued their ministrations.

"Dev, please let me," she whimpered, reaching behind her for him.

He allowed her to pull his face down for a kiss. "This is all for you, Meggie," he murmured against her lips. "I want to give this to you."

By then, she was flying with only Dev's arms keeping her on earth. Megan's eyes widened with wonder as she blindly watched the satisfaction on Dev's face at the pleasure he gave her.

What seemed like hours later, she lay in his arms and took in several deep breaths. "That was..."

He smiled. "Yeah."

Megan turned around. Her smile was positively wicked. "And now, it's my turn to return the favor."

READING MAISIE'S JOURNALS gave Megan a new perspective on the townspeople, especially the women. Maisie wrote of an era in which there were only two kinds of women—the ones men took home to Mother, and the ones men didn't dare acknowledge. Maisie did most of her shopping in another town because women refused to wait on her and the men were too afraid of their wives to speak to her. Yet they saw nothing wrong in making the drive out of town and up the hill to the Victorian house with the lights blazing six nights a week for talk, pool, poker and a few other activities.

Megan secured one of the books in her tote bag and any time she left the house, she made sure to take the time to read on. She smiled as she read about the victory parties celebrating the end of the war. Barney's homecoming and his first venture into local politics.

The passage she read on this trip to town was not so cheerful.

May 7, 1948.
I haven't told Barney yet, but I am seriously thinking of selling the house and moving where no one knows about me. I have William in a private school near San Diego, so perhaps I'll move there. While I love Barney with all my heart, I know I can't go on with my life as long as I stay here. His wife miscarried for the third time, and they were told it would be better if they didn't try again. I feel for him because I know how much he wants children. He dared to ask if I would allow him to adopt William so he and his wife could raise him as their own. How cruel could he be? I told him I would never allow my son to enter a loveless household or be mothered by such a coldhearted woman. That was three weeks ago, and I haven't seen him since. I know I hurt and angered him, but I felt it had to be said. I'm becoming selfish as I become older. I want more than just one part of a man. I want it all. I tell myself it's for the best, but it's difficult to make myself believe it.

Reading about Maisie's pain put Megan in the mood for the ordeal that awaited her at the hardware store.

"This is not what I ordered." Megan glared at the clerk who glared back.

"It's what's written on the order blank." The stone-faced man pointed to the slip of paper. "There's no mistake."

She tore open the brown wrapping to reveal the wall-paper beneath. Garish red roses seemed to jump out and blind the viewer.

"Looks about right to me." The man smirked.

Megan planted her hands on the counter and leaned forward until she was staring him straight in the face. "Since you took my order, I had assumed Eunice St. Clair had passed the word. Obviously I was wrong. Let me make this perfectly clear. I don't like to be crossed, and I don't like mistakes. I suggest you get the right order in by tomorrow. If you can't do that, then just give me my refund now and I'll go where they can do it right."

"No refunds on special orders, and we don't make exchanges." He stared back impassively.

She resisted the urge to throttle him. "Where's your boss?"

"He's not in today."

"Naturally." Megan turned and dug through her bag until she found her Day Runner. She searched through the leather-bound book until she found the envelope that held all the receipts. She slapped her copy of the order on the counter. "*Your* mistake. *Your* loss."

The man barely glanced at it. "I can't settle that. Only the boss can."

Megan snatched the receipt back. "You will have the correct wallpaper and paint in here tomorrow or so help me, I will wallpaper your face with this," she hissed, shoving the rolls of wallpaper at him so hard the man stumbled trying to catch them as they knocked him backward. She stalked through the door, slamming it so hard the glass shivered in the frame.

Megan was too angry to go back to the house. Instead, she decided to make a few phone calls in hopes she'd cool down. Just to get it over with, she called her mother first.

"Megan, you've been gone five months on this ridiculous stunt. Do you realize you no longer have a job?" Ellen Abernathy demanded the moment she came on the line. "You should have just sold the property and been done with it."

"Mother, we've been through this," Megan said on an exasperated sigh. "Renovating the house is more profitable. It's just taking more work than we figured on. And we weren't able to get a large crew working for us."

"And I can understand why. Do you have any idea what that house was once used for?" Ellen demanded. "I did some investigating and learned it was once a brothel! I knew that boy was no good, and this is proof of it."

Megan took several deep breaths to dispel her fury. Why couldn't the woman let well enough alone! "Mother, don't you ever say that again." Her voice was low and threatening. "You know nothing of what went on up here."

"I know that you ruined the chance for a perfect marriage to Rob to take up with a whore's grandson," Ellen argued. "Your father and I refuse to allow that boy to try to destroy you again."

"I had no idea just how close minded you were until now." Megan spoke slowly. "All I have to say is that I am very ashamed you are my mother. And I'm very grateful that I didn't end up like you. Goodbye, Mother." Megan made it clear her words were meant to be final.

"Megan!" Ellen's protest was cut off as Megan hung up. This time her mother had gone too far, and right now Megan wasn't sure she could forgive her for a very long time.

Megan turned in the confining booth and smothered a scream when she found someone standing outside the folding door.

The sheriff, in all his khaki intimidating glory, stood in a spread-legged stance, as if he would draw his gun if she made one wrong move.

Megan had no problem looking equally as intimidating as she opened the door so violently the man was forced to step back.

"Your car radio not working, Sheriff?" She exited the booth.

"You enjoy making trouble, don't you?" the man stated without preamble. His hand rested on his gun as if he feared she might do something violent.

Megan couldn't help but note his posture and read the meaning. She resisted the urge to grin. Little did the man know how a sheriff who was convinced he was Dirty Harry could hardly intimidate her. Not after she just went three rounds with her mother.

"On the contrary, Sheriff, I live such a clean life that I could make a laundry-detergent commercial."

The man's eyes narrowed. "You've got a smart mouth, missy."

Megan stepped forward until their noses practically bumped. "And you sound like something out of a B movie . . . Sheriff," she added the last belatedly and deliberately. "I can't believe I've done anything to warrant this impromptu visit from you right here at a public phone booth."

"This is a town full of good people, Miss Abernathy. You L.A. people like wild parties, bright lights and lots of people. We don't have a movie theater in town or a night club, but that's fine with us. We're happy with what we have and don't go around looking for more. Maybe that makes us hicks in your eyes, but we don't mind."

Her eyes flashed dark brown fires. "Talk about stereotyping," she snapped, advancing on him until they were nose to nose. "I shouldn't even defend my lack of a wild social life—I doubt you'll believe anything I say. I'm usually in bed well before midnight—by myself I might add—because I'm so tired from running around with clients all day I couldn't live it up if I wanted to. My idea of a fun evening is reading a good book with the stereo on. That's why what I see here is a lovely, unspoiled town that any sane person needing to get away from the fast lane would want to stay in. Too bad the residents are so close minded that an outsider wouldn't have a chance of finding that kind of life.

"Let me tell you something. One thing I learned from my parents is that no law officer worth his salt makes assumptions without concrete evidence. Doing otherwise could get him in a lot of trouble." She punctuated her words with a forefinger tapped against the man's chest. She swept around him and headed for her car.

"Miss Abernathy." The sheriff's voice rang out just as she opened her door. She turned her head, a defiant look on her face. "You might just be the one to change my mind about people from L.A."

Her face softened. "Maybe there's hope for you yet." She got into her car and drove off. At least she was closer to getting the sheriff on their side, even if they were a long way from converting Eunice St. Clair.

DEV ALWAYS ENJOYED LOOKING at Megan—whether she was covered with plaster dust and cursing at a stubborn piece of wood, as she was doing just now, or covered with bubbles and lolling in that large claw-footed tub, as she tended to do every evening. If he had to choose between the two, the latter would win hands down.

He was surprised how much he tended to think about her nowadays. He knew he looked at her like a lovesick kid when she was around. But, hell, he couldn't help it! And it wasn't just the way she filled out her jeans or shorts, either. There was something about the way she moved, the way she sang to herself, uncaring how badly she sounded. And the way she would look up and see him watching and give him the most beautiful smile that made him want to pick her up and carry her inside. He knew there was a name for the way he felt. A simple four-letter word. So why didn't he just say it out loud? Better yet, why didn't he say it to Megan?

"What a wuss you are, Grant," he mumbled.

Things had changed the past few days. Megan had come back from town looking down in the mouth. All she would tell Dev was that she had had an argument with her mother over the phone and she doubted that Ellen Abernathy would be calling again soon. She refused to divulge the reason behind the argument, but he had a hunch it had had to do with him. He was just glad Megan had chosen to remain here rather than go back to L.A., as he figured her mother had probably ordered her to do. Yep, things sure had changed.

Still, the idea of Megan staying here, with him, on a permanent basis seemed so right. He thought of that morning when he had spied the small plastic case with its tiny pills inside. He'd wanted to throw them away. He'd wanted to indulge his masculine urges and see her pregnant with his child. Hell, he'd just plain wanted her with him all the time! If that wasn't love, he wasn't sure what was. He wished he had the nerve to say the word out loud to her.

"Stop standing there laughing at me and come over here," the object of his ardor ordered as she struggled with a plank they'd just torn out of the wall.

Dev walked over and lifted the plank as easily as if it were a toothpick. "You should have eaten your Wheaties today," he chided, carrying the board out of the room and down the stairs.

"Ha, ha, ha," she retorted, hot on his heels, dragging a smaller board behind her.

"At least the hardest parts are over."

"For whom?"

"For all of us. We've got electricity, running water, a phone, and a couple of the rooms are actually habitable. Before you know it, you'll be able to start hanging all those rolls of wallpaper stacked downstairs."

"The bathrooms still need new tile work," she reminded him. "And floors."

"Okay, okay." He laughed, holding his hands up in surrender.

Dev walked outside and tossed the plank onto the pile of scrap wood they'd kept at the back of the house. Megan followed suit.

She looked up, studying the sight she'd seen all too many times and tried to block out. This time she saw it in all its sorry splendor. Warped boards, peeling paint, sagging shutters.

"Do you think we've taken on too much, Dev?" she asked. "Even with all we've done so far, we've still barely made a dent in what needs to be done. While Harry and Charlie are wonderful, two extra sets of hands aren't enough. At this rate, the place won't be ready for another year."

He draped his arm around her shoulders. "Sure, it will. You just have to have faith. We're able to get more supplies from town without hassles, right? That's saving us a lot of time."

"Yes, but now I wonder if they're serving us because they want to report our activities to good old Eunice." She sighed. "It's bad enough having the sheriff driving by almost every day."

"He might change his mind after yesterday." Dev chuckled at the memory of Megan stomping down the hill to the sheriff's car and tartly informing him if he planned to stop by so often, he may as well earn his keep and pitch in.

"I figured he could use a hammer as well as any of us could," she told him.

"Okay, hotshot, time to work some of that energy off." Dev gently pushed her toward the door.

"I just want to see those lousy walls finished so I can start doing what I know best," she argued.

"Don't worry, I already have a pretty good idea what you know best, and it doesn't have much to do with painting and wallpapering."

"Someday, Dev Grant, you'll get yours," she threatened, throwing open the screen door and walking inside.

He caught it before it could snap back in his face. "I think I already have."

Chapter Twelve

April 5, 1952.

Everyone in town was so surprised when Barney reactivated his commission. It isn't fair! He's supposed to stay here and be safe; not go off to Korea and risk being killed. He's already done his duty to his country. There's no reason for him to go again. Although, I know why he's going. Rumor has it his marriage is basically over. I admit I'm a selfish woman and want Barney to myself, but I wouldn't wish unhappiness onto anyone. His wife can't help the way she is. Sometimes I wonder if she didn't marry him because of his family name and the dream of living in the governor's mansion one day. How sad if that's the only dream that makes her life worthwhile.

Barney came to see me before he left town. He wanted me to understand why he had to go, and he also wanted me to know he's going to ask for a divorce when he returns. While I want nothing more than to spend the rest of my life with him and give him all the children he wants, I know I can't. There're too many others to consider than just ourselves now. Barney has the chance to have the political career his family has always dreamed of. A career he couldn't pursue if he divorces one woman to marry the likes of me. But, for now, I smile and pretend to make plans I know can't come about. Because when I learn Barney is returning home, I will leave town and move near William's school. It's past time I let Barney get on with his life, because it's time to get on with mine.

Megan closed the journal. There weren't many more entries, but she didn't feel in the mood to read on just now. Now when she knew Maisie broke off her affair with the only man she loved. How did Barney take it? Did he allow her to leave gracefully, or did he argue with her? While Megan might only have Maisie's point of view to go on, she sensed the two had loved each other very much. How sad they hadn't been able to share a life together.

She glanced down at her watch. Dev, Harry and Charlie would be back any minute, and she had to put the journal back into its hiding place. While they were off buying lumber, she had decided there wasn't a better time to try to finish reading the last of Maisie's journals. Now she wasn't sure she wanted to read the last entries. The ending of an ill-fated love affair hit much too close to home for her peace of mind. Not when she realized how much Dev had come to mean to her over the months. She was afraid to call it love, but she didn't know any other way to label it. No, that was the coward's way out, and after reading of Maisie's bravery, Megan wasn't about to be a coward. It was love. But even after all she and Dev had shared, she wasn't sure he would accept her gift.

Of course, if she just happened to say it in just the right setting, she mused, settling back to lean against the wall. Candlelight, soft music, her dressed in something sheer and clinging. She could take a bath with the last of her bath oil, use the last of her perfumed body cream in all the right places, then her dusting powder. She smiled, visualizing the scene.

Dev would come in all dusty and tired, and there she would be, like someone out of a man's fantasy. She'd first urge him into the tub, where she would take great pleasure in scrubbing his back—and a few other places. Too bad strawberries weren't in season. She could dip them in powdered sugar and feed them to him between kisses, then wash them down with some fine wine. She suddenly frowned. No, champagne would be better, more romantic.

All right, his bath is over and she's dried him off oh so carefully and led him into their romantic bower. She grimaced. Sleeping bags aren't all that romantic, but she'd do the best she could. A back rub to start with. Too bad she didn't have any body oil. Then a front rub along with a few scattered kisses.

Her breathing escalated as the pictures rapidly shifted from PG-13 to R to X rated. She would give him the perfect romantic night.

"Yes," she breathed, feeling her pulse rate jump to an alarming rate. After all that had gone on, they deserved it. She deserved it! Here she was, wearing jeans without a designer label on the pocket, drinking domestic beer and eating food from paper plates. Except Dev had made it all worthwhile. So the least she could do was make something worthwhile for him.

She stood up and stretched her arms over her head. The sound of Dev's truck alerted her to the men's return. She thought about the evening she planned and smiled. A smile that just as quickly dimmed as she saw the work ahead of her.

"Oh, well, it was a nice idea," she sighed, pulling herself back to the present.

"If I was meant to have muscles, I could have paid good money to develop them at the health club," she mumbled, pulling her work gloves out of her back pocket. She had just stepped outside the room when she remembered the journals. She ran back inside and stuffed them back into their hiding place, then ran outside.

"About time you showed up," Dev greeted her as he and Harry maneuvered a long plank off the truck bed.

"Be still my heart. He's so romantic when he sees me after several hours apart," she mumbled, walking toward them. "No offense, but they're a bit long for me to handle."

"You don't have to," Dev assured her. "Just make like a traffic cop and make sure we don't step in a hole or something."

"Out of the way, missy," Harry ordered, walking past Megan, both arms loaded down with cans of paint.

Her eyes widened as she looked into the truck bed and saw just how much was there. "How much did you buy?"

"Hopefully, enough wood to replace the warped boards, nails and paint," Dev replied, pulling his T-shirt over his head and draping it over the side of the truck. "I got what we decided on. White for the house and dark green for the shutters."

Her first thought was sadness. Picking up paint for the exterior meant that job was soon coming and with it, the completion of the house. She felt sad at the idea of the project coming to an end so soon, and she worried that it could mean the end to everything.

She bit her lower lip as she gazed at Dev's bare chest. Memories of her earlier fantasy returned in full force. Maybe it was supposed to be nothing more than a fantasy. Or maybe there was a chance, as long as she was brave enough to reach out and grab it. And no one had ever accused Megan of being a coward.

Dev dipped his head to murmur in her ear as he walked past her. "Sorry I don't have any time for more than you ogling me, sweetheart. But don't worry, I'll make it up to you later tonight."

"In your dreams, bub." *And mine.*

His wicked grin always did crazy things to her insides. "It's as good a place as any to start." He picked up some supplies and headed toward the house, then abruptly stopped and turned back to Megan. "You know, I had a thought. How about we give each other a break and go out for dinner tonight?"

"If you think I'm going to refuse, you've got another think coming," she said promptly. "All I ask is someplace that's as close to civilization as you can find."

Dev nodded. "Got it." Hearing Harry call his name, Dev held up his hand in acknowledgement and shouted, "Coming." Then he returned his attention to Megan. "If you've got something that will show off those great legs of yours, wear it," he told her before trotting off.

"I guess this is the closest I'll get to my fantasy," she muttered, walking back inside the house. She skidded to a stop and broke out smiling. "Until we get back, that is."

MEGAN LOOKED AT THE DIRT parking lot littered with potholes and pickup trucks of varied colors and sizes.

"You've got to be kidding."

"Harry said they have the best steaks in town and that the music isn't bad if you're a hard-core country-western fan." Dev parked his truck off to one side, where he hoped he wouldn't get boxed in the way so many other trucks had been. "We might have made a mistake picking Friday night, but I figured we deserved a night out on the town."

"No offense, but this isn't what I picture for 'a night out on the town,'" Megan said as she waited for Dev to assist her out of the truck. "I think it has something to do with that sign hanging by the door that orders the customers not to throw up in the parking lot."

Dev eyed her short denim skirt and the poppy red T-shirt she'd worn that first day. "You cleaned up nice, Meggie."

She cocked an eyebrow. "Mr. Grant, you take my breath away with your flowery compliments," she said wryly.

"Just wanted you to feel at home." With his hand resting against the small of her back, he guided her toward the entrance.

Dev didn't notice anything out of the ordinary when they entered the wooden building—once he looked past the sign asking that dogs and guns remain outside. The air was thick with smoke, the music loud and the talk, punctuated with curses, even louder. Just the kind of honky-tonk he felt he'd spent half his life in, and the kind he was equally certain Megan hadn't stepped inside until that night.

With Dev directing, they made their way over to a corner booth. A waitress stopped by the moment they were seated and took their order for a pitcher of beer.

"No white wine for the lady?" Dev teased.

Megan wrinkled her nose. "Very funny, Grant. I may not patronize places like this, but I know enough not to order wine or mineral water in here. Actually, I was expecting tall bottles of beer served with dirty glasses." She fanned the air in front of her face. "I guess no one here worries about secondary smoke turning their lungs black." She looked around with great interest. There was no mistaking the postage-stamp-sized floor filled with dancers. The women were poured into tight jeans or even tighter miniskirts. The men were betting each other as to who could down the most beer in the least amount of time. "I know a sociologist who would have a field day in a place like this." She looked down at the menu. "All they serve is steaks or barbecued ribs and beer."

"Good thing you're not a vegetarian, huh?"

"The size of these steaks is more for lumberjacks than me."

"Don't worry, I'm starving, so I'll eat whatever you can't."

"You folks decide what you want?" The waitress, wearing a pair of denim cutoffs and a bandeau top, set the full pitcher of beer and two mugs on the table between them and took their orders.

"Wanna dance while we're waiting for our food?" Dev asked.

Megan eyed the dancers' intricate steps and shook her head. "I'll stick to disco, thank you very much."

"In case no one bothered to tell you, disco's dead," he informed her, deadpan.

"They once said that about rock and roll," she reminded him lightly. "There's still hope for white polyester suits and open-collar silk shirts with gold chains against a bare chest. And I'm only talking about the men!"

Dev made a disgusted sound. "No, thanks, I'd rather be a macho ingrate."

Megan placed her folded hands on the table. As she looked down at the scarred wooden surface, she realized there was a multitude of initials carved into the wood, along with phone numbers and a graphic description of their owners' best traits. "And here I thought these kinds of ads were only written on bathroom walls," she murmured, studying one that turned out to be very interesting. "Hmm, this one sounds intriguing."

Dev could easily read the upside-down description that fascinated her. He grunted and slapped his hand over the words. "Once upon a time, you would have sworn that was disgusting."

"I used to hate sushi, but now I eat it. Given time, you can get used to anything." She waved a hand toward the center of the room. "There was also a time I wouldn't have been caught dead in a place like this. Over the years, I've learned to be more flexible in my thinking."

Something flickered across his eyes, but passed too quickly for Megan to accurately read it. "So I'm just part of your new, flexible thinking? That it's okay to go to bed with your ex-husband as long as the sex is good?"

Megan sat back stung. "Is that what you really think?"

"We haven't really talked about it."

She seriously thought about hitting him. "And you consider tonight and this place a good time to indulge in it?"

Dev shrugged. "Just something I happened to think about. Before you know it, the house will be finished and we'll have to make some decisions. I've been thinking it might be a good idea to put ads in fishing and hunting magazines now. It's too late for this year's fishing season, but it won't hurt to get a head start on next year."

"Just as long as there aren't any moose heads in the dining room."

He nodded. "Okay, how about a big picture of dogs playing poker or pool?"

She wrinkled her nose. "I'll come up with something tasteful but suitably masculine."

Dev laughed. "I trust you," he said as the waitress arrived with their order.

When they were alone again, Dev gave Megan a serious look, and said, "You know, we talk about the house and we talk about current events, but we never really talk about ourselves, our thoughts."

She lifted her head. "Is there some reason for this sudden interest?"

He grimaced. "I never did give you much of a chance to really talk, did I?"

"You haven't wanted to do much talking the past month or so," she said dryly, enjoying his discomfort. An embarrassed Dev was something new, and she intended to enjoy this. "But I didn't try to talk much, either. Fine, what exactly do you want to know?"

"How did you feel after our divorce became final?"

She sucked in a breath. That was one question she hadn't expected. "Relieved," she said bluntly. "By then, I was ready to go back to school and I saw it as a chance to begin again. I figured I could reverse my mistakes."

The expression on his face was intent, as if her reply to his question mattered a great deal. There was also a hint of pain in it. "And you saw our marriage as a mistake?"

Megan knew the loud music precluded anyone overhearing their conversation, but she still felt uncomfortable talking about something so personal in a public place. "Yes, I did."

Dev looked away. The muscles in his jaw worked furiously. "Then if you hated me so much, why did you come up here? You could have handled your end up from L.A. Why bother to do all you've done these months?"

"I already told you. To make up for the past." She concentrated on her food. "To prove to you I've changed. Nobody's perfect, Dev. We were two kids who followed our hormones and ended up in a situation we soon learned was too much for us. At least we got out before it ended up worse. What if I had followed you all over the world while you built bridges and dams? How many jobs have you been on that didn't allow wives present? How many men do you know are divorced because of their work?"

"More than I can count," he ruefully admitted.

Her voice softened. "And what if children came along? What kind of pain would they have had to endure because of our stubbornness? Would that have been fair?"

His shoulders rose and fell. "No, no, it wouldn't."

"Then just count us as two more casualties. Look at it this way. We both took this time to grow up and learn more about ourselves. It made us the people we are today."

His eyes left her face and slowly trailed down her body, pausing over her rounded breasts. "And I like what you are today."

Megan hoped she wasn't blushing. After all, the man had already seen everything there was to see. Why get hot and bothered just because he looked at her as if he wished she was the main course! "Eat your steak before it gets cold, and I'll tell you about my wild days as a college girl."

"How wild?"

"Our sorority helped a fraternity put their president's bed on top of their frat house—with a very drunk president still in it. We even strung Christmas lights all around it. A police helicopter almost landed on it."

Dev chuckled. "You're kidding!"

She shook her head. "It was done when the president had had a few too many beers. He was convinced a rival fraternity did it, and no one ever told him different."

"Is that where you met Rob?" Dev's lip curled when he said the name.

She shook her head. "No, I met Rob a year ago. He's a very nice man, a perfect escort for concerts and gallery openings. My parents had been pushing for grandchildren, and dating Rob was easier than putting up with their heavy-duty matchmaking. It got so I didn't dare stop by their house for fear of meeting one of their 'friends,'" Megan said wryly.

"Your mother must be having kittens at the idea of you being up here with me."

Her face tightened. "My mother has no control over my life."

"So you didn't just stay up here to get your mommy and daddy's goat?"

Megan dropped her utensils onto the platter before her. "We're here to have a nice dinner out, not to fight about my family. Why don't you back off." Her cold gaze drove steel spikes into his heart.

Dev knew it was time to shut up. He'd seen more than enough proof of Megan's temper to know she didn't make hollow threats. "Meggie." He reached across the table and took her hand in his. He rubbed her fingers between his, looking uneasy. "I'm sorry if I upset you. I guess I tried for one thing, and it came out something entirely different. I wanted this to be like a date. Only problem is, my dating experience is pretty limited." He managed a weak smile. "Jungles and deserts don't give a man too much practice."

Megan looked into his eyes and felt as if she saw so much more than he might have wanted her to see.

"So far, so good," she said huskily, turning her hand over so that palm met palm. She laced her fingers through his. "You asked me out to dinner, I accepted." She looked around. "We went to someplace unusual, had a nice dinner and talked."

He grinned, still looking uneasy. "I guess this isn't what you're used to on previous dates."

"I don't believe in having preconceptions anytime I go out," she told him. "It's more fun to be surprised." Her warm smile wrapped itself around him. "And tonight has been the most fun I've had in a long time."

Dev searched her face, but didn't find anything other than sincerity there. "You're something, Meggie. Really something."

She continued smiling. "You know, the date isn't over yet. You still have to drive me home, walk me to the door..." She paused dramatically.

"And...?" he probed.

"And, perhaps, we could try a good-night kiss. And if you pass the test of a great good-night kisser, we could go on from there."

"Go on where?"

"Oh, maybe a nice bubbling hot spring where we could relax or do... other things."

"We've already concentrated on the relaxing part. Let's work on the other things for now."

Chapter Thirteen

"You two planning on getting married again?" Harry asked Megan as he helped her carry paint cans into the kitchen, placing them on the tarp-covered counters.

Her fingers paused in their task. "We really haven't discussed it." She opted for a casual tone.

"You make a nice-looking couple," Harry told her. "And it shows you care for each other." He fumbled inside his shirt pocket. "By the way, I found something I figured you might be interested in." He looked around as if afraid of being overheard. "I didn't think Dev would appreciate it, but I thought you'd like to see it." He held out a photograph that was creased and slightly yellowed from age.

Judging from the clothing and car in the background, the photo had to have been taken around World War II. A young-looking Harry with a wide grin on his face stood next to a young woman whose face glowed as she stared up at him. Another woman stood off to the side. She was dressed in a halter playsuit that displayed a slender figure. Her delicate features were feminine, but Megan easily identified Dev's smile and eyes. "This is Maisie," she whispered.

Harry nodded. "A bunch of us had driven out for a picnic. Maisie never felt right going with us, but we played on her sympathy about men going off to war and such. Some of the men's girlfriends went along. We never told them exactly who Maisie was, but I think some of them guessed, but as long as Maisie didn't make a play for their fellas, they really didn't care." He looked pensive as he gazed down at the aged photograph. "She'd been looking peaked for a while, and we thought a day out might cheer her up. She had the most beautiful smile."

Megan made an impulsive decision. "Harry, did you know about her baby back then?"

He nodded. "One night, a bunch of us were talking about our mortality, and Maisie must have been feeling it, too, because she told us she had a little boy in a private school. Never said who the father was or where the boy was. Just that she was glad she kept him and wished she could see him more than the two weekends a month. None of us there ever talked about it after that night. We figured that was her secret."

Megan opened one of the paint cans and picked up a wooden stirrer. The rich creamy yellow blended easily as she used the spatula-shaped object. "She left behind journals of her life here," Megan said in a low voice.

Harry's eyebrows lifted so high, they almost reached his hairline. He whistled under his breath and uttered a curse. "Pardon my French," he muttered. "She wrote about the town, the people?"

Megan shrugged. "It was mostly her personal thoughts. Her mother's death, her taking over the house, later on, her baby. Things like that," she said cautiously. While she experienced relief at divulging her secret, she still felt wary of saying too much after keeping it to herself for so long. "She didn't name names or anything that could be considered blackmail material if the wrong person had found them." *Except for her words about the man she loved so much and gave up.* Megan wondered if she could be that unselfish if she were faced with the same situation.

"Meggie, you hide those books good," Harry whispered. "If word got out about them, people could turn real ugly."

"But there's nothing inflammatory in them," she argued, surprised by his ferocity.

The older man leaned forward. "But she wrote about the boy's father, didn't she?" he guessed.

Megan instinctively knew she could trust him. "She only referred to him as Barney."

Harry's eyes almost bugged out of his head. "Barney?" he repeated.

She nodded. "That's the only name she wrote. She said that he later married and had something to do with local politics when he returned home from the war."

Harry turned away, shaking his head. "Don't tell anyone else about those journals," he whispered, urgency radiating from his tense figure.

Megan felt his tension enter her body. "Harry, you're frightening me."

"I'm not trying to frighten you, just make you more cautious," he explained. "There's things that shouldn't get out."

She made a wild guess. "It has to do with the identity of Dev's grandfather, doesn't it?" The expression on Harry's face told her it wasn't all that wild, after all. "You obviously know who he is. I could tell by the look on your face when I said the name."

Harry turned away. "Some of us thought that was the way the wind blew, but none of us ever said a word," he murmured, as much to himself as to Megan. "We figured she deserved what little privacy she could get."

Megan caught his sleeve. "Harry, who is it?"

He remained with his back to her. "Let the past stay buried, Megan. You'd only make things worse by saying anything."

"I plan on giving Dev the journals when I finish reading them."

A slow shake of the head told her he didn't agree with her idea. Then, as if her words had finally sunk in, he turned around. "You mean you haven't finished reading them yet?"

"Lately it's been difficult to find time to myself to read them without Dev knowing what I'm doing," Megan replied. Another thought occurred to her. "Do you think someone knows about the journals? And maybe the problems we've had have something to do with them?"

"I doubt it," Harry said without hesitation. "You have to realize that Eunice and most of the women of our generation were taught that women in Maisie's profession were lower than mud and should be run out of town because they tempted God-fearing men and broke up marriages." He snorted his contempt of such an attitude. "They never stopped to think you can't break up a good marriage unless it's meant to break up. After Irene and I got married, I explained to her I came out here to have a few beers and play poker, nothing else."

"And what did she say to that?"

He grinned. "She said I was welcome to stop by here as long as I only had a beer or two or sat in for a hand of poker. But if I ever climbed those stairs, I better sleep with one eye open from then on 'cause she'd come after me with a carving knife. And I don't think she would've cut out my heart with it, neither. That woman has a temper like you wouldn't believe, so I never gave her any cause to worry."

Megan burst out laughing. "It sounds as if this so-called sleepy little town wasn't so sleepy after all."

"Never said it was." He looked around and lowered his voice. "I mean it, Megan. Keep mum about the journals."

She leaned forward. "Harry, I hate to disillusion you, but you aren't mentioned."

"Never thought I was. But some people might not believe you if you said they weren't in them." He held up his hand as if to ward off any further words. "I don't even want to know where they're hidden. You just be careful with them."

Megan had already seen enough evidence of the town residents' reaction to the house reopening even as a hunting and fishing lodge. "Okay, I'll be careful, but when the time is right, I still intend to give them to Dev. He can't ignore Maisie's past forever. It isn't right."

Harry smiled and touched her shoulder. "You're a good woman, Meggie. You should seriously think about staying up here once the house is finished."

Which was exactly what had run through Megan's mind an average of every few hours for the past few weeks, since she realized the house would be finished before she knew it. As it was, she didn't want this time to end. "I've got my work in L.A., Harry."

He waved his hand dismissively. "Selling real estate don't keep your bed warm at night, missy. You just remember that come winter."

"I haven't been asked."

He chuckled at her forlorn expression. "Sweetheart, don't wait to be asked. Just forge on ahead and do it! Isn't that what you women's libbers do anyway?" With that, he stomped outside.

"Missy, little lady, sweetheart and girlie," she muttered, returning to her can of paint. "And they wonder why women hate nicknames."

"I HEAR YOU COULD USE some carpentry work done."

Dev studied the young man, who'd introduced himself as Seth Andrews, standing before him. Dev doubted his age was all that much past twenty.

"I've been needing help for several months now. Why are you here all of a sudden?" He knew he should appreciate the man's presence, but after everything they'd endured, Dev could only feel suspicion.

The man shifted his feet uneasily. "Everyone figured you'd get fed up real quick and leave. You showed them different."

"Damn straight," Dev growled. "Maybe one inn won't turn the town's economy around completely, but it could give it a much-needed kick in the butt."

The man grinned. "That's why I'm here. There's not all that much work around here, so I have to do a lot of traveling looking for construction work. My wife's expecting our first baby in about six weeks, and I don't want to be too far away when her time comes. I won't give you cause to regret hiring me, Mr. Grant. I'm good with my hands, and I follow orders. The main thing is, I need the work," he added with blunt honesty.

Dev chewed on the inside of his cheek. "We begin at seven and work until dark. Harry and Charlie can't handle a lot of the heavy work, so I've been doing what

I can, but it's piling up over my head. I need another pair of strong arms. To be honest, I could use more than one pair, but I've gotten used to making do with what I have. You'll also have to realize that working for me could give you problems in town. I'm not exactly Mr. Popularity."

Seth's face cleared when he realized that Dev was actually agreeing to hire him. "I'm not a stranger to trouble, and I can start now."

"Stay home with your wife today," Dev advised. "After tomorrow, you're going to be too tired to spend much time with her."

Seth grinned and headed for his truck. Before he climbed in, he turned around. "If you meant it about extra hands, I'll see what I can do."

"Fine with me, as long as they realize the first person to create trouble out here will have to deal with me."

Seth knew about the fight in town a while back and knew Dev wouldn't hesitate to protect what was his own. "We're not all like Mrs. St. Clair and her followers," he said. "There're some of us who would have been out here sooner, but as I said, we didn't think you'd last."

"I'm like a virus, Seth. I don't go away easy."

"You'll get your men."

"Well, what do you know." Harry whistled under his breath, walking up behind Dev as Seth drove away. "That was Lois Andrews's boy."

"Think I made a mistake in hiring him?"

"Naw, he's a good kid."

Dev chuckled. "A kid who's going to be a father pretty soon."

"Yeah, and her daddy weren't too happy about it. They've only been married about four months. Once

Seth knew Jenny was pregnant, he insisted on their getting married. Said his kid wouldn't go through what he did because his daddy refused to marry his momma," Harry expounded. "Seth's as reliable as they come. And if he rounds extra workers, they'll be just as reliable. He was pretty wild a few years ago, but Jenny straightened him out just by giving him love."

Dev felt a strange ache well up inside. He remembered a wild kid not all that long ago who thought he loved the right kind of girl. He wondered what would have happened if he and Megan had had children.

"You gonna get her to stay?" Harry's sharp eyes didn't miss much.

Dev didn't need to ask who the old man meant. "She wouldn't be happy up here away from bright lights and Rodeo Drive."

"Did you ever stop to ask her? She sure looks happy in there mixing paint and deciding how to furnish the rooms." Harry clapped Dev on the back. "Son, you're in love with the girl. Why not marry her again and give her some babies to keep her busy?"

The ache intensified to a gnawing pain. "Harry, you're walking on dangerous ground."

"You think I don't know the two of you aren't doing more than sharing a house? Something tells me neither of you would do that unless there was something serious between you."

"You know how it was before," Dev protested, looking off into the distance, where pictures of the past seemed to haunt him.

"Does that mean it has to happen again?" Harry argued. "Why not find out just what you two could have. Besides, I'd miss her."

Dev smiled. "You old coot, that's your real reason for wanting her to stay."

"She's easy on the eyes. Just think about it. Not that many people get a second chance at life. Don't screw it up." With that said, Harry wandered off, shouting for his brother.

Dev had thought about finding a way to persuade Megan to stay here with him. But what could he really offer her? She was the one who invested most of the capital used to rebuild the house. Yet she never said a word about it, never held it over his head when her ideas clashed with his. "You're crazy, Grant," he muttered. "She's only sticking around to protect her investment, nothing else."

So why didn't his words sound all that convincing to his own ears?

Because he couldn't believe them anymore. Because he wanted her to stick around for other reasons, mainly because of him. Because of them.

He'd been thinking more and more about Megan staying up here on a permanent basis. His biggest fear was what she would do if she remained. There wasn't exactly a big real-estate market up here. Would she be happy helping him run this place once it got going? Or would she soon grow tired of it—and him?

There was only one thing he knew for certain—he just didn't want her to leave. Not now. Not when they were so close to having more than probably either of them ever dreamed of having. He looked upward. "Hey, Gram, maybe you didn't do such a bad thing after all."

MEGAN QUICKLY GREW accustomed to the sounds of more than three voices shouting back and forth and of the many hammers working on the house's exterior while warped boards were pried off and the thundering sound of them being tossed into a pile resounded through the air. True to his word, Seth had brought six other men with him. Megan was even able to appropriate one of them to rototill the backyard, where she planned to plant a lawn and new rose bushes. With the kitchen now painted and papered, she felt ready to begin work on the main rooms.

"Meggie, here's the clear varnish you asked for." Dev carried the can into the rear room downstairs that she announced would make an excellent game room with a pool table, dart board and a few other diversions.

"Thanks." She smiled up at him from her seated position on the floor, where she was busy using a fine-grain sandpaper on the wood molding. "What do you think?"

He hunkered down and looked at the warm wood, still barely visible under several layers of paint. "I can't believe how much you've accomplished in here."

Megan warmed under his praise. "Yeah, I'm pretty proud of it." She sat back on her heels and began rubbing her neck. She groaned with relief when a stronger pair of hands began kneading the tight muscles into submission. "Mmm, don't stop," she moaned.

"Remember that tonight," Dev murmured, leaning over and nuzzling her ear.

As the tension flowed out of her muscles, his touch slowed until his fingers were caressing instead of massaging.

"You've got a work crew outside waiting for you to play boss, Mr. Grant, sir," Megan murmured when his fingers fanned out over her back.

"I'm playing boss here. Wanna hear about my benefit plan?"

"I can imagine what they are." She could feel the warmth radiating outward from his touch. No matter how many times Dev touched her, it was always the same. First the warmth, then the fire, until she wanted him so badly, she couldn't breathe.

His teeth grabbed hold of her earlobe and pulled gently. His body was hard and aroused against hers. "Maybe I should take an early lunch."

Her head lolled backward against his chest. "We had lunch more than an hour ago."

"An early dinner, then." His voice was raw in her ear while a hand made its way down to the front of her shirt. One button loosened, then two, then three. Cool air wafted between the folds of the shirt before his palm warmed her skin.

Megan fought the strong desire threatening to overtake her. "Dev," she whispered, melting against him as his thumb and forefinger teased her nipple.

"Dev!" This voice was louder and very male. "You about finished in there?"

Dev's hand stilled before reluctantly withdrawing. "Not finished, just postponed," he murmured, dropping a kiss on her ear. "Shall we finish this discussion later on?"

She gulped in a much-needed breath of air. "All right."

Dev's hands tightened on her shoulders for a brief second before he stood up and walked to the door. "Coming!" he shouted. And then in a low voice to Megan, he said, "I only wish I was."

EVEN WITH THE EXTRA HELP, Dev was so tired that night, he kept his eyes open long enough to eat dinner then mumbled something about resting a bit before he went upstairs for a bath. He stretched out on their sleeping bag and immediately fell asleep.

"So much for 'postponed,'" Megan murmured, smiling at his soundly sleeping figure. She picked up her flashlight and stole into Maisie's room for a bit of late-night reading.

May 7, 1953.
Barney is dead. I had no idea I would write these words. At least, not this soon. Now, when he was still so young. Not after he survived those bloody battles fighting the Japanese, only to become the victim of a Korean fighter pilot strafing the camp. The only man I loved, the only man I wanted to spend the rest of my life with is gone, and I wish I was dead, too. Thank God for William, because he is the only reason I can go on. Now there's no reason for me to stay here, no worrying about how I would tell Barney our time together is over. Now I'll just close up the house and go away to a place where no one knows me. I only regret that Barney won't have the chance to see William grow up; that his only offspring won't carry his name. Although, even that could have been changed if I were a greedy woman. She came to see me yesterday. I had no idea she knew about us until she explained that before Barney left, he told her he wanted a divorce so he could be with me and our son. And now that he was gone, she wanted his son and was willing to pay handsomely for him, as long as I agreed to stay completely out of his life and disappear from the area forever. I never thought of myself as a violent person, but when she calmly offered me a hundred thousand dollars for Wil-

liam, I wanted to put my hands around her throat and choke her until all breath was gone. I ordered her out and made immediate plans to leave. Not because of her, but because of me. Half of my soul is gone and I can't stay in the rooms where we shared so much love. I'm just glad I can look at William and see Barney in his face. Maybe someday I'll tell him about his father and the circumstances behind his birth. As for now, I'll just play the part of a respectable widow the way I did when I enrolled him in school.

Rest in peace, my love.

"Oh, Maisie." Megan blinked rapidly to keep her tears back. "I wish you had said who Barney is."

She turned the page, surprised to find a loose sheet of paper tucked in the back of the leather-bound book. She unfolded it and directed her flashlight on the words.

January 25, 1991.

I never thought I'd return here after so many years, but lately I've felt the need to visit the place that gave me so much happiness. Not that I haven't lived a full life since I left here to see my son grow up and have sons of his own.

I don't know why I kept this house. Perhaps as a symbol. After all, it's been in my family for over a hundred years. Now it's time for a change. My days aren't as comfortable and I feel my time growing short. I could sell the land to someone who wants to raze the house and destroy all the memories. But I don't think so. No, I'll leave it to my grandson, Dev. His letters lately have betrayed a dissatisfaction. I don't think he knows it yet, but

I recognize his unhappiness and perhaps, by the time he finds out about this house, he'll be ready to settle down in one place. And there's no finer place than here. The only problem would be Eunice, and she's a formidable woman. I know Dev can handle her, but I know of a woman who could handle her even better. Megan has grown up into a fine woman and would be the perfect opponent for Eunice, if she's still alive when this all comes about. Who knows, perhaps Megan and Dev will rediscover each other, but I sincerely doubt it because they are too different in personality. But then, so were Barney and I. Still, I know Dev will do what's right. He's not Barney's grandson for nothing, and if Eunice has any good sense, she won't go against her own husband's blood.

When my time comes, I hope Barney is there waiting for me. It will make the trip so much easier.

"Oh, no!" Megan breathed, feeling the horror well up inside. No wonder Harry had been so upset when she mentioned the journals and asked about someone named Barney. Barney had been Eunice St. Clair's husband.

She fumbled with the oilcloth as she tried to jam the books into their wrapping. Now she knew she could never show these to Dev. They would have to be destroyed the first chance she got.

"Meggie?" Dev stood in the doorway, looking adorable in his sleep-rumpled state. "What's wrong?" His gaze fell on the books she held in her hands. The guilt written on her face highlighted by the flashlight she'd dropped on the floor alerted him.

"Just doing some reading. I came in here so I wouldn't disturb you." She injected a light, carefree note in her voice.

His gaze swung from the oilcloth-covered bundle to the opening in the fireplace. He walked slowly toward her and hunkered down. He touched one of the unwrapped books, flipping open the cover to see Maisie's name and the date neatly written inside. He jerked his hand back as if he had been burned. He took a deep breath before looking through the books. It wasn't difficult to guess the contents.

"How long have you known about these?" His voice fairly crackled with suppressed fury.

"Almost since the beginning."

He clenched his hand in a fist, then slowly unclenched it. "What are they? Financial records? A list of her customers? Maybe a record of their likes and dislikes? Their favorite positions? How kinky they want to get? Is that it?" His shout echoed in the empty room.

Megan knew she had to remain calm because if she lost her temper, all would be lost. "They're her private journals, her personal thoughts, nothing more." She snatched the book from him and hugged it against her breast, as if protecting it. "I thought I should read them before handing them over to you."

His eyes swept upward, the cold rage in the pupils slicing her clean through. "Why? Because you knew I'd destroy them first thing? Or did you want to read all the gory details? Learn just what my grandmother did for a living? After all, they're probably better than most porn books out nowadays!"

"Because she was your grandmother and she might have written something very important in them," Megan said quietly, holding on to her temper by a thread.

"Because she loved you enough to leave you this house because she knew you would protect it."

Dev gathered up the books scattered on the floor, then reached for the one in Megan's hands.

She held on tight. "You need to read them, Dev."

"I don't need anyone to tell me what to do! Just give me the damn book so I can put all these where they belong—on a fire!"

She stumbled to her feet and backed away, still keeping the book close to her breast. "You can't destroy these. They're your legacy," she argued, feeling the last threads of composure leave her body. "They'll tell you what Maisie was like back then. The kind of person she was. Why she did what she did! You refuse to listen to Harry and Charlie talk about her, so read about her in these. Give her a chance!"

Dev sliced the air with his hand, spinning around. "Why should I read what I already know? My grandmother was a whore!" he yelled, his voice booming in the still night air. "She made her living on her back, and my father was a result of that! I guess I should be grateful she didn't just go somewhere for an abortion. I mean, a pregnancy can't be a good calling card on Saturday night, can it? I wonder how much her business went down during her pregnancy."

"Stop it! Just stop it!" Megan screamed. "Deep down, you know none of that is true, and I don't intend to listen to something that dirty."

"Why not? Look what you've been reading." He held up the books. While anger quivered in his voice, something akin to pain darkened his eyes. "No wonder you've been so hot to trot these past months. It's been your late-night reading material. How many new tricks did you learn, sweetheart? How much of what we did was a result of this instead of true emotion?''

Megan's chest heaved with indignation that Dev had the audacity to cheapen what they'd shared. She didn't even stop to think. She clenched her hand into a fist and drove it into his stomach, all her weight behind the punch. He expelled a harsh breath and bent over, wrapping his arms around his stomach.

''By all rights, I should have aimed a hell of a lot lower, since that appears to be where your brains are,'' she gritted out. ''You son of a bitch. Who the hell are you to judge Maisie? You never cared to find out about her, about her life up here. And all because you learned the woman you remembered as the grandmother you idolized did something your high-and-mighty mind refuses to rationalize. You never stopped to think there might have been an excellent reason for what she did.''

''There's only one reason a woman becomes a whore. Because she likes it.''

''You're wrong, Dev. But you don't care about that because you only see what you want to see. You don't care about hearing the truth.'' Megan's voice vibrated with anger. ''I don't think you ever truly cared about her, because if you did, you'd be willing to understand. She was a woman who loved one man so much, she was willing to give him up because she knew how wrong it was and because she wanted him to have the kind of life he was groomed for. She was a woman who loved her son so much, she enrolled him in a private school away from here so he wouldn't have to endure slurs about her. She was a woman who managed a business but was never actively involved in it. Harry and Charlie said as much, but you never listened, did you? She knew more about love than either you or I could ever imagine." Megan paused to take a breath. "And if you can't see that, I feel sorry for you because then you're not the man I fell in love with." She kept the book cradled in her arms as she walked out of the room. "After you finish destroying the books, you can look for another place to sleep. Right now, I don't even want to see your face. Now I need to go where there's fresh air." She stormed out into the dark hall.

Man I fell in love with. Despite all the words she'd hurled at him, Dev knew those would haunt him for the rest of his life.

He looked down at the books he still held. With curses pouring out of his mouth, he threw back his arm and pitched the books against the wall. The thump they made wasn't completely satisfying. He slid downward against the wall and sat there, slumped, for hours, with only the flashlight shining a mocking beacon on his tortured features. He was unable to think coherently as he wrestled with the knowledge he'd blown his second chance after all. Then he recalled just how this all started.

"She had no right. No right at all." Whether he was talking about his grandmother or Megan, even he wasn't sure. Because it seemed the two had somehow become one.

Chapter Fourteen

"Never knew two people could be so damn stubborn," Harry told Charlie as they sat on the truck bed, sorting nails into empty coffee cans. Dev, not watching where he was going, had knocked over several of the cans and promptly lost his temper. Harry had shooed him off before he could do any more damage. "For the past week, she's been walking around here with her nose up in the air, and he pretends she doesn't exist. When they do need to talk to each other, they use us as go-betweens. I can't count the number of times one of them has asked me to ask the other a question when they're both standing right there."

"This morning, she asked me to tell him two floor-boards were warped in one of the bedrooms," Charlie drawled, holding one nail up to see it better. "Then he told me to tell her he'd get to it when he could. They were standing within two feet of each other and acting as if the other was invisible. It was really pitiful."

Harry shook his head. "And here I thought they were getting along just fine. Every time they looked at each other, the air crackled like it does before a lightning storm. And now look at them." He sighed, remembering Megan's tight-lipped version of the battle and her admission that Harry had been right. She should have destroyed the books first thing. Now it was too late. "They should be thinking of getting married again and making babies, instead of actin' like they're strangers."

"They both have a wide stubborn streak," Charlie commented, picking up another nail and dropping it into a can. "They really need to work together again instead of battling like two wildcats."

"If you two are finished dissecting us, I'm sure I can find something more productive for you to do." A cold voice rained an icy shower on their heads.

The two men looked up to find Megan standing in front of them. Only the slight flush on her cheeks and flashing eyes told them how much of their conversation she overheard. They guessed just about all of it.

"I told you those books could cause trouble," Harry said, defying her icy regard.

She stiffened. "Mr. Grant will have to learn that there are things in this world we all have to deal with. All along, he has refused to accept his heritage, and if it hurts, too bad. I'm sure Al Capone's relatives survived bad publicity. So can he."

"Then maybe you should have worked with Dev on this from the beginning instead of hiding it from him," Harry said gently. "We all knew he had trouble with Maisie's past, but none of us forced him to face it. I was hoping he'd get curious enough to ask."

Megan blinked rapidly. Harry wasn't a man from the big city, nor did he have lots of degrees, but he was astute enough to know she was trying very hard not to cry, and that she was taking the rift harder than she cared to let on.

"By all rights, I should be back in L.A. right now, looking for a new job," she stated coldly. "I'm only staying because it makes Mr. Grant crazy to have me around, and because I intend to see this project through, whether he likes it or not."

Both Harry and Charlie winced under her biting tone.

"Yeah, well, you're real good at that," Dev said from behind her.

She stiffened. "I won't even dignify that with a reply." Haughtily, she turned on her heel and stalked off.

"Then that will be a first for you. Usually you enjoy getting in the last word!" Dev shouted after her.

"The way you two carry on, you should be in kindergarten," Harry said, undeterred by Dev's warning glare. "So she read your grandmother's journals. She wanted to find out about the lady and you didn't. She didn't do any harm."

"She kept it a secret from me."

"She was trying to protect you, boy."

Dev pulled in a deep breath. "Protection is the last thing I need. Megan has always gone ahead and done what pleases her, and the hell with the rest of the world. She needs to learn there're other people around with feelings to consider."

"Then I suggest you stop and think real hard, because she did consider your feelings. She knew how you felt about Maisie, so she didn't hand them books over until she could read them and make sure there was nothing written inside to hurt you."

A muscle in Dev's jaw jerked. "Since I wouldn't have bothered to read them in the first place, she had no right to make that decision."

"She loves you. Isn't that enough of a reason?"

He opened his mouth to hotly retort, then abruptly snapped it shut. Without saying another word, he, too, stalked off. The two older men couldn't help but notice that Dev walked in the opposite direction from Megan.

"It's gonna be Mount St. Helens all over again when they finally get talking to each other," Charlie told his brother as they watched Dev walk away, then stop to crisply issue instructions to one of the workmen.

"Yeah," Harry sighed. "But maybe they'll clear the air."

"Or blow each other up."

"STUBBORN WITCH," Dev muttered, stripping off his T-shirt and buckling on his tool belt. He picked up his hammer.

"No offense, Dev, but the last time you hammered nails, we had to pry them all out," Seth ventured.

Dev swore under his breath. "Better hammering nails than her head," he said grimly.

"You two fighting is something else to watch," Seth commented. "My Jenny looks as if she wouldn't hurt a fly, but when she gets her back up, there's no stopping her. Megan looks like a rare flower that would wilt if she heard a bad word, but there's a lot more to her than meets the eye."

"And a mouth the size of Texas," Dev inserted. "Along with a razor-sharp tongue that can cut a man down to size so fast, your head would spin."

"Loving that kind of woman is hell, but worth it."

"Love? Me love her?" Dev shouted, looking horrified at the idea. "I'd sooner love a cobra. Actually, it'd be more enjoyable. Women have a way of making men crazy," he spat out. "And they do it for fun, just to watch us squirm. Well, this guy isn't going to squirm for any woman."

"All I know is watching you two is better than watching TV." Adam, one of Seth's friends, grinned. "It's sure given me ideas on what not to say to my wife. Between the two of you, this place is going to be something else."

Dev threw up his hands and stalked off.

"You're not going to help us hammer nails after all?" Seth called after him with a hopeful note in his voice.

"No!"

Dev found himself at the hot spring before he realized the direction his feet had led him. He didn't care. He just wanted a place where he could lick his wounds in private.

"Why does she have to stick her nose in places she's not wanted?" he muttered, dropping to the ground.

Because she cares.

Dev groaned as the thought echoed in his brain. He knew he had overreacted when he'd found Megan with the journals and learned what they were. And he had rightly deserved her punching him, considering what he'd said to her. He only wished he could get up the courage to tell her he was sorry. Except now he was afraid she wouldn't accept his apology, and deep down he was still hurt and angry she'd kept the journals from him.

He'd seen Megan angry before, especially during their stormy marriage, but never anything like this. When she looked at him now, he felt as if he was nothing more than a speck of mud she wanted off the bottom of her shoes. It hadn't improved matters when he'd let her think he had destroyed the journals. In fact, they were stashed away in the bottom of his duffel bag. He still didn't want to read them, but he couldn't bring himself to burn them, either.

So now he was angry with himself and sometimes taking it out on others, all the while wishing there was a way to make up with Megan. He missed her laughter, her conversation, and he missed her lying beside him at night where he knew if he woke up, she would immediately sense him and turn over to glide right into lovemaking that always blew his socks off. He stared into the bubbling water he hadn't visited in over a week. Not since before his and Megan's blowup.

At this rate, the moment the house was finished, she'd be packed and out of there before he could say a word. And that was the last thing he wanted, even if he did spout off about how glad he'd be to see the last of her.

"Why do I let my mouth get me into so much trouble?" he groaned. "Okay, give me a sign. I don't want to lose her again. The first time was understandable. This time, there has to be a way to fix it. Just give me an idea how it can be done."

Unfortunately, the water didn't have any answers for him, and Dev already knew he didn't have any of his own. But that wasn't going to stop him from searching for one.

MEGAN WAS MISERABLE. The anger she first felt toward Dev had quickly dissipated after she stopped to realize the reason he'd been so upset. The thing was, she refused to voice an apology when she knew she was in the right.

"He is so inflexible," she muttered as she drove toward town in search of the only cure for this kind of depression: a very large hot-fudge sundae. With a double helping of hot fudge, real whipped cream and plenty of chopped nuts. The cherry was optional. "He claims he's changed, but he hasn't. He still refuses to listen to reason." She wasn't the least disturbed that she was talking to a tiny voice inside her head. "He refuses to accept his grandmother's past, and he resents the idea she put it down on paper. He didn't want to bother to find out exactly what she wrote about."

And you didn't take the time to explain it to him, did you?

"Explain what? I was lucky to be able to keep the one book."

You could have tried to reason with him instead of losing your temper and punching him in the stomach.

"He deserved it." She made a face in the rearview mirror. It may have been childish, but it made her feel better. "Besides, I almost broke my hand against that washboard stomach of his." She slowed the car and pulled into the rear parking lot that served the town's few shops, one being a drug store with an honest-to-goodness, old-fashioned marble-topped soda fountain that made the best hot-fudge sundaes Megan had ever had the privilege to gorge on. She went inside and sat at the counter.

"I thought women your age ate nothing but greens and worried about your weight all the time." The sheriff sat on the adjoining stool just as Megan prepared to dig into her treat.

"There're days when this is very necessary. Today is one of them." She closed her mouth over the heaping spoon and savored the rich flavors. "Better than alcohol."

When the clerk approached, the sheriff asked for a Coke. Then to Megan, he said casually, "I hear there's trouble in paradise."

"I hear there's been trouble there since the day the snake showed up."

The sheriff's lips twisted in a reluctant grin. "Cute, real cute."

"I try. So, who's on the outs now?" Megan dipped her spoon in again.

"You and Grant. Heard the two of you are at each other's throats all the time." He stuck a straw into his drink.

Megan was never so glad to have the ability to mask her thoughts and emotions as she was right now. She also wondered who had the big mouth. "That's news to me." She spoke as casually as her companion had.

"Funny that someone who resents his grandma the way Grant does would be willing to put all that time and money into fixing up her house. You'd think he'd want to just get out of there fast."

Megan turned her head in the sheriff's direction. "You love to beat around the bush, don't you?" she marveled. "Is it something they teach you at the police academy?" She held up a forefinger. "No, wait a minute, I bet you're ex-military. Marines, right?"

He grinned. "They're the best. I'm surprised you guessed so easily."

"Marines have the hardest heads, the most obstinate natures, and they never back down from a fight. I dated one once, and that's what he told me." She rolled her eyes. "As if I wouldn't have guessed."

The sheriff burst into laughter, startling some of the curious shoppers who had been lingering nearby, trying to unobtrusively eavesdrop on the conversation.

"The name's Wade, Megan."

She grinned back, deciding he wasn't so bad after all. "If you really want to shock the locals, ask for one of these," she said in a stage whisper, pointing to her sundae. "You can keep me company."

"You've got that one almost finished."

She studied her nearly empty dish. "No problem, I intend to have another." After giving her order to the clerk, she propped her elbows on the counter and rested her chin on her laced fingers. "Aren't you afraid of being seen with the enemy? I can't imagine Eunice would appreciate you sitting with me."

"No one owns me, Megan," Wade informed her. "When I took on this job, the first thing I told the town council was that I left the San Francisco P.D. because of politics. I didn't intend to deal with them here. As long as I do my job, we all get along fine. And as long as your boyfriend stays out of fights, we get along better."

"The way I hear it, Dev was provoked into hitting that creep," Megan pointed out.

"A smart man doesn't allow himself to get provoked," Wade explained. "Even if it means defending a lady's name."

"I would have drop-kicked the sucker."

"Yes, I believe you would have." He chuckled. "You're a contradiction—a lady with the heavy-duty connections who sometimes talks like a regular person." When his sundae was set in front of him, Wade stared at the rich concoction with faint distaste.

"Hey, it's really good. Trust me," Megan confided, dipping her spoon into the ice cream. "This makes any problem in your life seem little."

"Like the boyfriend?"

She ate two bites before she replied. "If you want to know something, why don't you come right out and ask. You might get answers easier that way."

"Okay, why are the two of you so stubborn in rebuilding that house?"

"Because it's too beautiful to be torn down," she said promptly. "And because, no matter what Maisie Grant did, she was still a part of this town and remembered fondly by many people—and not just the men, but some women, too. The thing is, most of them are too afraid of Eunice St. Clair to speak up. So the zealots who are convinced we're building some new place of ill repute spread dirt about us. Let me make something clear—we want to open a hunting and fishing lodge, nothing more. We've worked damn hard to see that house brought back to life."

Wade nodded as he took two bites of the rich sundae, then pushed the dish away. "I don't know how you can eat that stuff," he grumbled. "Okay, no orgies, no trouble, right?"

She nodded. "Right."

"Any trouble out that way and I'll come down hard," Wade warned. He stood up and dropped money onto the counter for his Coke and sundae.

"Hey, my treat," Megan protested.

"Nope, don't want the folks thinking you're bribing a cop." His dark eyes twinkled. "See you around, Megan."

Megan turned back to see the clerk start to pick up Wade's unfinished sundae. "Ah, ah, ah," she chided, sliding the dish in her direction. "No use in seeing it go to waste."

By the time she finally slid off the stool, Megan felt a little queasy from the three sundaes she'd consumed and immediately headed for the part of the store that offered something in the way of relief.

She had just paid for her purchases when Eunice St. Clair entered the store. The woman stared coldly at Megan, then abruptly turned on her heel and walked out.

"Oh, well, can't make friends with everyone overnight," Megan murmured, heading for the door.

Once inside her car, Megan leaned over and popped open the glove compartment where the last journal lay safely hidden. Her fingers stroked the leather cover. She hadn't seen what Dev had done with the other books; she knew she couldn't bear to watch him burn them. She only mourned the fact he'd never really known about his grandmother. Nor would he ever care to find out. She considered this book the important one in many ways and still vacillated over what to do with it. When she came to her decision, she knew it could backfire on her, but deep down she felt it was still the best way to go. She decided to proceed before she lost her nerve.

Megan slowly drove out of the parking lot and headed for the outskirts of town, firm in her resolve and praying hard she was doing the right thing.

"TO WHAT DO I owe the honor of this visit?" Eunice asked, remaining seated in her chair after Megan had been ushered into the parlor by the housekeeper.

Megan didn't wait to be invited to be seated. She had a hunch Mrs. St. Clair would prefer she be ushered out as swiftly as she had been ushered in.

"Let's call it old business." She took the chair directly across from the older woman.

Eunice arched an eyebrow. "Oh, really? I can't imagine we have any old—or new business, as a matter of fact—to discuss. Unless, of course, you've decided to sell the property to me. Naturally, the price will be greatly reduced."

Megan reached into her tote bag and pulled out the leather-bound book. "To make a long story short, I discovered journals belonging to Maisie hidden in a fireplace," she explained. "They deal with her life from the time her mother died and she took over the house until the time she left here."

Eunice's face turned paper white. Other than her loss of color and the tightening of her hands on the arms of her chair, no one would have guessed she came dangerously close to losing her composure. "I can't imagine they would be of any interest to me."

"Not even where Barney is concerned?"

If Megan hadn't been watching the older woman closely, she would have missed the way Eunice's lips trembled for a scant second before she tightened them into a thin line.

"How much do you want?"

Megan blinked at the automatic assumption of blackmail. "I don't want money, Mrs. St. Clair."

"Then why did you come here? To taunt me? To see if I'd break down?" It didn't take a detective to see how upset Eunice was or how much effort it took for her to keep hold of herself. Even in her agitated state, she held her head high. "I'm sure your ex-husband will enjoy relating this little story around town."

"Dev doesn't know." Megan's voice gentled. "Mrs. St. Clair, Maisie saw no reason in telling anyone who the father of her baby was, and I believe in doing the same. It's really no one's business."

"Then why are you here?" Eunice demanded, leaning forward in her chair.

Megan held the book out. "To give this to you. Do anything you want with it. I didn't make copies of the pages, and I don't intend to tell anyone what I read."

Eunice's fingers twitched as if she wanted very badly to accept the book but was still suspicious of Megan's motives. Even the sincerity ringing true in Megan's voice and in her eyes didn't reassure her. "Why?"

"Because the way I see it, Maisie and Barney aren't the only victims. You were, too."

The older woman reared back. "I don't need anyone's pity!"

"And I wasn't offering it. If there's anyone who doesn't need pity, it's you. Considering what you must have known all those years, you still managed to hold your head high and carry on. Maybe there were mistakes made all the way around. I don't know, because I only know Maisie's side. But you have to have been hurt by what went on between them. Why should you be further hurt by something that happened more than fifty years ago?"

Eunice reached out and gingerly accepted the book. She placed it in her lap and folded her hands over it. "Then you know I refused to give him a divorce to marry her. That his parents and I threatened him with all sorts of dire happenings if he dared to leave me. He was willing to give it all up for her—his political future, his reputation, everything. I couldn't understand how he could be so stupid." She blinked furiously. "Perhaps if I had given him a child, things might have been different, but it wasn't to be. He wanted to adopt the boy, but I refused to have *her* child in this house."

She looked off into space, into the past. "There was no reason for him to go to Korea. He did it because he could no longer bear to be with me. He told me he wanted a divorce when he returned, and for the first time in my life, I lost my temper. I told him I would rather he never came back than embarrass me with a scandalous divorce. I've been haunted by those words ever since," she whispered, looking down at the book that held her long-kept secret.

Megan felt sorrow for the woman. "We all say things we don't mean," she said softly. "But he didn't die over there because of what you said. He died because he was in the wrong place at the wrong time."

Eunice looked up. "Did she write in here that I went to her afterwards and asked to adopt the child?"

Megan nodded. "That's why she left town."

"She gave all the women who worked for her a generous severance pay and closed up the house without a word to anyone, save Ezra. Even then, any communication was handled through an attorney in Los Angeles so no one knew where she was. I think she wanted it that way. It wasn't until you and Mr. Grant came up here that we realized she'd moved to San Diego. To be honest, back then I wouldn't have cared where she had gone." Eunice's voice dropped to a trembling murmur. "I blamed her for Barney's death because it was easier than blaming myself."

Megan's heart went out to the woman who had lived with guilt and bitterness for so many years that it had consumed her like a disease. At the same time, she doubted Eunice would remain in this vulnerable state for long. She was right.

Eunice lifted her head and eyed Megan with a great deal of caution mixed with suspicion. "I suppose you're pleased with yourself now. Learning all my deep, dark secrets."

"No, because we all have something we don't want anyone to know about," Megan freely admitted. "I know you wish you hadn't told me, but it must have festered inside you for so long that you finally felt you had to get it out or allow it to completely poison you. If I had wanted to hurt you in some way, I wouldn't have brought you the book. I would have handed it over to the local paper." She leaned forward in her chair, keeping her fingers laced in her lap. "Dev is hurting just as much because he had no idea of Maisie's past, and he's having a great deal of trouble coming to terms with it. He's grown bitter and angry at the woman he once loved and revered. Maisie never entertained the men. She only handled the administration end. According to her journals, the only man she was with was Barney, and that was long before you two were married. She never wrote his last name or gave any hint as to his identity, so I had no idea who he really was until the last journal."

"Barney was his middle name," Eunice explained in a low voice. "He was always referred to as William."

"The name of his son."

Eunice nodded. Her hands twisted together with the agitation that ran through her fragile body.

Megan sensed it was time to leave. She stood up. "The book is yours to do with whatever you wish," she said. "As far as Dev is concerned, it was destroyed. There's no reason for him to know. He's already destroyed the others without reading them. All I ask is that you let him open the house and give it a new life. There's no reason to bring up the house's history, although would it be so bad?" she probed gently. "We're all drawn to places that have a notorious past. And whether you like it or not, the town needs the business."

Eunice's lips trembled. "You don't know how much it hurts to love a man who doesn't love you back."

"I know how much it hurts to see the man you love hurting and you're powerless to help him."

Eunice eyed the younger woman speculatively. "It appears the rumors that the two of you are getting together again are wrong."

Megan shook her head. "No, there're many reasons why that can't happen," she said sadly.

"Then you'll just repeat history."

"Don't they always say history repeats itself?" Megan said wistfully. "Goodbye, Mrs. St. Clair. You were a formidable enemy. I hope, with time, you will become Dev's friend. He'll need them once I'm gone." She walked out of the room and headed for the front door.

"Megan." Eunice stood in the parlor doorway, calling out as Megan turned the doorknob. "I . . ." The older woman swallowed, looking as if the words were difficult to form. "Thank you."

Megan's answering smile was wan. "You may find this hard to believe, but I figured you'd be the safest place for the book. Don't disappoint me."

The older woman nodded. As Megan walked outside, she was aware of Eunice standing in the open doorway watching as Megan got into her car and backed down the driveway. Megan took one last look at the house. Eunice was still standing there. She only hoped she hadn't made a mistake leaving the book with Eunice. Something told her she hadn't.

Chapter Fifteen

"You get any more down in the mouth, boy, we'll have to bury you."

Dev looked up when something cold and metallic nudged his arm. He smiled and accepted the can of beer Harry held out. The three men having a beer together at the end of the day had become a habit. "I look that bad?"

"Worse. Why don't you just tell her you're sorry and get it over with?" Harry suggested. "Hasn't this cold war between the two of you gone on long enough?"

"How do you know it wasn't her fault?"

"Hell, boy, with women it doesn't matter whose fault it is, the man always apologizes," Harry said with a long-suffering sigh. "I should know. The last time anything was Irene's fault—according to Irene, mind you—was October 1957."

"Don't listen to him," Charlie piped up. "He'd lay down his life for that woman. He just hates to admit it."

Dev absently rubbed his abdomen where he could still imagine the ache from Megan's punch. He had no idea the woman could pack such a wallop. The purple bruise had been a good reminder to keep out of fighting range with her. "No, I think it would take more than an apology this time." Funny, he never imagined he could talk so freely to these two men. They had little in common other than their work on the house and their knowing Maisie. But now he realized something else bound them together. They all truly cared about one another.

"She can't understand why I don't want to talk about Gram," Dev said in a low voice, popping the tab on the beer can and lifting it to his lips. The cold brew soothed his dry throat.

Harry sat down on the redwood bench next to Dev. "The last thing you should feel about Maisie is shame," he said sternly. "She was a lady through and through. There wasn't a man around here who ever treated her any differently. In fact, none of the women here were treated shabbily because Maisie wouldn't allow it. You loved her before you knew all about this, didn't you?"

Dev nodded reluctantly.

"Then what's the problem?" Harry demanded. "None of what happened before had anything to do with you or your dad."

Dev thought of the journals still tucked in the bottom of his duffel bag. He still thought about burning them, but found the idea of tearing the pages out and throwing them into a fire strangely distasteful. Instead, they were better off just out of sight.

It was bad enough without Megan. Oh, she was around, but she had let it be known she had no use for him and that the farther away from her he stayed, the better she liked it. Trouble was, he missed her. The nights without her sleeping next to him were long and lonely. Yet every time he came up against her, he found himself using biting words instead of suggesting a truce.

"Maybe it's better this way," he muttered, finishing his beer. "Now she can leave here without any regrets." Pain colored his voice.

Harry shook his had. "Son, you can be downright dumb at times. If I were you, I'd come to my senses real quick before you lose Meggie again."

"I didn't lose her the first time," he argued.

"Maybe so, but you're older now and her parents aren't around to make any trouble, so make the most of this time. Break out a bottle of wine, light some candles and put on some romantic music. If you do it right, she won't have a chance."

Charlie snorted. "You've been watching Oprah and Phil again, haven't you?" he accused his brother.

"It worked with Irene. It can work with Meggie," Harry argued, turning to Charlie. "And I'll have you know I heard it on Arsenio. Some musician used it when he proposed. Okay, the marriage didn't last long, but the woman ate it up."

Dev groaned as he reached into the cooler for another beer. "I can't believe I'm hearing all this." But no one heard him as the two men continued their argument as to who had the best ideas for a romantic setting. Dev decided he'd just come up with his own idea and hope it would work.

MEGAN DIDN'T RETURN to the house until well after dark. She parked her car and got out, stretching her arms over her head to relieve the kinks from driving all over the country while she tried to clear her brain.

"I should have finished painting the upstairs bathroom instead of wasting gas," she chided herself, looping her tote bag strap over her shoulder.

"It's already done."

She turned around to find Dev standing outside the back door. The light from the kitchen backlit his body, leaving his features in shadows so she couldn't read his expression.

"Seth's wife had their baby today, so I let the guys off early to celebrate."

"Boy or girl?"

"Girl. Seth could only say over and over again that she looked like Jenny and that he was going to spoil her rotten."

Megan ducked her head. "That's wonderful," she said softly.

Dev looked at her, feeling his stomach tie up in knots at the idea of her carrying his baby. He suddenly wanted to run upstairs and pitch her birth-control pills out the window. He tried to tell himself that was nothing more than a macho thought that gave no consideration to her feelings. But the almost wistful expression on her face hinted that maybe she wouldn't mind it so much after all.

"Are you hungry?" he asked.

Megan laughed as she thought of the three sundaes she'd consumed. "I haven't given much thought to food, I guess."

He stepped to one side as she walked into the house. The tantalizing smell of roast beef permeated the air. She looked quizzical. "You cooked a roast?"

"More like tried out the new microwave," he admitted. "I cheated and already ate a piece to make sure I wouldn't poison you." He gestured awkwardly toward the table. "Why don't you sit down."

Their meal wasn't the sharing they'd had in the past, but it held none of the simmering anger that had colored the air lately, either. They approached each other cautiously as they ate their dinner and casually spoke of the day's happenings.

"All the shutters will have to be replaced. Seth told me he knows of someone who can get them at a good price."

"I was able to order mattresses for those two brass beds we kept. They'll arrive next week. I also got the names of three antique shops that might have furniture in keeping with the house."

Dev toyed with his food, then finally set down his utensils. "Do you really want to talk about the house, Meggie?" he asked quietly.

She kept her eyes downcast as she twirled her fork through her vegetables. "It might be safer." Her voice was just as quiet.

Finally giving up any pretense of eating, Dev pushed his plate to one side. "Meggie? Look at me. Please."

She slowly looked up.

Dev wondered what she'd say if he explained he wasn't used to baring his soul to anyone. That the words he wanted to say hurt a lot. Not that they would hurt her. They hurt him.

"I can't apologize for losing my temper about the books. I still feel I was right about them," he said in a low voice, keeping his eyes directed on hers. "You knew from the beginning I didn't want to know about that part of Gram. I didn't listen to Harry and Charlie talk about the old days, and I hated anyone who brought them up. Seeing those books just seemed to make it worse, as if the words made those times even more real than I wanted to imagine."

"Did what Maisie have here make her a bad grandmother to you?" Megan asked.

He shook his head. "No, but you have to admit it doesn't go with the image of my grandmother who took me to the park on Sundays and made me homemade chicken soup when I had the measles," he explained. "She played bingo on Tuesday nights and bridge on Thursday afternoons. When I went through my rebellious state, she talked Dad out of sending me away to military school, all the while saying it was in the Grant genes. Along with my parents, she attended all us kids' school functions, and when my mum was sick with the flu, Gram was brave enough to oversee my brother's tenth birthday party. We could always talk to her about anything." He gave a wry smile. "Even sex. Now I know why nothing shocked her."

Megan reached out and laced her fingers through his. "That's what I've tried to tell you," she murmured. "The Maisie who lived in this house wasn't your grandmother but another woman. Maybe that's saying she had two different lives, but there's nothing wrong with that, is there? The important one is the one she spent with you. The loving memories you have of her."

Her smile touched his heart. He closed his eyes. "It's still hard to take in, to admit. Dad and Gram were always very close. I don't know how he would take this."

"He doesn't need to know."

"He'd find out the first time he came up here. There's no way of keeping it quiet."

"Then you be the one to tell him, but you also tell him all the wonderful things you've learned about her. Don't let him think the worst about her the way you've tried to do," Megan advised.

"I burned the journals." He hated lying, but he still couldn't bring himself to tell the truth.

Megan winced. "I wish you hadn't. I had hoped you'd read them." Her face settled in sad lines.

"What did you do with the last one?"

"It's destroyed." There was a strange look in her eyes when she said it.

Dev brought her fingers to his mouth. He brushed his bearded chin back and forth across her knuckles. "No more fighting?"

"I won't if you won't."

"I don't like sleeping alone anymore, Meggie," he murmured. "I don't like knowing if I wake up in the middle of the night I won't find you curled up next to me, trying to warm your feet against mine. I don't want to make war, I want to make love."

She stretched out her index finger and rubbed it across his lower lip. "I think I could handle that."

"Meggie, I'm sorry for yelling at you. For accusing you of things."

"I'm sorry for hitting you."

He winced at the remembered punch. "I could have sworn you used brass knuckles."

"You were acting like a fool. You deserved it," she freely admitted with a tiny smile lifting her lips.

"I guess it says a lot that we can sit down and reasonably discuss our differences now."

"Because we're all grown-up now?" she teased.

He grinned. "Maybe because we're a hell of a lot closer to it than we were fifteen years ago. Before, we both flew off the handle and yelled. Now we fly off the handle, yell, then calm down enough to talk things over." He kept her curled fingers close to his lips, pressing light kisses on them between words. "I'm tired, Meggie. Tired of moving from a steamy jungle to a hot desert with little relief in between. Tired of not having a home to call my own except for a small mail box at corporate headquarters. One by one, the engineers I started out with have settled down with wives and kids. Admittedly, there were a few who couldn't handle a desk job and ended up divorced. The others are happy with their white picket fences and dogs in the backyard. I used to think they were crazy." He turned his head and rested his cheek against her hand. "I'm changing my mind."

"It's a complete turnaround from your former lifestyle," she whispered. "Are you sure you can truly handle it? You can't walk away once you start, Dev. It wouldn't be right."

He lifted his head and stared at her with pleading in his eyes. "It wouldn't be so bad if the right person worked with me."

Her tongue appeared and dampened her lips. "Don't dance around, Dev. You're going to have to come right out and say it. The one thing that will work is honesty."

"Then stay here with me."

If those weren't the words she hoped for, she gave no indication.

"It's not as if you've got a job waiting for you back in L.A. You've put a lot of yourself in fixing up the house. It's only right you should be here to reap the benefits. We're almost finished. I've contacted some magazines to place ads, and with luck, we'll see some response." He took a deep breath, as if preparing himself. "I love you, Meggie. Would it be so wrong for us to give it a try? To see if we could make it this time? I don't want to lose you."

He was so intent on hearing her answer, he didn't notice the sorrow that briefly flickered in her eyes before it was just as swiftly erased. If marriage was on his mind, he hadn't given voice to the thought.

"Dev, could we forego the rest of dinner and go upstairs?"

His features sharpened. "Are you sure?"

She took a deep breath and nodded. "About as sure as I can be."

When they reached the second floor Megan discovered Dev had done more than paint the bathroom that day. Instead of going to the room they had been using, he led her down the hall to the master bedroom, where she found Dev's belongings set in a neat pile in one corner of the sitting room.

"I wasn't going to overstep my bounds by putting my stuff in the bedroom," he explained. "But I'd hoped you'd feel sorry enough for me that you wouldn't mind." He tried a hangdog look that didn't quite catch.

Megan tried not to laugh as she looped her arms around his neck. "Devlin Grant, if you're trying to look pitiful, you're failing miserably."

He rested his hands on the graceful curve of her waist and just looked down at her, studying her features with an intensity that left Megan tingling with anticipation. The guards were down, and his blue-gray eyes now glittered hot and molten with desire.

"I remember the first time we made love." His voice was raw with need as his breath warmed her lips before he brushed his mouth over hers in a light kiss. His hands roamed upward, his thumbs just barely skimming the sides of her breasts.

Suddenly he grabbed her hand and pressed it hard against his groin. "Do you feel it, Meggie? It's just like that night. I still can't get enough of you."

With her eyes lowered and cheeks flushed a dusky rose, she looked like a young girl who was trying to get up the nerve to take that all important step with a boy. Except this time, she knew what that step would entail and she already knew how much she wanted him. "But we're not on that deserted beach now, Dev, and we can control our urges," she said huskily.

"I've never had much control where you're concerned." He drew in a ragged breath. "Oh, Meggie. I was so crazy back then because I didn't know very much and I was afraid you'd laugh. I always saw you as somebody special, someone I wanted all to myself." He groaned when her hand moved away, until it started unbuttoning his shirt. She feathered kisses on his chest, her warm breath misting every square inch of bare skin the open fabric revealed.

Dev gripped her arms and pulled her up against him. "Oh, Meggie, I was so afraid we'd lost this."

She tipped her head back and looked up at him with flames burning in her eyes. When she spoke, her voice came out like liquid velvet. "No, Dev, we couldn't lose something we never threw away."

In one fluid, swift motion, he swept her up into his arms, cradling her against his chest, and carried her into the other room. Two sleeping bags had been again zipped together, with the top folded back invitingly.

"I see you've done a bit of rearranging," she murmured, nuzzling his ear.

"I'm only sorry I don't have any champagne," he said, lowering her onto the bags.

"We don't need anything but each other, Dev." She fingered his nape, feeling the coarse hairs prick her fingertips.

He stretched out next to her, curling one leg over hers. He cocked his head to one side as he toyed with the button on her blue top before loosening it and pulling it over her head. He drew in a sharp breath at the sight of her bare breasts. He was equally leisurely in removing her cotton pants, pulling them down her legs and leaving her garbed only in her lacy bikini panties.

Megan tipped her head back, crying softly as Dev's tongue laved her nipple into a hard aching nub. "You are so beautiful, Meggie," he murmured. He ran his hands over her bare shoulders with a reverence that brought tears to her eyes. "Warm, giving, all I ever need."

She reached down to unsnap the buttons to his jeans. "I'd feel much better if those were off," she breathed, pushing on the waistband.

Dev reared back long enough to shuck his jeans. Megan smiled at the realization he wore no underwear. When he returned to her, covering her body with his, she felt his erection hot and hard against her belly.

"No one could ever fascinate me the way you do, Meggie," he told her, his dark eyes boring into hers. "I'll never love another woman the way I love you."

"And I know I'll never find anyone that could replace you," she murmured, touching him with loving hands and dropping kisses on his neck and throat before biting down gently. She laughed throatily when he jumped and then groaned as she wrapped her fingers around his pulsing warmth and gently caressed him.

"You little witch." He threw his head back and grimaced with pleasurable pain as she continued her ministration.

But it was Megan who soon began moaning when Dev touched her, dipping his fingers inside the moist heat and starting up that rhythm that left her moving with him.

When he finally entered her, for a tiny fraction of a time, he felt as if he was dying. As if he was finally home.

Megan's eyes opened and looked into his as he possessed her. They echoed all the passion and desire her body displayed. She raised her hips to welcome him further, and soon they were lost in the way they had been so many times before.

Megan's breath caught in her throat, and Dev looked as if he could die at any moment. Except when the time came, instead of dying, they both reaffirmed life. And love.

Chapter Sixteen

Megan awoke just as the gray early-morning light began turning pink and blue with the rising sun. She lay there for several moments, feeling warm and secure with Dev's arms wrapped around her as if he wouldn't let her go. How many times had he whispered those same words to her during the night?

Except this time, she didn't feel secure the way she truly should. Instead, she felt ready to cry. She snuck a glance at Dev's sleeping features and eased herself out of his arms. She stilled when he mumbled, but he merely fell back asleep. Keeping her eyes on him, she quickly dressed, then crept downstairs.

When the coffee was made, she took a cup outside and sat on a bench overlooking the patch of earth that would soon be a new rose garden.

The lightening sky brought not joy for the new day but sorrow, because she knew she would have to say a great many words that would hurt both of them. Words she didn't want to say but that had to be said if they were to have a chance with each other again. Tears filled her eyes, threatening to spill down her cheeks.

"You idiot." She sniffed as she chided herself. "For a woman who just spent the most incredible night of her life with the man she loves, you should be upstairs in his arms, smiling like crazy. Instead, you're down here alone, feeing miserable and hating yourself." She hunted through her pocket for a handkerchief. When she couldn't find one, she muttered, "The hell with it," and used the sleeve of her windbreaker to wipe her nose.

"Your mother would have a fit if she saw you do that. Try this instead." A wrinkled, but clean, handkerchief passed in front of her face.

She accepted the offering and blew her nose. "Thank you."

Dev straddled the bench so he could face her. "Something tells me we might not think of last night in the same way."

Megan wiped her nose again and kept her head down. She was too afraid to look at him. "That's not it."

"Then what is it?" He bit out the words. "I don't know why, but I assumed I'd wake up with you still in my arms and we would naturally take up where we left off when we both fell asleep a couple hours ago. Instead, I wake up alone, and you're out here crying. What's wrong, Meggie?"

She looked straight ahead, not seeing the hurt look in his eyes at her silence.

"Talk to me, dammit!"

She still refused to look at him. "All…" She paused, biting her lower lip to keep it from trembling. "All we have going for us is great sex, and that isn't enough to keep us together. It certainly wasn't enough for us the last time."

"Correct me if I'm wrong, but didn't we both admit how much we loved each other, or doesn't that count? I don't think you said it in the heat of the moment."

"No, I didn't," she admitted softly, remembering how many ways she had told and showed him she loved him. "But sometimes love doesn't work out, either." It didn't work for Maisie and Barney, she thought with painful clarity.

Dev made no move to touch her, as if sensing that would only make matters worse. He cleared his throat. "So what exactly are you trying to say?"

Megan knew she had to say the words before she changed her mind. "The house is almost finished, and I think I should go back to L.A."

"Why?"

Megan steeled herself against his plea. She told herself to be strong. Easier said than done. "Because... there's still a lot to be resolved," she began haltingly.

"Such as what?" It was clear he wasn't going to make this easy for her.

She looked down at the handkerchief she was twisting between her fingers. "When we first arrived, we might not have hated each other any longer, but we weren't too sure we liked each other, either," she said softly. "You came up here with the intention of looking over Maisie's house and selling it. I came up here because I wanted to make up for what happened during our marriage and divorce."

Dev swore under his breath. "Don't give me that bull that all those nights together were your way of apologizing, because I won't accept it."

She flinched. "No, that was purely between us. Look, we've proved we could work together without killing each other, and we've proved the sparks between us are even stronger than before. But that's way up here away from everything familiar to both of us. We've been together for months, and we created our own little world away from reality. I think we need to step back and take stock of ourselves. To see if what we have here is real.'' Her lips barely moved as she spoke the damning words.

Dev arched his arm over his head and threw his coffee cup toward a nearby tree. It shattered on contact.

''You're just running away,'' he said through clenched teeth. ''You don't want anything more than some good sex, especially nothing close to a commitment, so you decide it's easier to run back to that fake life-style of yours that was killing you and the hell with something good and real between us!'' His words pounded against her senses.

She blinked rapidly to keep the tears from falling. Her eyes burned from her efforts. ''I'm trying to give us some breathing space, to give us a chance to know this is the right thing,'' she murmured. ''I don't want us to go through what we did before. The next time could be much worse.''

He grabbed her arms and forced her to face him. ''Who says we will? Do you doubt us that much?''

''No, just me.''

Her honesty stung. She could see it by the raw pain in his eyes.

''We still have our differences, Dev,'' she whispered, silently pleading with him to understand. ''All along you've refused to give Maisie a chance. Refused to hear anything about her. You shut out the woman who loved you and deeded you this house, something that once upon a time must have meant a great deal to her. I used to be one of the most close-minded people alive, but I was willing to find out about her, not because of her past, but because she was a part of you. I need to settle things about my old life, and you need to settle things about an important member of your family. We can't begin something new until we settle the old.''

Dev's fingers turned punishing as he held her in a bruising grip. ''Meggie, I love you. I don't want you to leave.'' There was no mistaking the sorrow in his voice, as if he already knew any plea was useless, but that he had to try anyway.

Megan wanted to cry because she knew how difficult it was for a man like Dev to beg. ''I have to.'' Her voice cracked. Her body was stiff with tension as she strove hard not to break down in front of him.

He released her so suddenly, she almost lost her balance. When she looked up, she saw raw pain mingled with fury in his eyes. ''Damn you. Just go, then.'' He got up and walked off into the trees. Within seconds, he was out of sight.

With Dev gone, Megan didn't bother to hide her tears. Now she allowed them to flow freely down her cheeks. ''Oh, Dev, it has to be. I want us both to be sure about this.''

She cried the entire time she packed all her clothing and carried it out to the car. Deep inside, she hoped Dev would return and force her to stay. She also prayed he wouldn't. It was hard enough to leave without him making it worse.

When she pulled away from the house, she didn't look back.

DEV WALKED UNTIL HE reached the hot spring. He sat on a rock, skipping stones against the water's surface. He could feel the pressure in his chest expand until it threatened to explode.

''She loves me, I know it,'' he said out loud. ''So why does she want us to split up?'' He skipped another stone. "I know what I want. Why can't she? She has to see how good we are together. That we belong together, dammit!" he shouted to the trees. No answer was forthcoming.

Memories crowded his brain with breakneck speed. The first time he saw Megan, the first time they made love, their wedding, the day her BMW rolled up to Maisie's house, the first night in the hot spring...

For some reason, he and Megan had been given a second chance. Was he going to let her blow it?

Dev jumped up. "No way is she leaving here," he said with a determined air. He strode back to the house, oblivious of tree branches hitting him in the face. "If I've got to talk until I'm blue in the face, I'm going to convince Meggie what we've got is very real." He began walking faster, almost running, as his spirits lightened.

"Meggie!" The screen door slammed shut behind him as he hurried through the house and up the stairs.

It didn't take seeing her things gone to tell him she had left. The absolute silence and the absence of a presence he'd grown used to told him loud and clear. Dev scanned the room and his belongings. He found no note. He dropped to the floor and seriously thought about crying. Then he collected himself and rummaged through his duffel bag until he pulled out the journals. He stared at the cover of one of the books for a long time before he opened it and began reading.

"YOU LOOK LIKE HELL." Ellen Abernathy walked past Megan. She looked around the living room littered with papers and boxes and turned to her daughter. "What's going on?"

"I'm spring cleaning, and thank you so much for that compliment, Mother," Megan said dryly. "Want some coffee?"

Ellen sat on the couch, pushing a stack of papers to one side. "I'd prefer some answers. You've been back for three weeks, you haven't bothered looking for another job, and I happen to know that at least three agencies are trying to persuade you to join them. What exactly is wrong with you? All you've done since you returned from that horrible place is wander around this apartment like a lost puppy. When are you going to snap out of this ridiculous depression?"

Megan brushed a stray hair away from her face. "I am not depressed."

Ellen's gaze started from the top of Megan's tousled hair, over a face without a speck of makeup and down to clothing that looked as if it should have been thrown out years ago. Megan's eyes had dark shadows under them as if she hadn't slept well. "I have never seen you look so unkempt."

Megan smiled. Next to Ellen's immaculate appearance, she supposed she did look pretty ratty. "I'm cleaning, Mother. I didn't think I needed to worry about power dressing." She plopped onto a bar stool. "So, why aren't you in court putting the bad guys in jail?"

"Is it a crime to want to visit with my daughter? I thought we could have lunch together, but since you aren't dressed..." She arched an eyebrow. "So tell me, when are you going to stop looking like a ragpicker's child and return to your normal self?"

"Maybe this is my normal self."

Ellen opened her purse and took out her cigarette case. After lighting up, she studied her daughter with the same merciless gaze she used on difficult witnesses. "I can't believe you did it," she said flatly.

"Did what?"

"You know very well what. You fell in love with him again. You're not house cleaning. You're preparing to move back up to that remote place. Didn't the past teach you anything?"

"Yes, it did," Megan replied gently. "It taught me that we were too young and immature to go into something as serious as marriage. It taught me that love needs to be nurtured in order to grow and that if two people are willing to work together, anything is possible. Even to seeing an old run-down house come to life again."

She smiled. "Oh, Mom, if you could have seen what we did to that house. It looked so terrible when I first saw it that all I could visualize was a bulldozer putting it out of its misery. But Dev saw something else. He saw a firm foundation and a strong frame that only needed some love and caring. He looked beyond the exterior and saw a chance to make it beautiful again. With that kind of enthusiasm, it was easy to share his dream. And to answer your question, yes, I did fall in love with him. Maybe not again, because I don't think what we had back then was love." Megan faced her mother. "But I do know it's what we have now."

"Then why are you here?"

"Dev needs to be left alone to do some thinking. I want him to be very sure I'm what he wants," she explained.

Ellen asked the question Megan had ignored these past weeks. "What if he changes his mind?"

Megan didn't allow her mother to see how much the question hurt. "Then I pick up the pieces and go on with my life."

Ellen leaned forward and crushed out her cigarette in the ashtray. "No running off and getting married this time. If the two of you do insist on marrying again, you'll do it right."

Megan smiled. "I wouldn't have it any other way."

Ellen stood up and smoothed her skirt down over her trim hips. "We'll have lunch tomorrow. Be at my office at twelve-thirty, and please dress properly." She kissed her daughter on the cheek as she walked out. "And if you insist on giving us grandchildren, make sure they take after our side of the family!"

Megan had to laugh. Only her mother would make that kind of statement.

Megan looked around as she tried to figure out what to do next. She already knew what she wanted to do. She wanted to pick up the phone and call Dev. So far, her own phone had been silent. She didn't want to think that he had finally seen the light and was now relieved she had left.

"I'll give him one more week," she decided, sliding off the stool.

"IF YOU DON'T SLOW DOWN you're going to collapse," Harry predicted, watching Dev balance himself on the ladder as he painted the new shutters, the final touch to the new exterior of the house.

Dev didn't look down. "I'm too close to finishing to stop now. How does the rose garden look?"

"You know very well how it looks—as if it's been there for a hundred years. Dev, why don't you go down to L.A. and bring her back where she belongs?"

"Not until everything is finished." Dev didn't explain that he had made the decision when he first found Megan gone. He wanted a finished product to bring her back to. He wanted to tell her he'd read Maisie's journals and discovered he had a very special lady for a grandmother. Now he regretted that he hadn't been able to tell her so in person. He looked down at Harry. "Did you find someone to restore that painting I found in the attic?"

Harry nodded. "Actually, Charlie did." His face creased in a broad smile. "She's going to look beautiful when it's done."

Dev thought of the day he had spent in the attic. Most of the items there were only fit for the junk pile, but one of the few treasures he did unearth was a large oil painting of Maisie dressed in a dark blue velvet evening gown. What caught his attention was the light shining in her eyes and the smile on her lips. It was the look of a woman deeply in love. After reading her journals, he learned of her love for a man she couldn't have and the son she bore him. While he didn't know the man's identity and sensed he could learn the name from Harry if he pressed, he hadn't. He already realized that that identity had been revealed in the last journal, which Megan had destroyed. It didn't matter. Time had let him discover nothing mattered except Megan. Once he had something concrete to offer her, he'd be in L.A., asking her to come back.

"She was right," he said out of the blue. "She said we needed the space to better know what we wanted. I thought she was wrong. I wanted to hate her."

"Hate's just the other side of love," Harry said quietly.

"Yeah, well, that was something else I had to realize. From the beginning, I wanted to hate Maisie for what she did and had up here, but I found out I couldn't. Because if all this hadn't come about, Meggie and I wouldn't have met again. I learned what fate meant. She's had her time to figure things out, and I've had mine. With luck, by the end of next week, we'll be finished except for furniture, which I want to leave up to her." He was afraid he was babbling, but he didn't know how to stop. Too many nights without Megan's company had left him lonely and even a bit afraid she might have discovered she wanted her old life back after all. That was something he dared not think about too much.

"Maisie would be proud of what you've done," Harry said. "And I bet she'd be happy for you."

Dev carefully descended the ladder. "You're a good friend, Harry," he said sincerely.

The older man shuffled his feet in embarrassment. "Hell, you're Maisie's blood. 'Sides, some of us are hopin' you'll revive our old poker games." He winked.

Both men turned at the sound of a car engine straining as it climbed the hill.

"Expecting anyone?" Harry asked.

Dev shook his head. He watched a dark sedan appear at the top of the hill. "Looks like trouble."

Harry sighed. "And it's been so quiet, too."

Eunice St. Clair carefully climbed out of the car and walked toward the two men.

The first thing Dev noticed was the lack of disdain on her face as she looked beyond him at the house.

"You've done a lovely job, Mr. Grant," she said quietly, walking to one side to glance at the rose garden that was partially visible from the front of the house.

"If I didn't see it with my own eyes, I wouldn't have believed you could perform such a miracle. You are to be congratulated."

"Uh, thank you." Dev stumbled over the words. What was she up to now?

She smiled at his wary expression. "The war is over...Dev. I understand you've applied for all the necessary licenses to run a lodge, and now that I've seen what you've accomplished, I can believe you weren't just playing at this. I wish you a lot of luck." She glanced around. "Is Megan around?"

"Ah, no, she's not. She's in L.A." He was still stunned by Eunice's words.

"Then please tell her I stopped by." She paused. "Someone said Megan would be a formidable adversary for me. She was right."

She turned away, then looked back at Dev. "I'm sure your lodge will do well. After all, you have the genes to succeed here. Perhaps the day will come when we can talk about things." With that, she returned to her car and drove away quickly.

"Whew!" Harry pushed his cap to the back of his head. "Boy, I'd say all is forgiven."

Dev watched the dust swirling around the retreating car. "I'd say it's more than that, but I'm not exactly sure what, and I don't even want to try to figure it out." He didn't see the small smile flitting on Harry's lips.

"So, you finishin' the shutters today?" the older man asked.

"Or die trying."

Dev moved the ladder to the next window and was preparing to climb up when he heard a heavier engine than the one in Eunice's car.

"Must be our day for company," he mused. "At this rate, I won't get them finished."

This time, a slate blue four-wheel-drive truck appeared at the top of the hill. A small trailer hopped along behind it. Dev froze when the truck stopped and a familiar figure hopped out.

This wasn't the Megan with the French braid and designer clothes he had first seen here. This was Meggie, a riot of curls around her face, dressed in a black T-shirt and faded jeans that lovingly clung to her slender frame.

"What—" He stopped because he couldn't think of any words.

"Devlin Grant, you are the most stubborn man I know!" She advanced on him. "How much time do you need to come up with what we already knew? Are you so hardheaded you refuse to accept the truth that's practically smacking you in the face?" She poked him in the chest with her forefinger.

He looked down and grabbed the punishing hand topped by pink polished nails. "Didn't waste any time in getting your claws rebuilt, did you?"

"They are a necessity, not a luxury, and don't you dare get off the subject," she snarled. "We are getting married, Devlin Grant. We are getting married as soon as possible."

Hope blossomed. "You're pregnant?"

"No! I'll have you know that our children will be conceived *after* the wedding. Damn you, you could have called!"

"I wanted to finish the house first."

Megan spared a quick glance at the house with its gleaming paint job, rebuilt front porch and bushes lining the new flagstone walkway. "It looks finished to me."

Dev couldn't believe the scene unfolding around him. "You could have come back."

"I *am* back!"

"You could have come back sooner!"

"I had things to settle before I could come back," Megan retorted. "It's all gone. I sold my condo."

"Yourself?"

"Of course, myself! Why give another real-estate agent the commission when I have a license? And I got a great price for it, too," she said proudly. "I transferred my bank accounts, and I sold my car and bought the truck. I figured it would be of more use up here."

Dev whooped for joy as he picked Megan up and swung her around in his arms. "Meggie, you constantly surprise me."

"Good. I don't want you to get bored."

"I don't think that will ever happen." He lowered his head and gave her a kiss to make up for all the days they were apart.

"Wow, you are lonely, big boy," she breathed once they parted. "By the way, wasn't that Eunice St. Clair's car I saw coming down the hill?"

He nodded. "Yeah, she came by to make peace." He tipped his head back in thought. "She knows about my father, doesn't she?" He suddenly covered Megan's lips with his fingers. "No, don't tell me. Maybe it's better this way. I read the journals, Meggie, and I learned a lot. No wonder you felt you had to leave. I wasn't offering you everything the way it should be. I guess I was still a little afraid of putting it all on the line. Yet you weren't afraid. And I'm not anymore."

"Oh, Dev. This time apart killed me, but I kept telling myself it was for the best. I guess it was."

"Yeah, well, don't break out the crow pie yet," he teased, swinging her around again. "So, hotshot, what's in the trailer?"

Megan was taken aback by the sudden change of subject. She slid out of his arms. "Anything I didn't want to throw out that I felt we could use. Along with some things I picked up for the house."

He found himself unable to stop grinning. "Deer and moose heads and piles of beer cans for the corners?"

"In your dreams! Maybe we'll be catering to hunters and fishermen, but there's no reason why their wives can't come along and have something more civilized to look at. I'm here to make sure they have a pleasant place to stay," she haughtily informed him.

Dev couldn't stop looking at Megan. He doubted there was ever a more beautiful woman. And she was all his! "Harry, you going to be my best man?" he asked without taking his eyes off Megan's smiling face. He saw the light dawn in her eyes at his words, then saw a hint of tears. "Trust you to break out the tears now that you've got me where you want me," he teased, hugging her tightly.

"With pleasure!"

Dev looked down at Megan. "I was coming down to get you, you know," he murmured.

She tossed her head back. "Too bad. You took too long and I was getting impatient."

"Something tells me this marriage won't be boring."

"Something tells me this marriage will last a great deal longer than the last one," she replied, sliding her arms around his waist. "I'm going to make you toe the line, Neanderthal. You won't have a chance."

"Well, then, I'll just have to overcome that yuppie part of you with a lot of loving, won't I?" Dev then did what he deemed necessary after his unorthodox proposal. He kissed her with everything he had.

"Think we should go off somewhere and plan our wedding?" Megan asked softly.

"Hell, no. We'll work on the important stuff first. We're going off and planning our honeymoon." He grinned.

Harry chuckled as the couple walked into the house, arm in arm. "Yep, I was right about those two. They *are* better than TV."

H A R L E Q U I N
American Romance®

American Romance's yearlong celebration continues. Join your favorite authors as they celebrate love set against the special times each month throughout 1992.

Next month, fireworks light up the sky when Anne Haynes and John Westfield meet in a special Fourth of July romance:

JULY

S	M	T	W	T	F	S
			1	2	3	4
5					11	
				17	18	
19	20			23	24	25
26	27	28	29	30	31	

**#445
HOME FREE
by Cathy Gillen Thacker**

Read all the books in *A Calendar of Romance*, coming to you one per month all year, only in American Romance.

If you missed #421 HAPPY NEW YEAR, DARLING; #425 VALENTINE HEARTS AND FLOWERS; #429 FLANNERY'S RAINBOW; #433 A MAN FOR EASTER; #437 CINDERELLA MOM; or #441 DADDY'S GIRL and would like to order them, send your name, address, zip or postal code, along with a check or money order (please do not send cash) for $3.29 for #421 and #425 or $3.39 for #429, #433, #437 and #441, plus 75¢ postage and handling ($1.00 in Canada), *for each book ordered*, payable to Harlequin Reader Service to:

In the U.S.
3010 Walden Avenue
P.O. Box 1325
Buffalo, NY 14269-1325

In Canada
P.O. Box 609
Fort Erie, Ontario
L2A 5X3

Please specify book title(s) with your order.
Canadian residents add applicable federal and provincial taxes.

COR7

HARLEQUIN
American Romance®

COMING NEXT MONTH

#445 HOME FREE by Cathy Gillen Thacker

John Westfield's million-watt smile seemed honest, but was his interest in Anne Haynes political or personal? After all, she held the key to a scandal. Would she tear New Hampshire's first family asunder and shut the door to John's governorship—or would she lead them all to home, hearth and happiness . . . and the greatest of all star-spangled dreams? *Don't miss this Calendar of Romance title.*

#446 THE TROUBLE WITH TERRY by Jacqueline Diamond

There was magic to Terry Vogel. He could charm children and animals, and he made every day a celebration. But Karen Loesser was too busy for charm and romance. That is, until he moved into her house . . . and into her life.

#447 DAYE AND KNIGHT by Patricia Cox

Something happened on the island of Hawaii when Michael Daye and Jo Knight met. In fact, Jo swore she heard the loudest fireworks ever! But although Michael was one pretty good male specimen, he had one small flaw. With a devilish gleam in her eye, Jo set out to prove that opposites attract in the most exciting and unexpected ways. . . .

#448 BEWITCHED by Saranne Dawson

When the feud between two rival aunts—and witches—began to burn again, Samantha Bridges's only hope was to consort with the enemy. But wasn't Deke Jacobs a sinister witch-in-training himself? Samantha had decided to take the heat, not set herself afire. But Deke's burning gaze was sorcery of the most sensual kind.

Take 4 bestselling love stories FREE

Plus get a FREE surprise gift!

Summer Reading At Its Best

In July, Harlequin and Silhouette bring readers the Big Summer Read Program. Heat up your summer with these four exciting new novels by top Harlequin and Silhouette authors.

SOMEWHERE IN TIME by Barbara Bretton
YESTERDAY COMES TOMORROW by Rebecca Flanders
A DAY IN APRIL by Mary Lynn Baxter
LOVE CHILD by Patricia Coughlin

From time travel to fame and fortune, this program offers something for everyone.

Available at your favorite retail outlet.

BSR

OVER THE YEARS, TELEVISION HAS BROUGHT
THE LIVES AND LOVES OF MANY CHARACTERS INTO
YOUR HOMES. NOW HARLEQUIN INTRODUCES YOU
TO THE TOWN AND PEOPLE OF

One small town—twelve terrific love stories.

GREAT READING... GREAT SAVINGS...
AND A FABULOUS FREE GIFT!

Each book set in Tyler is a self-contained love story; together, the
twelve novels stitch the fabric of the community.

By collecting proofs-of-purchase found in each Tyler book, you can
receive a fabulous gift, ABSOLUTELY FREE! And use our special
Tyler coupons to save on your next TYLER book purchase.

Join us for the fifth TYLER book,
BLAZING STAR by Suzanne Ellison, available in July.

Is there really a murder cover-up?
Will Brick and Karen overcome differences and find true love?

FREE GIFT OFFER

To receive your free gift, send us the specified number of proofs-of-purchase from any specially marked Free Gift Offer Harlequin or Silhouette book with the Free Gift Certificate properly completed, plus a check or money order (do not send cash) to cover postage and handling payable to Harlequin/Silhouette Free Gift Promotion Offer. We will send you the specified gift.

FREE GIFT CERTIFICATE

ITEM	A. GOLD TONE EARRINGS	B. GOLD TONE BRACELET	C. GOLD TONE NECKLACE
# of proofs-of-purchase required	3	6	9
Postage and Handling	$2.25	$2.75	$3.25
Check one	☐	☐	☐

Name: _____

Address: _____

City: _____ Province: _____ Postal Code: _____

Mail this certificate, specified number of proofs-of-purchase and a check or money order for postage and handling to: HARLEQUIN/SILHOUETTE FREE GIFT OFFER 1992, P.O. Box 622, Fort Erie, Ontario L2A 5X3. Requests must be received by July 31, 1992.

PLUS—Every time you submit a completed certificate with the correct number of proofs-of-purchase, you are automatically entered in our MILLION DOLLAR SWEEPSTAKES! No purchase or obligation necessary to enter. See below for alternate means of entry and how to obtain complete sweepstakes rules.

MILLION DOLLAR SWEEPSTAKES
NO PURCHASE OR OBLIGATION NECESSARY TO ENTER

To enter, hand-print (mechanical reproductions are not acceptable) your name and address on a 3"×5" card and mail to Million Dollar Sweepstakes 6097, c/o either P.O. Box 9056, Buffalo, NY 14269-9056 or P.O. Box 621, Fort Erie, Ontario L2A 5X3. Limit: one entry per envelope. Entries must be sent via 1st-class mail. For eligibility, entries must be received no later than March 31, 1994. No liability is assumed for printing errors, lost, late or misdirected entries.

Sweepstakes is open to persons 18 years of age or older. All applicable laws and regulations apply. Sweepstakes offer void wherever prohibited by law. Prizewinners will be determined no later than May 1994. Chances of winning are determined by the number of entries distributed and received. For a copy of the Official Rules governing this sweepstakes offer, send a self-addressed, stamped envelope (WA residents need not affix return postage) to: Million Dollar Sweepstakes Rules, P.O. Box 4733, Blair, NE 68009.

✂ HA3C

ONE PROOF-OF-PURCHASE
To collect your fabulous FREE GIFT you must include the necessary FREE GIFT proofs-of-purchase with a properly completed offer certificate.

(See inside back cover for offer details)